Pandemic

A Novel

by

J. A. Lourenco

This book is a work of fiction. Characters, corporations, organizations, and institutions in this work are the product of the author's imagination or, if real, are used fictitiously and without any intention to describe their actual conduct

PANDEMIC

Cover Design by Judy Bullard

ISBN:0615762948

ISBN-13:9780615762944

To Helena, my wife and my best friend,

with love

Preface

The human race is a complex mosaic, shaped less by intelligence, instinct, or ethnicity than by emotion. For every saint, philanthropist, or humanitarian with the dream and the drive to make the world a better place, there is a thug, a tyrant, or a terrorist with a wicked dream of his own. History is full of examples where altruism and generosity are overshadowed by malice, vengeance, or envy. If nothing else, September 11, 2001, proves that evil can hatch dark dreams and carry out unimaginable vicious deeds.

At the dawn of a new century, we find conditions never before experienced by humankind. The technological advances of the last century have allowed human beings to enjoy longer and healthier lives, to live more comfortably, to travel faster, to produce more food, to communicate instantly to anyone anywhere on the planet, to store and share huge amounts of information, and in many cases to breakdown political or social oppression and to establish democratic rule of law. But the same scientific breakthroughs have also allowed a human population explosion, created record amounts of pollution, exterminated countless animal and plant species, produced nuclear, chemical and biological weapons, and permitted the rise of a new breed of goon, the international terrorist.

Overcrowding, global pollution, and ecological stress are serious problems, which fortunately or unfortunately are not immediately catastrophic. They are progressive calamities, and we will watch them turn increasingly more desperate until we learn to live with them or decide to reverse them. However, the manmade weapons of mass destruction are an open Pandora's box that no one will ever be able to close.

Fiction often presents a view of the future, but more often than not it underestimates the magnitude of future events. In the biological realm, history's reality is already ahead of the fiction. Throughout time, naturally occurring diseases routinely changed the course of history and kept human population under control. Along with war, the plague was the number one societal concern in Europe throughout the middle ages, with recurring epidemics causing widespread death and devastation. Old World infectious diseases killed more than half of the natives of the Americas during the sixteenth century, opening the way for conquest by the Europeans. The Spanish Influenza of 1918-1919 was responsible for more deaths during the two years following the First World War than the war itself. Smallpox killed more people during the first seventy years of the twentieth century than any war in history. And today, the world chooses to ignore the AIDS decimation of third world nations because... well, because they are mainly poor.

Also ahead of the fiction is the scientific reality. While progress in healthcare and vaccine technology are preventing most large-scale epidemics and saving millions of lives, widely available genetic information and advances in microbiology make it possible for average scientists to manipulate existing bioagents. They can change their pathogenic behavior, they can render them immune to known vaccines, or they can build totally new pathogens by combining virulent characteristics from different bugs. Recently, scientists at a university in New York created a living and reproducing poliovirus from ordinary inert chemicals purchased from a mail-order supplier. The skills required to do so are within the reach of most molecular biologists, and the needed equipment and chemicals can be obtained for the price of a small car.

Today, new and more virulent pathogens are being developed by modern day Huns who strive to use them for evil purposes. The combination of bioengineering knowledge and suicide terrorism will forever keep governments and societies on high alert. And the worst-case scenario will someday become reality. Because there are too many people dreaming the unthinkable. Because it is possible. Because it is easy to plan and attempt, particularly if you don't mind dying while carrying it out. Because the destructive power of the new tools is unprecedented. And because the avoidance precautions and countermeasures in place only need to fail once.

One day, perhaps before this new century is over, our defenses will fail and a sudden, unstoppable bug will start devastating the citizens of our rich countries. The fabric of our society will likely disintegrate, because our economies and our way of life do not support the disruption, and because our pampered psyche is not ready to cope.

J. A. Lourenco
October, 2003

Pandemic

CHAPTER 1

The sudden ringing startled him awake. David Reiss turned on a light and picked up the phone while trying to focus on the alarm clock by his bed. 4:43 on a Monday morning! Who in God's name was calling at this hour? His wife pulled the covers over her head and turned her back on him.

"Hello," he said, his voice hoarse from sleep.

"Dr. Reiss?" an accented voice asked at the other end of the line.

"This is he."

"I am really sorry to call at this hour. I know it is very early in the United States."

Reiss could not place the voice or the accent, but the Director of the Centers for Disease Control and Prevention in Atlanta was becoming wide awake. This was an international call, and few people had his home number. Someone calling him directly at this ungodly hour could mean only trouble.

"No problem, I assume it must be important," Reiss said.

"I wouldn't call if it weren't," the woman replied. "My name is Claudia Senna. I am a doctor in Rio de Janeiro and an advisor to Brazil's Health Ministry. We met at a conference last year in Orlando and . . . "

"I remember you, Dr. Senna," Reiss interrupted. "What can I do for you?"

"We have two very sick men at a hospital here in Rio. This, of course, is not unusual, but what is unusual is the nature of their sickness. Both show clinical signs of severe hemorrhage. Both had painful prodromal symptoms, and both now have heavy bleeding of the gums and nose, hematemesis, and melena," Dr. Senna explained.

"Any idea of what it is?" Reiss asked, now fully awake. Vomiting blood, black liquid stool, and heavy internal bleeding were all signs of some of the worst hemorrhagic viruses known to man, like Ebola hemorrhagic fever for example. But severe hemorrhaging cases were more common than many people suspected, and their cause often remained unknown. However, if they happened in clusters, there had to be a common cause that demanded investigation.

Dr. Senna took a deep breath. "I fear we have disturbing news. The laboratory at the hospital ran a number of specimen tests, and we are quite sure that the patients are infected with an Orthopox virus."

"You mean the *Variola* virus?" Reiss asked.

"We can't be sure of that yet. We have used light and electron microscopy on the samples, and we can't distinguish between *Variola*, mousepox, monkeypox, *Vaccinia*, or others. But we are certain it is a pox-family virus."

Dr. Reiss froze. If it was *Variola*, the smallpox-causing virus, where did it come from? The CDC received a few scares just about every day. All were taken seriously, and luckily the vast majority were false alarms. However, this one sounded more serious than most. He remembered Dr. Senna well now – a thin, tanned, attractive woman in her fifties. The Brazilian doctor was highly professional and would not be calling if she weren't reasonably sure that some cause for concern existed. From what he had heard, he needed to be worried.

"And the symptoms fit smallpox," Dr. Senna continued. "In addition to the bleeding, both patients have extensive rashes. In one case, the skin has turned rubbery and dark purple."

Reiss thought for a few moments. "Your description matches hemorrhagic-type smallpox," he conceded. "Let's hope it isn't so. If you have smallpox in Rio de Janeiro, it's not only very contagious, it's also a serious emergency."

"That's correct, Dr. Reiss, and this is why I am calling you. One of the patients is an American, and we would like your help to ensure that this outbreak does not spread to other cities or countries. We at the Health Ministry are already involved. We are mobilizing all the appropriate local and government agencies and have contacted the World Health Organization."

After a pause, the Brazilian doctor added, "We are not panicking yet, but we are taking no chances and starting all worst-case surveillance and countenance procedures. We will send you a specimen, although we expect to know with certainty what we are dealing with before you receive the sample."

"Anything unusual about the two patients?" Reiss asked.

"It's carnival week here, and nothing is unusual. They arrived in Rio four days ago. We believe that both were already sick when they arrived, which is troubling because one came from São Paulo and the other from Chicago. That's about all we know."

"Where are the patients now?"

"We've moved them into isolation."

"Have you tried to retrace their steps?"

"It's part of the procedure we are following and we need your help in Chicago," Dr. Senna replied. "We are getting a team ready to look for all contacts immediately, both here and in São Paulo. Obviously, we start with the families and co-workers. It won't be easy because of the Carnival mayhem, but we expect to have more information by the end of the day, which should help us determine how to proceed."

Dr. Reiss thought for a little while. The Brazilian appeared to be following all the appropriate procedures.

"Very well, send me all the information you have on the American. I'll get a team to work with you. I don't need to tell you how to do your job, and we shouldn't panic. Please keep me informed of anything relevant," the CDC Director said.

"I will keep you updated, Doctor, and thank you."

"Thanks, and let's hope for the best." Dr. Reiss hung up. He walked downstairs to his home office, turned on his PC, sent an e-mail to Dr. Venkatraman, his Assistant Director at the CDC, and copied Dr. Emile Gastineau, his colleague and friend at the Pasteur Institute in Paris. He then went back upstairs to try another hour of sleep.

But this Monday morning would be anything but restful. His cell phone rang before 6 A.M.

"Hello," he said sleepily, becoming awake again and trying vainly to let his wife sleep for another half hour.

"David, were you asleep?" another accented voice asked.

"That's what normal people do this early in the morning, Emile," Reiss said, recognizing the French accent.

"Sorry to wake you up. When I saw your e-mail I thought you were already working."

"Well, I was on the phone with the Brazilian doctor for a while, then tried to go back to sleep."

"I'm sorry, I could have waited a couple of hours before calling, but this is important."

"Anything to do with my e-mail?"

"Unfortunately, yes," the head of the Pasteur Institute answered. "I got a call from Italy a few minutes ago. An Italian man is in critical condition at a Rome hospital. According to the information I received, he is oozing blood from every orifice in his body. It apparently started with pain, vomiting, and a rash, and it has escalated into severe hemorrhaging. Not very different from your Brazilian subjects."

"Any idea as to a diagnosis?"

"Negative. They are running tests in Rome, and I expect to get a specimen in about two hours."

"Anything unusual about the patient?"

"Not really, except that he has been traveling. He spent the past week in Santiago, Chile, and returned to Rome the day before yesterday with a connecting stop in Miami. The symptoms are similar to the ones in Rio, but it seems unlikely that these people's paths ever crossed."

They chatted for a while about the two cases, but they lacked enough information to draw conclusions.

"Maybe it's just a coincidence," Reiss said in an attempt at optimism before hanging up. He didn't need to tell Dr. Gastineau to make sure that the Italians treated this seriously. He hated coincidences, or rather, he didn't believe in them.

It made no sense to go back to bed now. He picked up the phone again and called Dr. Venkatraman.

"Dave, glad you called," Venkatraman said. "I was just about to call you. We have another hemorrhagic case."

"I know. I've just spoken with Emile Gastineau."

"Gastineau?" Venkatraman's voice showed surprise. "How did he find out so quickly?"

"The folks in Rome called him. They're sending him a specimen."

"Rome? They have a case in Rome?"

"Isn't that what you're referring to?" Reiss asked, his heart suddenly skipping a beat.

"No, I am talking about New Jersey." Venkatraman was starting to share his boss's alarm. "A hospital in Morristown has a thirty-one-year-old woman with many of the same symptoms. Dr. Frank DuBois, from the University of Medicine of New Jersey, has run tests and thinks it could be smallpox."

"Oh, my God," Dr. Reiss almost screamed. He was usually reserved and cool, even when alarming news of unusual bugs came across his office, but he was shaking now. "We've got to put an emergency response in place," he finally said. "Call Morristown and tell them about Brazil and Italy to make sure they take this seriously. We need a specimen here, but they must inform all appropriate agencies at once and get people into isolation. Call our senior team together. I'll be in the office in less than an hour."

It was now after 6:30. Reiss took a quick shower, shaved, got dressed, gulped down a corn muffin and a glass of orange juice, and drove the twenty-five minutes to the office. He had barely sat at his desk when the phone rang.

"David, have you heard about the women in Tel Aviv?" the voice on the phone asked without bothering with introductions. Again, Reiss recognized the French accent. "This is getting to be a real nightmare," Gastineau added.

"What about Tel Aviv?" Reiss asked, pressing the phone's speaker button as Venkatraman walked into his office.

"Three women, all prostitutes at the same bordello, same general description as the other two events," Gastineau replied.

"The other *three* events, Emile," Reiss corrected him. "We have one case here in the U.S."

"*Merde*," the Americans heard on the speakerphone. The expletive captured their feelings, and they didn't need to speak French to understand it.

"Look, Emile, we're sending an emergency communication to the World Health Organization and to every health ministry on the planet," Reiss said. "We must assume it is smallpox and start all applicable emergency response procedures."

"We have potential outbreaks in four countries on three continents in a matter of six hours. It has to be a deliberate attack, and this could be just the tip of the iceberg," Venkatraman said, stating the obvious and voicing everyone's fears.

"That's why we must move fast and get every health professional around the world looking for the right symptoms,"

Reiss replied. "We can't afford contagious people waiting for hours in emergency rooms and infecting everyone around them just because the doctors don't know what's happening."

They hung up. Then Reiss dialed the Director of the FBI, and together they called the Secretary of Homeland Security.

CHAPTER 2

The lot, at the edge of the Great Swamp Wildlife Refuge, had been an illegal dumping area for construction debris and other waste long before the house was built. A letter from the EPA had stunned the Wilsons with the news that their property might be contaminated and that tests would be run to verify it. Now, on a late August afternoon, Anne DuBois and Sarah Wilson watched in astounded silence as environmental personnel poked holes and took samples from Sarah's front yard, from under the same lawn where the two had always played. The facemasks and white suits that covered the workers from head to toe were in surreal contrast with the bathing suits worn by the girls, who had been running barefoot on the grass, chasing each other with water balloons just before the men arrived. They stared at the workers with utter disbelief and Anne wondered aloud if they could be astronauts that had somehow landed on the wrong planet.

The lot was indeed contaminated and needed to be cleaned, environmental officials informed several weeks later. The following spring, the trucks and bulldozers arrived, the property was excavated, the contaminated topsoil was trucked away, and new soil was brought in as a backfill. The ground was raked, seed was spread on the new surface, new grass took root, and by the summer the girls were again running and playing in the yard.

But the white suits returned and again removed earth samples for analysis. Again the heavy machines arrived and once more the yard was dug up and the replacement soil was hauled away. As it turned out, the EPA contractor had illegally taken the backfill dirt from another hazardous waste site.

More testing was done, this time both in the yard and inside the home, and environmental officials informed the Wilsons that their property was still contaminated. They were ordered to vacate, and Sarah moved with her family to a different school district.

The girls had always been each other's best friend. Anne was pretty, intelligent, often sensitive, and quiet. She was also headstrong – once she made up her mind, arguing with her became an exercise in futility and contradicting her led to resentment and stubbornness. Still, growing up in an affluent New Jersey neighborhood, there was nothing to indicate that she could become, in her late twenties, a radical environmental activist. The youngest child of Frank and Doreen DuBois, Anne excelled in school, stayed out of trouble, and kept mostly to herself. Her brother Bruce, three years older, had his own friends and rarely paid any attention to her. Anne played with other kids at birthday parties and school breaks but, except for

Sarah Wilson, she never invited them home to play or went to their homes after school.

With Sarah it was different – they did everything together. Sarah, a pale, skinny girl of Anne's age who seemed to catch every cold before anyone else, was perfectly happy following her friend's lead and playing whatever game Anne chose. The two had been in the same grade since kindergarten and were as close as sisters. They would do their homework together and Sarah would often spend the night with Anne, almost a second child to the DuBoises as Anne was to the Wilsons. That is, until the white suits tore them apart during junior high.

Anne was bitter and became fascinated by environmental issues as she entered high school. How could people go on damaging the world around them and not be bothered by it? Chemicals, all chemicals, were the problem, she decided. The discussions with her father, a doctor specializing in infectious diseases, and especially with her mother, a materials scientist working on semiconductor research, became quite lively. When, during an innocuous dinner conversation, she found out that her mother was using ozone-depleting Freon by the gallon as part of her work, Anne threw her napkin on the floor, pushed away from the table with such fury that her chair tipped over, and darted into her room, slamming the door. For weeks she refused to talk.

A few months later, she learned about a high-school science program sponsored by her mother's employer. One of the projects studied the use of a natural, non-polluting orange peel extract to replace Freon as a solvent in semiconductor production. Anne quickly enrolled. She demonstrated such dedication and ingenuity in the testing and refinement of the new product that her name was added as an inventor on a patent filed by the company's engineers.

Her science work gave rise to an almost obsessive concern: global warming and the survival of life on earth. She believed all the environmental doomsday scenarios for the planet and failed to understand people's lack of concern. When the time came to choose a college she told her parents and teachers, "I want to be a paleoclimatologist."

"What's that?" they all asked.

"Paleoclimatology is the study of climate changes over time," she replied. "I'll prove that global warming is real. More importantly, I'll show that it's happening at an unprecedented rate and that our society is the culprit." She was fascinated by scientists who studied, among other things, buried petrified trees and ice layers in glaciers to determine climate conditions through the ages.

"By studying how and why the climate has changed over the millennia, we can show that the present pattern of environmental abuse is catastrophic," she explained.

She enrolled at Ohio State University, where such work was already being done. There, Anne quickly joined a group engaged in environmental propaganda and protests. She became convinced that economic development and technological advancements were the primary factors in global warming and pollution and responsible for the destruction of plant and animal species.

Over time, she began to believe that the fundamental principles of Western culture and religion were at the root of the problem. The assumption that mankind had a divine right to control and dispose of all creation was allowing humans to destroy it without remorse. The belief in the sanctity of human life above all other life forms was justifying the unchecked explosion of human population to the detriment of all others. Humans were becoming the major blight on earth and heading toward self-destruction.

By her junior year in college, Anne's ideal of protecting the environment through paleoclimatology had escalated into an aggressive activism. She became a member of a radical environmental group and quit school. Her last visit to her parents ended in a shouting match, and she stormed out of the house after accusing her mother of being an environmental terrorist. Anne vowed never to return.

In Oregon, she joined other environmentalists in fighting the logging industry. In Alaska, she battled the oil companies drilling in the fragile arctic tundra. Then she traveled to Brazil where she spent nine months preaching against the destruction of the Amazon rain forest and fighting for the rights of primitive Indian tribes. The experience was a revelation. In her view, the Amazonian Indians represented the proper placement of humankind in earth's ecosystem, a species in equilibrium with its environment and surviving on its natural defenses and adaptation without relying on modern technologies.

And the more she thought about them, the more she became convinced of what the goal of the environmental movement should be – to reestablish ecological balance by forcing humankind back to levels of population and activity that would allow the thriving and well-being of all species.

Anne concluded that her struggle needed another focus. Speeches, and marches, and fires, and sabotage, even the occasional bomb, were not the solution and accomplished little.

Worse, they were counterproductive, as they only inflamed public opinion against those like her trying to save the earth. She needed a more effective, more dramatic plan if the forces of technological destruction and human over-population were to be controlled.

***

Raful Shomali had never planned to become a radical or a militant, and he certainly was not a religious fanatic. He had left his native Palestine for the United States as a child, after the Six-Day-War had destroyed his family's home in Gaza and their property had become no-man's land. His parents settled in Chicago, where other Palestinians already resided and where many refugees ended up. His father purchased a small grocery and liquor store and provided quite well for his family. They were Catholic, even if they didn't practice much, especially after their arrival in the States.

Most everyone simply assumed Raful was a Moslem, and he never bothered to confirm or deny it. If American ignorance presumed that all Arabs were Moslem, so be it. In time, even Shomali would identify himself as a Moslem, particularly when he saw how they were portrayed in the media. He knew that public opinion included him, so why fight it?

He earned a master's degree in biochemistry at the University of Illinois, then joined a biotech firm based in Virginia. The company was a repository of viruses and bacteria and a supplier of biological specimens, some genetically altered for pharmaceutical, agricultural, and biochemical research. Shomali became an expert in gene splicing and eventually, in recombinant viruses for vaccine development. He married a Greek-American woman right after college, but the marriage lasted little more than two years, luckily without children.

At a pharmaceutical conference in 1998, he met a fellow biologist, Nur Ahmad, a Johns Hopkins doctoral student. Raful and Nur, a Moslem of Filipino descent, became friends.

Nur had been born shortly after his parents' arrival in the United States. His family was fleeing abject poverty. They had settled in Seattle and, as a youngster, he had tried to fit into the Filipino community there, but he had felt more ostracized by his mostly Catholic compatriots than by non-Filipinos. He had made friends within the Moslem community and by the time he was a teenager, his radical views were well known. When he finished his undergraduate degree at the University of Washington and moved to Baltimore, he had developed a fairly wide circle of friends and acquaintances, many of them in Europe and Asia, who shared his ideas.

Nur Ahmad was passionate about America's policy in the Middle and Far East. He recognized the U.S. military, economic, and scientific superiority and strongly resented it. As a high school student, he had seen the Gulf War as an intrusion in the affairs of Moslem countries, undertaken for the sole purpose of assuring the flow of cheap crude oil and preventing economic hardship in the West. He viewed the continued U.S. military presence in the region as a callous disrespect for Moslems and a desecration of the Islamic faith.

On September 11, 2001, Nur secretly cheered the destruction of the World Trade Center. Later, he privately wished for the defeat of the American forces when they invaded Afghanistan.

"The Americans are just trying to maintain their economic imperialism over poor nations," he vented to Raful.

When the U.S. supplied military support to the Philippine

administration in response to terrorist kidnappings of American tourists, Nur seethed. "Another excuse to subjugate the Filipino Moslem minorities," he fumed.

Nur became more vocal and often shared his views with Moslem friends. He praised the activity of the Filipino guerrillas, like the Moro Islamic Independence Group (MIIGro), and believed that terrorism and guerilla war were the proper ways to challenge the established authority.

"Hit-and-run raids and kidnappings are absolutely legitimate defense mechanisms for oppressed minorities," he told Raful.

"What about the blameless victims caught in the middle? Why do they have to pay?"

"History is full of national heroes and liberators, even Nobel peace prize winners, who resorted to violence to achieve ultimate freedom. Sometimes innocents have to suffer. The end justifies the means."

"Terror shouldn't be the first option. We should exhaust all peaceful alternatives before turning to violence."

"You're naïve, Raful. The only way to get the attention of the established oppressors is by getting them off balance and undermining their comfort level."

Shomali did not share the extremist views, but he did enjoy the lively exchanges with his friend. Nur's excitement was contagious and over time, it began to influence Shomali's thinking. Could American foreign policy, which he had always perceived as well-intentioned, be mere self-serving meddling? Could military action in support of allies be only an arrogant preservation of western capitalism? Still, Raful did not dislike America or Americans. America had been good to him and his parents. He had experienced a much more comfortable life growing up in Chicago than he would have ever had if they had stayed in Gaza.

His hatred was focused on Israel and the British. He didn't remember life in Gaza and wasn't interested in returning to Palestine, but years of listening to his parents had left him with a deep-rooted rancor toward those who had stolen his ancestral land and identity. Raful thought of the Jews in the Middle East as thugs who would kill or enslave an entire population in order to confiscate their land. And he despised the British because he considered them responsible for setting in motion the events that had resulted in the establishment of the State of Israel – in fact, stealing the land from the Palestinians in order to settle a group of ruthless Jews.

***

Raful's emotional confusion following the World Trade Center attack was a revelation to him. He was battling the flu on that day and had stayed home from work. He was sipping his morning coffee with the TV on when the first images of a smoldering WTC tower flashed on the screen. Like most people, he assumed it had been an unfortunate accident, but when a second plane hit the other tower, he knew it had been a deliberate attack.

He stayed glued to the TV all day, stunned by the destruction of two of most significant symbols of American power: the financial district and the Pentagon. As it became clear that the events had been the result of a well-coordinated undertaking, he was not horrified but rather, in awe at the wicked genius and guts of those who had planned it.

He was sorry for the dead and their families, but felt no

deep pain. He watched the news of the event almost as if it were a documentary – it had happened, it had been tragic, great physical structures had been destroyed, a nation's sense of security had been shattered, lots of people were dead or hurting, but although he wanted to feel genuine grief and indignation he experienced only an eerie emotional detachment. Instead, as he understood the planning that had gone into carrying out the attack, he was truly impressed by the patience, the boldness, and the thoroughness of bin Laden's preparation.

The upheaval following the attack mesmerized him. The grounding of the airlines and the collapse of the travel and tourism industry, the sell-off on Wall Street, the fear of workers and security officials at the Empire State Building, the Sears Tower, and other highly visible structures, the emotional response of Americans and many others around the world, were all genuine revelations. Raful was astounded by the pain and helplessness shown by western society and felt a totally unexpected sense of vindication: the U.S. and the western world were now getting a taste of what his family had experienced in Gaza when nobody had given a damn.

I'm spending too much time listening to Nur, he told himself.

When the anthrax scare broke out, Raful watched in disbelief as the world panicked. A bunch of spores sent over the mail by some nut had killed a few unfortunate people, but what chaos it had generated! Government buildings evacuated for weeks, post office centers closed for decontamination, mail carriers wearing gloves and masks, tragic scenarios all over the media. Copycats sending a little baking flour inside a plain envelope could close whole businesses for days. And not just in the U.S. – from London to Sydney, from Tokyo to Buenos Aires, entire police and fire departments were tied up for weeks responding to reports of suspicious letters received by celebrities, politicians, or mere citizens.

Then a question struck him. What if, instead of an amateur, the person who had started the anthrax scare had been smart and patient and had planned the biological attack with the zeal used by bin Laden's team? The thought wouldn't leave his mind, and Raful could visualize the possibilities. Someone knowledgeable and bold, choosing the right agent, the right delivery system, the right time, and the right location, could create worldwide hysteria that would make the WTC destruction look like child's mischief.

Raful spent the rest of 2001 observing the changes in U.S. society. He would often find himself imagining what he, the biochemist, could do if he truly wanted to. He had access to tools that would be more effective than any nightmare anyone could dream of. A nuclear bomb could destroy a city, maybe even render it uninhabitable for a few decades, but so what? Earthquakes and volcanoes did the same, and wars had created anarchy throughout history – after the immediate shock, the world moved on. A chemical weapon could kill or disfigure a large number of people in minutes, but chemicals struck only locally and dissipated quickly, and the long-term effects were irrelevant. But a well-planned biological attack could generate unprecedented panic and affect mankind in a way that only those working in the field could imagine. It could create such chaos that the fabric of society would rip apart and a new dark age would arrive.

He spent hours fantasizing and putting together what-if scenarios. It was a mental exercise that pleased him, but it became an obsession that at times frightened him – he knew it was feasible, and were he a madman, he could actually carry it out.

***

For Raful, the U.S. 'war on terrorism' response was predictable. He heard the war speeches and followed the military activity in Afghanistan without great emotion. It was just the logical sequence in the real-time documentary.

"The American President's rhetoric, this whole patriotic sentiment, it's just an opportunistic way to stop the late-night ridicule and shed the stigma of a controversial election," an agitated Nur Ahmad would tell him. "He's taking advantage of a tragedy for his own personal and political benefit."

Shomali did not buy it completely, but could not discount the argument. With the economy faltering, the chance to redirect the nation's anxiety toward a foreign terrorist group was a godsend for the new administration. He had heard theories from some Islamic groups that the Israelis had actually planned the attack in order to divert attention from their eradication of the Palestinians. But as much as he hated the Jews, he was not ready to give them credit for such a brilliantly carried-out plan. Yes, the Islamic radicals had done it. They had turned the western world upside down and deserved to be proud of it, regardless of the consequences.

Only one thing would make his blood boil: the British Prime Minister's constant posturing as if he ruled the world. Shomali just couldn't take it. The U.S. was the most powerful nation on earth, and if the President or the Secretary of Defense were arrogant, at least they had power on their side. The Israeli military stepping up the killing of innocent Palestinians and destroying entire communities under the pretext of fighting terrorism was something they had done for half a century, so it was no more outrageous than it had ever been.

But the Prime Minister's behavior was something he couldn't stomach. The ruler of a has-been power was acting as the moral authority and the voice of reason on everything from the war on terrorism to the socio-economic deterioration of western African nations to the Israeli-Palestinian conflict. This revolted Shomali. The Prime Minister's constant globetrotting and condescending speeches in foreign countries, including a stop in Gaza, made him sick. His hatred of the British became visceral, the kind of hate one feels, not for a thug, but for the relentless little punk who harasses you because he has the backup of the big bully.

CHAPTER 3

"Raful, can we meet?" Nur's voice on the phone betrayed anxiety.

Raful Shomali was under a lot of pressure at work. A number of unforeseen process problems had forced the rethinking of a major project. Given the deadlines, his schedule had become considerably tighter and he anticipated unusually long workdays ahead.

"Okay, but I don't have a lot of time."

"It won't take long. I can meet you for lunch."

"That's a long ride," Shomali answered.

"It's not that bad, only about 80 miles. I should be able to make it in less than two hours. Can we do it tomorrow?"

"That'll be fine."

"It's settled, then. And by the way, I'm bringing a friend."

"Oh? Anyone I know?"

"No, but a very interesting person. I'll see you tomorrow."

Shomali hung up. Over the last few months, Nur Ahmad had become even more vocal about the U.S. policy on anti-terrorism. He had long suspected that if it wasn't a ploy to disguise problems at home, then it was just an anti-Moslem campaign. The latest threats to overthrow Saddam Hussein convinced him that he had been right all along.

Despite his tight schedule, Shomali was actually happy that Nur had called. He needed to take his mind off work. Besides being overloaded, his long-term career prospects were getting him frustrated. His year-end performance review was an almost exact duplicate of the previous year. It had all the standard words – 'dedicated,' 'competent,' 'valued team player,' 'meeting performance objectives,' 'an asset to the department,' 'excellent work ethic.' But it lacked keywords that he knew were mandatory if he were to ever become a technical supervisor, passwords like 'leadership potential 'and' far exceeding objectives.'

He had been around for a while and was now convinced that he would never become a supervisor, regardless of his performance. At his company, as in many research facilities, there wasn't much of a chance of moving ahead without a PhD. It wasn't a set rule, but it just did not happen in biological research. No matter how good your work or how many patents you were awarded, you were perceived as not competent enough to manage high-visibility scientists or to represent the company at conferences and seminars, toe to toe with university professors and Ivy League PhDs.

Hard work and dedication are getting me nowhere, Shomali thought. He knew he was good. No, he was very good!

The work of a biochemist was not exclusively theoretical, or even mainly theoretical. A lot of it was detailed experimentation, careful analysis, and learning from past work. In the lab, it was also common sense, a lot of intuition, even an art. On that front, nobody was better than he was but unfortunately, that was irrelevant.

Having lunch with Nur would be a good distraction, although wanting to meet in the middle of the week was a bit odd. Shomali assumed that his friend simply wanted to vent off some more steam.

***

It was early February, and Punxsutawney Phil had just predicted another six weeks of winter. But then, Phil was an overgrown rat with a lot of hype. Winter had been quite bearable except for a snowstorm just after Christmas. The sunny day, with temperatures in the mid fifties, already foreshadowed the arrival of spring.

Nur made it from Baltimore in just over two hours, having stopped in Washington to pick up his companion. The traffic around Baltimore and Washington was fairly light, and they arrived at the parking lot of Shomali's employer by 11:45. A few minutes later, he appeared and they shook hands.

"Raful, this is Anne DuBois. Anne, my friend, Raful Shomali."

"It's a pleasure to meet you, Raful," Anne said cordially. "I've heard a lot about you."

"The pleasure is mine," Shomali replied, "but I've heard nothing about you," he added with a smile, guessing that this pretty lady might be Nur's latest romantic interest, even though his friend had never mentioned a girlfriend.

They walked to a nearby Italian restaurant, one of Shomali's favorite eateries, breathing in the crisp air and talking about the weather.

The place, narrow and deep, was almost empty, and they sat at a small corner table next to the only window. Nur looked around. Their table was separated from the rest of the dining area by a large refrigerator filled with a variety of soft drinks.

"As you may have guessed, I didn't drive all the way here just to chitchat," Nur said as a young waitress handed them menus.

"Anything to drink?" she asked.

"We'll just get something from the machine, thanks," Shomali replied.

"We have a proposition for you," Nur said as if he had not been interrupted.

Shomali realized that he had been wrong. Not only did this meeting have a clear purpose, he could see Nur's eagerness to get to the point.

"It must be important," he replied with a smile.

"It is." Nur looked straight at Raful and said, "Anne and I have made a decision that will change our lives. It wasn't a spur of the moment thing. We'll move ahead regardless, but we're hoping you'll join us."

"Join the two of you?" For a second there, Shomali thought that Nur might be talking about marriage, but his friend's serious tone told him otherwise.

"Yes, the two of us and a few others. First, I need to tell you what this is about and find out if you want in. You'd be perfect for our team."

Shomali was getting a bit uncomfortable. Given his friend's

fanaticism, he guessed that any proposal had to be at least borderline extremist. It was not at all clear to him that he would become an active participant in whatever Nur had in mind. However, if this lovely young lady was part of the plan, it couldn't be all that extreme, could it? He was indeed curious to learn what off-the-wall, life-changing plan Nur Ahmad had now conceived.

He got up, went to the refrigerator, and pulled out a Sprite. "What would you like?" he asked before closing the refrigerator door.

"I'll have a Coke," Nur said.

"A Coke is fine," Anne replied.

He grabbed two more cans, sat back at the table, and looked at them with an expression that indicated he was ready to listen.

"Anne is an environmentalist who believes, correctly I may add, that the world is going insane with all the over-population in the poor nations and the pollution and waste in the rich ones," Nur said. "Rather than complain or preach about it like some, or sit back and do nothing like most, she decided that she could do something about it."

Raful now looked at Anne with more curiosity. Obviously, it was not physical attraction that had paired these two, even though they actually made a good-looking couple. Nur was approaching thirty, of median height, trim and fit, with dark skin, sharp features, short black hair, and intense black eyes. Anne appeared to be of about the same age. Thin but not skinny, her dirty blond hair was shoulder length, and brown eyes dominated a long face. Pretty without being a classic beauty, she wore no make-up and didn't need it.

"Anne has been in Washington for a few months now," Nur continued. "She's really dedicated to her cause, and her enthusiasm is contagious. She gave me the push I needed to make my decision."

"We met for the first time only two months ago," Anne interrupted. "A mutual acquaintance introduced us."

She looked at both men with an expression that said here we go. Then she stared straight at Raful, leaned forward, and folded her arms on the table.

"Raful, are you aware of animal studies that show outbreaks of disease when a population goes beyond sustainable levels?"

Her question was so unexpected that he didn't know what to respond. Shomali realized that there was more to this lady than the first impression he had received. He was about to say something, but she didn't wait. "This has been shown with coyotes, deer, mice, and others. It's a beautiful natural defense mechanism to maintain ecological balance. It protects a species from a more painful fate, like death by starvation, and prevents it from interfering with the well-being of others sharing the same ecosystem.

"The problem is," she continued, "the population of one species has been able to explode while managing to escape the natural laws of ecology. That species is now destroying the habitat for all living things on earth." She paused. There was no need to mention what species she was referring to.

"Have you ever seen a satellite picture of the earth showing urban development in the so-called civilized world?" Again she didn't wait for an answer. "I have. Around the big cities it looks like canker on an apple. And it keeps spreading, not just in size around each city, but in the number of cities around the world. It won't take long for this entire planet to rot." Anne maintained eye contact with Shomali.

He didn't know where she was going with this. He knew that, with over six billion people, planet Earth was stressed. He had read somewhere that there were more people living today than all the humans that had died since the appearance of *Homo sapiens*. This had made an impression, even though he didn't know if it was accurate, but he was not concern by human over-population. By many accounts, the average person was doing much better today than ever before. Although not everyone had access to today's healthcare and technology, most people were not worse off now than the average person a century ago when such things simply did not exist.

It was clear, though, that Anne had a more pessimistic view. "The present world mess is a result of western scientific advances. You're supposed to think that progress has benefited every human on the planet. The argument is that enhanced crops are feeding more people and allowing the population of even poor nations to grow and survive. The argument also states that better medicines and new vaccines allow many diseases to be controlled, resulting in a healthier population worldwide. The argument even says that enhanced technologies are making life easier and more enjoyable for everyone." She looked intently into Shomali's eyes. "You know that the argument is total bullshit, don't you?"

"How's that?" Shomali felt like she had been reading his thoughts and was about to contradict them.

"Don't be dumb, Raful," Nur interrupted. "You know very well how it is. It's a self-serving theory for the Americans and the Europeans, maybe even the Japanese. Some believe it because they need a moral justification for their apathy, others use it to maintain the status quo."

The waitress came back to take their orders. When she left, Anne continued. "It is undeniable that better crops and medicines have allowed the populations of third-world countries to explode. But compared to a century ago, do you think there are less people now living in misery? Think again. In the mid 1800s, the great potato famine killed one million Irish over four years. Today, hunger kills the same one million people every six weeks and nobody gives a damn. And today, more people live in abject poverty than the entire population in the early 1800s.

"And how about the benefits of technology? Just consider that one in every two people has never made a single phone call." Anne's brown eyes remained focused on Raful as she smiled sarcastically. "That's twice as many people as the world's population when the telephone was invented."

Shomali still didn't know where these arguments were going, but he couldn't help but smile and to some extent, agree with their logic. Whatever the proposal, it probably had something to do with correcting all the wrongs created in recent years. He looked at his friend.

"Nur, since when did you become a concerned anthropologist? Did you want to meet me to discuss the ills of world population?" he asked with a half smile.

"No, but I want you to understand why I'm doing what I'm doing. We've talked before about the injustices and atrocities levied on the weak by the powerful, but I never thought I could do much about anything. You're gonna think that I'm totally mad, but I've given this a lot of thought and am now convinced that I can do something. Anne and others helped me reach that conclusion."

He paused and shifted in his chair before continuing. "I'm also certain that I'm doing the right thing. Global economies and lifestyles are totally interdependent these days, but the only ones benefiting from the status quo are the rich. They'll have you believe that their scientific advances are making this world a better place for all, but they look at the rest of the world merely as suppliers for their cheap clothes and electronics and consumers for their weapons and fast food." Nur slammed his soda can on the table, spilling the Coke.

Shomali's smile vanished. His friend was not only serious but also angry, angrier than usual. And that could only mean that his proposition would be more radical than Raful had anticipated.

"So what are you gonna do about it?" he asked.

"Help Mother Nature," Anne replied. "We'll speed up the restoration of balance on earth and undo the madness of the last two hundred years."

Nur nodded and added in a low voice, "We can do it without you, but it'll be easier with your help."

"That's a grand objective, but how do you plan to achieve it?"

"Raful, listen to me." Nur leaned forward and looked around to make sure no one was watching them. "Earth's population is growing exponentially, but that's not the main issue. The issue is that as more people are born and survive, more are condemned to live with poverty, and hunger, and war, and disease. You don't have to believe me; just look at the statistics. Those who benefit are the elite few who live in the rich nations. Many of their populations are not even increasing because it's a stupid thing to do when you analyze it. But they need the rest of the world to propagate in order to maintain their economic dominance. In the meantime, they're depleting natural reserves, destroying the world's forests, extinguishing species as never before, polluting the atmosphere, the ground, and the oceans, and slowly turning the apple into a putrid mush, to use Anne's analogy."

The waitress brought their lunch. Nur took a bite of his pizza slice. "Everyone knows this, but no one acknowledges it," he went on. "The west has everything to gain from continuing with the present global status. How else would the large multinationals survive? And there are enough corrupted governments and dictators in the Third World putting their Swiss bank accounts ahead of their people's well-being, so they don't care. The minority, who can do something, isn't interested, and the majority, who would be very interested if they knew how, can't do anything. In the midst of this madness, Islam is being ridiculed and Moslems are being chastised as the black sheep in the global family. It's a pathetic world!"

The religious and ethnic angles were there all along and had to be Nur's primary motivation. Shomali knew it from prior conversations. The environmental argument was Anne's hot potato, but it was also the added justification his friend needed to go over the edge. However, Raful still wondered what they had in mind.

"But where do I fit into this grand plan of yours?" he asked, twirling his fork in his fettuccini.

"You know that I have friends in the Philippines and in

other parts of the world with whom I stay in touch. We often share ideas but mostly, we share frustrations."

Raful was well aware of it.

"About two months ago, a friend visited me accompanied by Anne," Nur continued, "and that's how we met. As a result of that visit, I decided to leave the university and move to the Philippines. An important project is underway, and Anne is part of it. I can and want to help, and we need someone with your knowledge and practical experience. That's why I'm here."

"Wait a minute! Are you asking me to go to the Philippines?"

"Well, yes. I know it sounds crazy, but it's a chance to become part of history and do something really meaningful," Nur replied. "It's not like I'm offering you a job. Think of it as a mission, or a calling. I want to tell you what we're planning and give you an opportunity to consider it. I know you well enough to believe that you'll at least understand why we are taking the risk."

Shomali stopped eating and looked at the two people before him. He was baffled.

"As I said, in early December, Anne and my friend, Shariff Usman, visited me in Baltimore," Nur continued. "He's a university biology professor in the Philippines."

"I met Shariff in Manila about three years ago during a protest against the government' intention to implement a new Philippine development plan sponsored by the International Monetary Fund," Anne interjected. "The government's desire to achieve 'newly industrialized country' status was prompting a sellout to the capitalistic interests. The plan would have resulted in additional deforestation, destruction of pristine habitat and already endangered species, and further subjugation of indigenous populations." Anne paused and took a sip of her Coke. "Shariff is a member of the Filipino Moslem minority, just like Nur's family," she continued. "He's connected to MIIGro and was fighting the imperialistic intrusion of the World Bank to avoid further atrocities to his people. Our paths crossed, and we realized that we had common goals."

"Like me," Nur said, "Shariff wants to level the playing field among world nations to avoid the subjugation of the poor by the rich. Anne wants to reduce human population and restore ecological balance."

"Maintaining the Earth healthy and wild is more important than preserving individual human life," Anne said, nodding. "The only means to achieve these goals is through some cataclysmic event, and we believe we've found a way."

Raful was becoming very uncomfortable, very quickly.

Nur continued, "Last August, just a few weeks before the WTC attack, Shariff traveled to Afghanistan where he met a Russian researcher from the old Soviet biological weapons research labs. The Russian had been able to smuggle out several biological specimens that the Afghans were trying to turn into weapons. Unfortunately, the work conditions weren't the best, and the Afghans were scared of working with the dangerous viruses. As luck would have it, the Russian agreed to move to the Philippines with his specimens just before the American invasion started in Afghanistan."

Nur stopped when he saw the waitress approaching. "Anything else?" she asked.

"Coffee, please," he requested.

"Make it two," Shomali said, dazed.

"Nothing else, thanks," Anne told the waitress.

Shomali now had a pretty good idea where all this was going, why he was being sought, and the purpose of the 'mission'. His daydream was becoming a nightmare. The fantasy he had imagined since the anthrax outbreak was now becoming a ghoulish reality thanks to a bunch of terrorists on the other side of the globe, and his friend wanted him to become part of it. He wanted to pinch himself to make sure this was not a bad dream.

It suddenly dawned on him that he could be in real danger. The two people before him were associates of a terrorist organization and were trying to recruit him. They had met with a foreign national associated with international terrorist groups. What if the FBI had followed Shariff as he entered the U.S.? Nur might be under surveillance right now and he would immediately become a suspect by association. The thought left him white, and a cold chill ran down his spine.

"Are you okay?" Nur asked, seeing the sudden change in Raful's expression.

"Are you out of your mind?" Raful whispered, visibly upset. "You're planning to become a terrorist and without warning, you're trying to recruit me in public. Do you want the Attorney General to parade us all in front of the cameras to make propaganda examples of a radical environmentalist, a Palestinian, and a Filipino?"

"Calm down," Nur told him. He had expected his friend's reaction. "Nobody will recruit you to do anything unless you want to. And there's no better place to meet than in a public setting. We are just friends having lunch. I'm sure no one knows that I'm here or what I'm doing. And aside from you, we haven't told anyone what we shared here today. Actually, Anne was quite concerned about talking with you, but I convinced her that you could be trusted to keep quiet, even if you didn't join us.

"I suppose that many people will call us terrorists," he continued, "but what we're doing is a world war, not terrorism. It's a war to re-establish a balance that was lost generations ago."

"It's a war to save this planet from the plague that we humans have become," Anne added.

"I'm becoming a soldier in that war," Nur continued. "What I propose, because I think you can understand the rationale, is that you, too, become a soldier. You possess skills that can help us win the war. I don't expect anyone will ever call us heroes. With luck, no one will even know that we were the ones who did the world a favor. Hell, we'll probability die in the process. But the goal is noble."

"What you're proposing is to develop and deploy a weapon with the potential to kill many innocent people," Raful replied, twitching in his seat and still upset.

"What I'm proposing is a means to restore some sanity to this world," Nur replied. "There are always casualties in war. Or perhaps I should say 'collateral damage,' as our government puts it when it kills innocent civilians. This will be no different. Yes, there'll be lots of deaths in Manila, and Karachi, and Cairo, but the way I see it, we'll be doing those poor folks a favor – their lives are so miserable that they're almost better off dead."

He stopped, and there was a brief moment when no one spoke. Raful was stunned and at a loss for words. Nur folded his arms on the table, leaned forward, and continued. "As it is, many are already dying from diseases that haven't been eradicated only because they don't affect the rich nations – tuberculosis alone kills six thousand people every day. Malaria kills another three thousand, mostly children. There is a whole host of other infectious diseases that even the World Health Organization calls 'neglected diseases,' but they are all neglected since they affect people the world has forgotten. Another killer bug is not going to make a difference to them. In the west, the story will be different. All the rich bloodsuckers will see their world turned upside down and this time they won't be able to avoid the pain. They're used to seeing their wars on TV, with those suffering staying thousands of miles away. Now we will bring them a war they can't escape."

"Have you stopped to think about the consequences of a bio-attack?" Raful asked, trying to interject some sanity into the arguments. "Once you start, it's not like you can sit at a negotiation table and call a truce. It'll be out of anyone's control, and no one can fathom how it'll end."

"I know, and that's the beauty of it," Nur countered. "Every time a conflict arises, the more powerful nations can either resolve it by force or just get out if public opinion turns against it. Sometimes they'll stop it halfway in order to have an excuse to keep meddling into some poor nation's affairs. The ongoing war on terrorism is a perfect example. There will always be a few courageous individuals who won't merely sit back and take the abuse. They'll fight back the only way they can. They'll strap dynamite around their bodies or hijack a plane, and they'll kill themselves along with a few others on the other side. Nobody can ever stop that. But do you think the Americans want that to end? Of course not."

Nur stopped to catch his breath. He looked around, then

continued. "How else could they justify the U.S. presence everywhere? They're already in Afghanistan and Iraq, they're moving into the Philippines and Somalia, and they're desperate to get into Iran and Syria. They'd love an excuse to rush into most of the other Islamic countries. We need to stop this madness. We need to bring the war to this country, to Washington and to every other city in America and Europe, so that they stay home and mind their own business."

The waitress arrived with their coffees. Nur stopped long enough to allow her to leave.

"I know this plan sounds too radical," he went on, "but a major biological outbreak will happen sooner or later anyway. As Anne said, we're just giving nature a push. There've been outbreaks throughout history, and the conditions today are as good as ever for it to happen again. People are much more mobile and are spreading microbes that otherwise would never leave their habitats. Drug-resistant mutations are becoming more prevalent because of antibiotic misuse. But it's a good bet that an outbreak will happen because someone will unleash it deliberately."

Nur looked into Raful's eyes. "You know better than most that this scenario is more than likely, it's probable. Your own company sells genome databases classified by every conceivable characteristic, from antibiotic resistance to virulence. It's not a question of if, but when. If not me, then someone else will do it. If threatened nations have the capability, they'll use it as soon as the Americans try something stupid. And how long do you think the North Koreans will sit on their bioweapon arsenal while their society disintegrates? Since they're an 'axis of evil,' they may as well prove it."

Shomali sipped his coffee and listened. His thoughts were going in all directions. He had toyed with the idea of a major outbreak, but only as an intellectual exercise, like a couch athlete dreams of winning a medal at the Olympics. He had no intention of acting upon it. But here in front of him was a man who not only dreamed but was also training for the event and working with a team. If he succeeded, the world might soon be dealing with a major tragedy.

"Raful," Anne said, "I know that what we're doing will cause a lot of pain, but the cat is out of the bag – it'll happen eventually, just because it's possible and relatively easy, and because too many people can already do it. One of the things I've learned is that there are other groups working on similar things. In Holland, for instance, there is a team linked to Al-Qaeda, which includes a university professor, working on aerosol transmission of *Yersinia pestis*, the bacterium that caused the plague. In Iran, Russian biologists have been working for years on a secret project. As we speak, Japanese radicals are in Africa trying to collect Ebola samples from the latest outbreak there. Your own company ships viruses and bacteria to anywhere in the world, including genetic information on deadly bugs that can be used by any biologist with half a brain. Some labs will even sell recombinant bacteria already containing altered genes. This won't go away. We're only one of many teams, and if one doesn't succeed, another will."

Shomali kept listening and said nothing. He knew that Anne and Nur were correct in at least one thing: it was very likely that someone would soon free up a nasty pathogen. It was the perfect terrorist tool – it could be deployed anywhere in the world, and the perpetrator would be long gone before anyone noticed. By the time it was discovered, it would cause pandemonium and be almost impossible to trace.

The 2001 anthrax scare was a perfect example. The CDC and the FBI had spent countless hours investigating and still did not know who had done it, where the sample had come from, or even if they were dealing with a single culprit. The experts had learned that they knew little about the spreading and infectious characteristics of the bacillus and knew even less about the psychological behavior of the affected populations.

"I don't expect you to give us an answer right away because I suspect that right now, it would be no," Nur said as he finished his coffee and pushed the cup aside. "I'll give you a few more details and then let you digest all this for a few days."

Nur rested his chin on his hands and kept his eyes on Shomali. "I'm leaving for the Philippines at the end of the month," he continued. "I need a few weeks to prepare, as I probably won't return. I'm joining Shariff and the Russian who are already setting up a lab. The plan is to develop a genetically modified version of a known pathogen and make it resistant to current vaccines. Ideally, we'll also develop a vaccine for the engineered strain, if nothing else to prevent our team from getting infected, but this isn't the major focus. It'll probably take a couple of years, but we'll make history."

"Don't you think you'll get caught?" Raful asked finally. He had been quietly listening to Anne and Nur and felt confused by his own thoughts and emotions. "From what I've been seeing in the news, the President is sending additional forces to the Philippines, and the government there is aggressively going after MIIGro. Eventually, they'll find someone who'll spill the beans."

"MIIGro is already structured so that destroying one piece won't kill the network," Nur replied. "We'll work independently from the rest. Only a few people know about us, and those who do are unaware of our location. Shariff knows what he's doing and has enough funds to last him for a while. The lab will be located far from the present targets. The government and the Americans are going after MIIGro in Basilan, Jolo, and other southern islands, which isn't where we'll be working. We have a great cover, won't be conspicuous, and will be mostly alone. The chances of being discovered are very slim."

The waitress brought the bill and Nur took care of it.

"Raful," he pleaded, "Give it some thought. You can be a real asset to us and become part of something big. And don't be squeamish. You can become a soldier in a holy and just war against those who oppress the weak. Some may call you a terrorist, but do you really care? Do you really believe that those people have the moral high ground and that because they shun what you do, your work is somehow shameful? We're not part of them. We're living a lie. You and I, we're hypocrites taking advantage of the easy life in the West, a lifestyle acquired with the blood and sweat of our brothers in poor nations around the world. By our behavior, we're worse than them and allow them to point at us and say, 'We're not anti-Islam, we're not anti-Arab. Just look how happy they are living among us.'"

They left the restaurant and walked back in silence. In the parking lot, Nur turned to his friend and extended his hand. "Think about it. I'll call you next week. I know this isn't like asking you to join the Boy Scouts, but I believe it's a much nobler calling. I gave you most of the details I can share right now, but call me if you have any questions."

“Or me,” Anne interjected, handing him a small piece of paper bearing a phone number. “I’ll be in Washington for a while.”

“Regardless of your decision, we’ll always be friends. I trust you’ll keep this information to yourself,” Nur said, shaking Raful’s hand again. He turned and walked to his car, followed by Anne. They drove away without waiting for a response.

Raful Shomali stood there watching the car disappear. He hadn’t uttered a word since leaving the restaurant.

CHAPTER 4

Shariff Usman drove his van onto the unpaved driveway on the side of the factory's main building and went past the side entrance. The outside of the building was unassuming. A one-story masonry structure with peeling paint that had once been white, it looked like most other buildings in this industrial area located about twenty miles outside Manila. "Sharusman Manufacturing Company" was painted on a semicircle above the entrance on the street side. Thirty people worked inside. For the most part, they lived away from the industrial park and commuted by bus daily, some from Manila and others from nearby towns.

The van continued on a flat dirt road that led beyond the small parking lot into a wooded area, toward an enclosure some 300 yards away. The place, fenced off with uneven boards and tree branches nailed into wooden posts, could easily pass for a large chicken coop or pigpen when seen from the outside. As the vehicle neared the fence, a gatekeeper appeared and opened a rustic gate. Shariff drove through and parked in an open area to the right of the entrance.

"Good morning," he greeted the young man who was closing the gate.

"Good morning, Doctor," the guard replied. As owner of the company and a university professor, the employees treated Shariff deferentially, which tickled his vanity.

Inside, the compound was certainly not a farmer's yard. A rectangular area approximately seventy by one hundred yards, it held three separate buildings along the back. They were invisible from the driveway because of the enclosure and the abundance of vegetation growing alongside the fence, and because the compound sloped slightly downward toward the rear.

Shariff exited the car and walked across the compound toward the largest of the buildings, designated Building 1, a long but narrow structure on the far left with two single doors and three small windows on the long wall. The cobwebs and accumulated dirt on the glass and windowsills indicated that they had not been opened recently.

Shariff entered a vestibule and closed the door behind him. The vestibule was formed by a floor-to-ceiling transparent plexiglass barrier separating the outer wall from the rest of a large laboratory. It was a narrow hallway about three feet wide and twenty feet long that ended in a closed door on the left and a steep flight of stairs on the right. The stairs were partially obstructed by a coat rack holding strange orange and white clothing. Next to the rack were several shelves holding a variety of plastic gloves and facemasks. A two-by-six-foot opening had been cut into the plexiglass, forming the only access to the lab. A shower head hung from the ceiling just outside the entrance, and a flexible shower hose rested on a hook on the wall. Thick linoleum flooring extended from the vestibule into the lab under the plexiglass partition, and a drainage hole covered with a PVC grille had been cut into the floor, directly below the shower head. Two large plexiglass panels, supported by hinges and folded against the outer wall, could be swung into the hallway on either side of the drain to create an enclosed shower area.

Shariff knocked on the partition to attract the attention of a man sitting in front of a microscope and facing away from the entrance. The scientist looked back, got up, and walked over. He wore a full-body orange suit, rubber boots and gloves, and a transparent plastic helmet. A small battery-operated motor was strapped to his waist, pulling ambient air through a filter and pressurizing it inside the helmet.

"How's it going, Alexander?" Shariff asked, speaking through a slot in the plexiglass fitted with a filter, after pushing aside a hardcover that usually sealed the opening.

Alexander turned the little motor off. The rush of air around his face had not allowed him to hear the voice coming across the opening. He cupped his hand behind his ear to ask Shariff to repeat his question, which he did.

"Not good," Alexander replied. "It'll take us years to come up with anything that works, if we're lucky. We should just go ahead with what we have."

***

Alexander Managadze was not naïve and could appreciate the irony of the situation. The team was trying to develop a vaccine for a new virus, but the real purpose of the work performed over the past eighteen months was not to save people but to kill. That had been the story of his life.

Born in Georgia in the old USSR, he held a degree in microbiology from Tbilisi State University. He had rejected a teaching post at the university to accept a job with Biopreparat, the Soviet weapons program. By the late 1980s, he was a team leader at the famous Vektor lab conducting biological research with a number of nasty viruses, including Marburg Ebola and *Variola major*.

Much of his work involved genetic modification of existing viruses to determine the pathological changes in their behavior. He also assisted in the development of hybrid biological organisms, created by combining genetic portions of different viruses in an effort to achieve single pathogens with multiple virulence traits found separately in nature.

Managadze had always been aware of the purpose of his research. He knew the potentially destructive power of what he was creating and, had he forgotten, he would have been reminded by the death of several technicians due to carelessness on a number of occasions. But he lost little sleep over it. He was part of an important program, relatively well-funded, and closely monitored by the military hierarchy who thought his work crucial to the defense of the country. He had been told that the enemy was doing the same and that they needed to protect themselves. Clearly, they could turn his work into powerful offensive weapons, but they were also developing vaccines against the various bugs and the only way to do so was by developing the virulent organism first.

Then, in the early 1990s, his world crumbled. The Soviet Union fell apart and most of the funding stopped. He and many of his colleagues were still working, but payment was sporadic. The improvements needed to maintain the safety of the research team were not happening for lack of funds. Accidents became more frequent, morale dropped, and many of his colleagues left. And he, Alexander Managadze, a native of the newly independent Republic of Georgia, was trapped in frigid Siberia, doing work that people were now more concerned about than interested in.

He had to get out, and the logical decision was to return to Georgia. However, after contacting former colleagues and friends back in Tbilisi, he came to the painful conclusion that he couldn't find meaningful work back home. Georgia was in no better shape than Russia, all the research and educational funding had been cut to the bone, and many highly-skilled scientists were working at menial jobs or looking for employment in the West. American and European companies had already discovered the wealth of expertise inside their old nemesis, in a variety of technical fields. These experts could be hired for a song, and western firms were actively courting key talent. The pay was low by western standards but huge for Russians.

One afternoon, Managadze was approached by one of his colleagues. "How would you like to leave this place?" Vladimir Ilyenko asked, sitting next to him in the cafeteria.

Managadze knew that there was a reason for the question. He and Vladimir had been colleagues for many years and had never talked except for work-related issues.

"And go where?" Alexander answered.

"Europe, I think."

"You think? You're going away but still don't know where?"

"I have an offer from a recruiting agency in Amsterdam. I don't have all the specifics, but it has the guarantee of decent pay and a signing bonus greater than my combined salary for the last three years."

"Sounds good. Are you going to accept it?"

Vladimir nodded.

"Do they have other positions available?" Alexander asked, a bit envious but also hopeful. The foreign agencies often used internal referrals in their recruiting efforts.

Vladimir nodded again. "They asked me to suggest another scientist and from the job description, it appears that you have all the right qualifications. I'll recommend you if you're interested."

Only after accepting did Alexander learn that, as part of the deal, they needed to find a way to take a biological sample with them. Specifically, the Marburg Ebola virus had been requested. It was a nasty hemorrhagic virus notorious for causing the death of one researcher after a laboratory accident. Alexander was uncomfortable with the idea, but he also knew that others had already left and taken similar samples. Record-keeping and biological security were so lax that only those who actually worked with a product knew what existed, in what quantities, and where. On several occasions, he had already found product missing and had a pretty good idea of where it had gone.

He decided to ignore his scruples and did not object when Vladimir took the Ebola. Worse yet, he found himself retesting *Variola* samples on his last day at Vektor. What the heck? he thought. He would be very careful. No one, not even Vladimir would know about this. Besides, he had no plans for it. I'll end up just burning it, he told himself. The freeze-dried *Variola* virus was merely a souvenir after fourteen years of service and dedication.

The new job turned out not to be in Europe at all. The recruiter was part of a group tied to Al-Qaeda, and the two scientists found themselves in a clandestine military camp in Pakistan. They were given a building and three assistants, but there was no lab that could remotely handle deadly viruses. The scientists requested the minimum lab equipment needed for their work, but it took a long time to arrive. And just when it finally did come, they were forced to evacuate the camp in a hurry, leaving everything behind.

They were taken to a different camp, this time in Afghanistan, which was bigger and designed mostly for military training exercises. Several militant groups, including MIIGro rebels, passed through the camp to study and train, using the tools and techniques of Al-Qaeda. Although the camp included a lab for chemical weapons experimentation, it still did not have the conditions required for biological research, considering the kind of organisms they planned to study.

"I can't do this," Vladimir told Alexander after several frustrating months sitting around and observing young men come and go. "I thought I could, but I can't. These people are terrorists on the run."

"What did you expect?" Managadze responded. "That much was evident when they asked for Ebola."

"I know, but at the time, all I wanted was to get out of Vektor and earn a living. I have been doing some serious thinking lately. I have a wife and a child at home. I need to feed them, but I can't collaborate with people who will kill them indiscriminately."

Alexander was also frustrated but had no family to worry about. He had always focused on his work since leaving Georgia, had never found time for courtship, and somehow didn't miss it. Surprisingly, he enjoyed the changes in the physical environment. Were he not a microbiologist, he might have been an anthropologist, given the pleasure he got from learning about different cultures. He would love to travel if he could afford it. This curiosity had led him from Georgia to Russia and had been a factor in his decision to join Vladimir.

When Vladimir left, Alexander stayed. After all, where would he go? To Georgia? To do what? He had not been there in almost sixteen years. His parents were dead and he had no other close relatives. He didn't know if he would do any real work anytime soon, but he would stick around for now and maybe something might develop.

It was then that the Filipino showed up. Shariff had a plan if he were interested.

For Managadze, the invitation to go to the Philippines was an opportunity to visit a different country. He liked his work as a microbiologist, but it was not scientific curiosity that motivated him anymore. He was now a mercenary, he realized. Not with guns or grenades, but with viruses, and he would work for whoever was willing to pay him. And, like most mercenaries, his conscience did not bother him much. Yes, by helping the groups he was associated with, he would probably help kill some people, maybe a lot of innocent people, but if not him, someone else would. So why worry about it?

And so Managadze found himself an employee of Sharusman Manufacturing Company in Manila.

"This is not bad!" he told Shariff, surprised by the quality of the lab facilities. "You should have seen how they wanted me to work in Pakistan."

Shariff certainly knew what was needed and had the funds to set things up. Through his position at the university, he could procure and purchase the required equipment with some degree of safety. When Alexander first arrived at the compound, most of the equipment had already been delivered and the basic laboratory facilities had been assembled.

Electrical current and a water line had been pulled from the main factory building. A deep septic tank had been built behind the compound and septic connections had been run to all three buildings. In the attic of each building, a vacuum pump had been installed, exhausting through the roof, pulling the air from the building through a hole in the ceiling, and creating a negative-pressure working environment. Also in the attic, a one-hundred-gallon PVC tank had been mounted, and an outlet pipe ran from the tank to a flexible shower handle through the ceiling wall. Fixed shower heads with pull-down chains had been installed and connected to the water lines, and linoleum floors had been laid down in all buildings. Appropriate plexiglass partitions had also been built.

"We still have a lot of work to make the lab operational," Shariff said, "but I couldn't bring in just anybody to do it. It would raise too many questions. We must finish it ourselves."

"It's actually better this way," Managadze replied. "I can set the equipment the way I like it."

In less than two weeks, Alexander and Shariff had assembled a working lab. They set up two double-chamber CO2 incubators and two large biological safety cabinets. They had an autoclave to sterilize lab equipment, a light microscope with high-powered objectives, a clinical centrifuge and a high-speed centrifuge, a speed-vac, several ovens, a liquid nitrogen storage tank, a refrigerator freezer, personal protection equipment, and an array of tools. The PVC tank above the laboratory was filled with a 10% sodium hypochlorite solution, a slightly stronger version of regular household bleach. It was a powerful disinfectant that would kill any virus on contact and would be used for decontaminating tools and protective gear after working in the biological hot space. All seams, cracks, and openings in the laboratory walls were sealed with layers of sticky tape, and high-efficiency particle arrestor (HEPA) filters were installed in the vacuum vents in the ceiling. HEPA filters cleaned the air passing through them by trapping any airborne viruses.

"It would be nice if we had an electron microscope," Managadze said.

"We can use the one at the university," Shariff answered.

"Don't they have a technician in charge of the machine? It's an expensive and complicated piece of equipment and not everyone knows how to use it."

"There's an operator, and I'm in good terms with him. I've often used the electron microscope on my own, after hours."

"Excellent. Do you also know how to prepare the specimens?"

"Of course. Don't worry about testing. Whatever we don't have here, I can get through the biology department. I can also obtain any biological samples or research materials we need."

Alexander looked around when they were finished, clearly pleased.

"Not a class IV biological research lab, but certainly adequate for the purpose," he said.

"We still need to be careful," Shariff reminded him.

***

Shariff had toyed with the idea for some time. He would put it aside, but he would always come back as it always seemed to make sense. Finally, during a New Year's Eve party and after more than a few drinks, he had offered to buy the fledgling company from its founder who was struggling to get it off the ground. Thus Dr. Usman had started the new millennium as the proud owner of Sharusman Manufacturing Company.

Since then, he had reduced his workload in the biology department. Well respected, he had been able to remain on the faculty on a part-time basis while managing his company. The university connection was important as it gave him access to the various biological suppliers without raising suspicion.

He was not a revolutionary, in the sense that he would not pick up a gun and shoot someone, or blow up some military outfit, or sneak a bomb into an embassy. He was afraid of guns, and bombs, and grenades, but he truly believed in the activities of friends who did just that. Many of them had given up comfortable lives to dedicate themselves to MIIGro and its principles. He admired them. They had the guts to fight for the survival of the Moslem way of life in a country increasingly exploited by the economic imperialism of the West and controlled by a Catholic majority that forced its beliefs and morality on the Islamic minority.

But he could still fight, couldn't he? Maybe not in the jungle of some isolated island, but right here in Manila under the establishment's nose. He had a brain and knew how to use it. He had knowledge acquired abroad, but very useful right here at home. He was a biologist and knew of many agents that could be used as weapons. They wouldn't go off with a bang but, without a whisper, they could be much more effective. Some could be bought in the open market with complete detailed genetic information, and he could probably put together an unsophisticated weapon good enough to create some havoc. But he was also very aware of the advances and potential of genetic and biological engineering. He didn't have all the expertise required, but he could perhaps find the right experts to work with.

Shariff had approached a former high-school friend, now a leader with MIIGro, and had explained in general terms what he could do for the cause. He was not surprised by how well his idea was received, but he was amazed when he was handed more than enough cash to put the plan in motion, and more was promised if needed.

He had also been told about Alexander Managadze.

His plan had rapidly moved into high gear. He leased a new location for the factory and brought in a former student to help him revamp the company. They purchased additional manufacturing equipment, set up the new factory, hired a few more workers to replace those lost in the move to the new location, and in three months, the new Sharusman Manufacturing Company was ready for business.

No one knew it, but the isolated compound in the woods was the major reason for moving the factory.

Shariff hired Hector Garcia, a young business graduate, as marketing and sales manager reporting directly to him. Given that profit was not the main objective, the company was able to launch a successful marketing campaign based primarily on aggressive pricing and quickly captured a significant share of the national condom market. Sharusman was a legitimate and outwardly successful firm and Dr. Shariff Usman a successful entrepreneur.

***

Alexander was pleased with the arrangements, including the little apartment set up for him next to the lab. Although he liked to travel, he was somewhat of a recluse when working. Staying at the compound made his time more efficient and allowed him to work the odd hours he preferred. It also minimized the eventual curiosity about the role of this foreigner in the company.

Shariff decided to share his plans with Alexander, who could not be so dumb as to not guess the general purpose of his work. If he had no qualms about what he was doing, he might as well know the details. The whole project would make more sense, and he might even be able to help reshape and refine the plans as they moved forward.

As expected, Alexander showed no surprise, resentment, or moral concerns about the assignment. He accepted it matter-of-factly and asked intelligent questions about the process.

"Have you considered using a different agent?" he asked.

Shariff had planned to use the Marburg Ebola virus. It was the reason the Russian was here – he had immediately applicable experience working with the deadly pathogen and most importantly, he had a sample.

"I thought of many bioagents that can effectively do the job, but once I learned of the work you were doing, it became settled in my mind," Shariff replied. "I'd be hard pressed to find anything more appropriate."

"Smallpox would make a bigger splash," Alexander retorted with a smirk.

"Yes, it would, but the chances of getting that virus are slim to none. It's not like I can call one of the supply houses and get it delivered overnight."

"I've got a specimen," Alexander said, looking at Shariff for a reaction.

"You must be joking!"

"I don't joke about serious matters. I've had it since I left Russia. I used to research the *Variola* virus at Vektor labs and took a sample when I left. I've taken considerable care not to lose it or kill it, and I'm pretty sure it's still viable. You're the first person I've told this because I think it's a better choice for your purpose."

Shariff Usman was speechless. Smallpox, one of the most vicious and deadly diseases ever to afflict humankind, had been eradicated decades ago by a worldwide, concerted effort of identifying and isolating every case until none remained. The only samples of the *Variola* virus in existence were thought to be in research labs in the U.S. and Russia. Rumors abounded that the Russian samples were not as secure as they should be and that some might have been removed, but no such rumors had been confirmed. And now he had one right there, available for his project and brought in by a scientist who had actually studied it and knew the virus better than almost anyone alive.

"I also have useful documentation on its genetic composition and on the behavior of some of the genetic engineered versions we developed in Russia," Alexander added. "I brought it along with my other papers. I think that information will be immediately applicable here if you want to try it."

"Are you kidding? Of course I want to try it," Shariff said when he could finally speak. "It'll make this project quite fascinating and much more effective."

"Well, it's yours. For a price."

Shariff should have guessed. Managadze was a mercenary. Maybe there was some thrill in it for him, but he was there for money, pure and simple.

They agreed on a purchase price on the assumption that the *Variola* virus was still alive.

Alexander went into the lab to awaken the virus and to confirm its viability. Two days later, he summoned Shariff to the laboratory where a slide had been setup under the optical microscope. Shariff could see tiny specs of something on the growth cells, but the magnification was not high enough to make out the features of the viruses multiplying in the sample. He needed to use the electron microscope.

He borrowed some of the fixing resin from the microscope technician at the university. Back in the lab, Alexander zapped a small sample with ultraviolet light to kill the virus without destroying its shape and transferred some of it into a plastic vial. Shariff encapsulated the dead virus by pouring the quick-drying resin over it. He could now transport the specimen safely out of the lab and prepare it for viewing in the electron microscope.

After slicing the hard resin into tiny wafers and mounting one into the appropriate copper holder, he loaded the sample. Shariff worked late in the evening to avoid interfering with the regular work schedule and to avoid questions from the technician or anyone else who might come by.

He fiddled with the adjustments on the electron

microscope for a while. He knew how to use it but didn't have the practical expertise of the technician who worked with it daily. Eventually he got it. The greenish screen showed the typical rectangular bricks of interlocking proteins hiding the virus' genetic material in their center. He stared at it in awe. He had never seen it live, of course, but he knew what to expect. He took a few black-and-white Polaroids, removed the sample, and wiped all tools, holders, and counter with a commercial disinfectant.

Back in the lab, he showed Alexander the pictures.

"What did I tell you? They're alive, trust me," Managadze said with a broad smile.

"They're beautiful under the microscope," Shariff replied. "Tiny hand grenades." It was a good description, physically and figuratively.

"As you know, there are vaccines for smallpox," Alexander said, still examining the photos. "Most people were never vaccinated, and those who were probably didn't get the needed booster shots because the virus is no longer a perceived threat. But the richer nations will quickly identify the outbreak for what it is and have the resources to produce and distribute the vaccine rapidly."

He paused and looked up at Shariff. Then he turned his attention back to the Polaroids and continued, "Those who'll suffer the most are the people already hurting in overcrowded and poor cities like Manila."

"What are you saying?" Shariff asked, puzzled. "First you suggest it, and now you tell me it's not such a good idea. What do you have in mind?"

"There's something we can try, but it'll require more time

and expertise. Of course there's no guarantee that it'll work, but now that I have seen this facility, I think it may be worthwhile."

"What are you suggesting?"

"That we develop a recombinant *Variola* virus. I am convinced we can do it here, and if we are lucky, we can develop an engineered strain as virulent as the original but resistant to the existing vaccines."

"How long will that take?"

"Hard to tell. I think one year, give or take."

Shariff thought about it. It would delay the implementation of the plan, but it was an intriguing idea. They could cause major damage before anyone even knew what to do.

"Do you really think you can do it?"

"With the right help, I believe so. Ideally, in addition to you and me, we would have two or three microbiologists with practical knowledge of virus bioengineering and vaccine development. I assume you want to protect a few people before you let anything loose."

"That's the idea. It makes no sense to die if you don't have to."

It was not exactly the idea. Shariff did not worry about dying. It would be nice to have the vaccine, but it was not mandatory for carrying out the plan. He was a soldier and like any good soldier, he was ready to die for his cause.

"Exactly," Managadze replied, "We'll also need testing subjects."

"You mean people?"

"Of course, I mean people! We need to test the effect of both the virus strains and the vaccine samples. You could use animals for some of it, but there's no way we can avoid testing on people." He looked at Shariff. "Some will probably die, and all will suffer to some extent. Will that bother you?"

Shariff was stunned. God, this Russian, or Georgian, or whatever the hell he is, is actually a cold, ruthless bastard, he thought without letting his expression betray his reaction. This man was certainly the right person for the job but still, it was startling how businesslike he could be with such a subject.

Shariff was not a wimp. After all, the whole thing was his brainchild and the purpose was to cause panic and terror. But the idea of bringing in unsuspecting people, of seeing them, meeting them, feeding them, and then inflicting on them a lot of pain, was not something he contemplated lightly.

"No, it doesn't bother me," he lied. "Let me give it some thought."

Alexander's new virus and his suggestion made the most sense. Even without re-engineering, the introduction of *Variola* back into the population would have global ramifications. But Alexander was also correct in his assessment that those getting the brunt of an outbreak would be the miserable folks in the slums of Calcutta, Karachi, Bangkok, and Manila, while the U.S. and Europe would quickly rush to immunize their people and could have the virus confined in just a few weeks. Developing a vaccine-resistant strain would distribute the pain more evenly.

He needed to locate additional expertise.

CHAPTER 5

The e-mail to Nur Ahmad was answered almost immediately. "What are you doing working at this hour? It must be 3:00 A.M. in Manila."

"I'm glad to hear from you. Yes, it's the middle of the night but it's been an interesting day, and I couldn't sleep. Anyway, I must talk to you," Shariff e-mailed back.

"What's on your mind?"

"I want to meet with you in person. Will you be available next week? I'll be traveling to the U.S., specifically to Washington, and I can visit you in Baltimore."

"Sure. It'll be a pleasure to finally meet you. Just let me know when."

"Okay. I'll e-mail you with more specifics in a few days. Look forward to seeing you. Regards."

This was not something Shariff could do over the phone or via e-mail. It had to be done face to face.

Amazingly, there had been no resistance when he asked for additional funds for his project. His contacts at MIIGro appeared quite pleased with the direction of his plans and perfectly willing to fund them. It was obvious that the chaos in the West after September 11 had created excitement among many militant groups. They now realized what upheaval planning and patience could generate. They had access to money and were willing to use it to support new ideas. Shariff's proposal, while not entirely new, had more potential than most.

The scrutiny at U.S. airports was now much tighter, but Shariff thought he was relatively safe. He was certain that his association with MIIGro was unknown to any intelligence agency. He had traveled to Afghanistan under a false passport, wearing a full beard, spectacles, and a turban, using an alias known only to the militant group, and only two people at MIIGro knew his true identity. He was now traveling to the U.S. as a university professor, clean-shaven and in western clothes, ostensibly to attend a scientific conference. He expected to raise no flags with the INS.

He met first with Anne at a hotel in Washington. Her reaction was just as expected. She was excited and eager to become part of the team and the two drove to Baltimore to meet with Nur.

Shariff was not so sure about him. They had never met personally, although they had often exchanged thoughts. Shariff's concern was that Nur might be sympathetic in principle but not gutsy enough to act on his ideas. And Nur could kill the whole project if he were to blow the whistle.

Still, Shariff had to take the risk since he needed Nur's knowledge and help. He had to convince him to join the project and recruit additional biological expertise. There were few experts willing to give up a comfortable career for a radical cause, so Shariff was coming in person to explain his plan, hoping to give it more credibility. He also hoped that his power of persuasion would play a role. In addition, he was bringing Anne DuBois along, an American partner, to demonstrate that he was not some crazy lone ranger but a member of a wider movement. Clearly there was no guarantee, but knowing what he did about Nur, he was confident that the young man would agree to join him.

He was correct – Nur Ahmad was impressed and excited. He also developed a quick rapport with Anne, and the decision to join the project was made immediately.

Shariff returned to the Philippines while Nur went to work on two fronts. One, to identify an expert able to understand and willing to embrace the cause. And two, to prepare for a life change.

The latter was relatively easy. He owned little to tie him down and rented a small apartment with cheap furniture. Nothing in it had any emotional value, and much of the preparation consisted of gathering information on the *Variola* virus. He needed it to guide the direction of the research ahead of him.

He would not tell his family. They rarely talked anyway. His radical ideas had made him the black sheep of the family and his father had long ago written him off as a lost cause. Even his success in school had not improved their relationship. His sisters, with whom he spoke only sporadically, would eventually realize he was missing but would not be overly worried.

Deciding on the right person to approach was more

difficult. Shomali immediately came to mind, but he was a high risk. Although Raful was a friend and sympathetic to social injustices and political oppression, there was no way of knowing what he would do if he were to become aware of terrorist activity. Yet, Nur knew no one else with his practical experience who could remotely sympathize with the project. If he was going to recruit someone, it had to be Raful.

So Nur stepped up his extremist rhetoric to get a better read on his friend's reaction. He was pleasantly surprised – Raful was actually making unsolicited comments about biological warfare.

"Imagine if that clown actually knew what he was doing," he had said while discussing the panic caused by the anthrax letters. There was also his rancor toward the British. "Why don't you mind your own business instead of insulting us?" he had screamed at the Prime Minister's televised speech in Gaza. And he appeared much more ready to agree with Nur's views than he had in the past. With time, Nur became certain that the Palestinian would not betray him even if he refused to join the team.

He drove to Virginia with Anne to extend an invitation to Raful. Three weeks later, Nur Ahmad had joined Alexander Managadze and Shariff Usman in Manila.

***

For weeks after the meeting, Raful could think of little else. Normally, the heavy workload would keep him in his lab until very late, but nothing was normal about his state of mind lately. He was unable to concentrate on his work and would just leave by mid afternoon and go home. The hell with it, it's not like I am jeopardizing a promotion, he told himself. He would fix a quick dinner, watch TV, and ponder Nur's crazy proposal.

"The whole thing is insane," he would mumble. How could Nur become part of a terrorist group? How could he even consider becoming a killer? How could anyone in his right mind drop everything he had worked for and engage in an activity that would cause only suffering to countless victims?

He would get angry. How did he dare assume that I'm so morally confused as to join his suicide mission? Raful would ask himself. He thought about going to the FBI. He was neither a terrorist nor an assassin, and that was the project's whole purpose: to kill people. He should just blow the whistle on the crazy operation going on in the Philippines and get rid of the nuts planning it. The authorities would search the Johns Hopkins records, go through Nur's e-mail and hard drive with a fine tooth comb, and tie him to Anne and the environmentalist maniacs and to the professor. The FBI might even be able to retrace Shariff's steps over the last several months, find his terrorist contacts, and dismantle another radical group. Case closed.

Or was it? What conversation or e-mail records would the FBI uncover that might incriminate him? He, Raful Shomali, would become a suspect by association. Even if he had done or said nothing that could be considered extreme, the FBI might find past exchanges with Nur where radical ideas and hatred were expressed. He would be interrogated, placed under surveillance, maybe even incarcerated. The Attorney General was on a mission and would not miss an opportunity to make an example. Imagine, a Palestinian nabbed in America for planning terrorism – the Israelis would love it! He would lose his job since no company would tolerate a biochemist performing genetic research if there were the slightest suspicions of a connection with terrorism. As he contemplated this scenario, he became enraged. "Nur really put me in a fucking quandary."

He could not go to the FBI. Besides, what good would it do? He had to agree with Anne and Nur on at least one point – they were not the only ones dreaming of cataclysmic bugs. Rogue nations, organized terrorist groups, religious fanatics, environmental extremists, even lone lunatics were striving to use bioagents to undermine the foundations of society. He had often wondered who was buying all those pathogens sold by his employer and what for. Although his company's customer list was a well-protected secret, he knew that orders were being filled for many germs that should be well guarded. Sooner or later, one of these wackos would succeed.

Because of his internal turmoil, Raful was failing to meet his deadlines at work. His director called him and blasted his recent job performance.

The news on TV also frustrated him. More than that, it made him mad. Apart from the never-ending reports on the fallout of September 11 and the war in Afghanistan, the main topic was the suicide bombers and Israel's retaliation in the Middle East. A segment from British TV showed someone in the House of Commons demanding that the Palestinian leader arrest the bombers. It didn't matter that they were all dead and that the Palestinian government was corralled in a ruined building with all communications cut off and surrounded by Jewish soldiers. The British were again criticizing the Palestinian people for defending themselves in the only way they could. Why didn't they demand that Israel stop building settlements in illegally occupied land? That would stop the suicide bombers!

Maybe it was time for him to stop dreaming about what he

could do, and do something for a change. Nur was offering him the opportunity to build a weapon that maybe, just maybe, would restore some order to a world out of whack. And it was just that – a weapon to fight back, no different from the sophisticated tools in the U.S. and British arsenal. If they could use the most advanced technology to develop ever more complex and deadly weaponry, why couldn't he? Nur was right, he was too squeamish. He was sure that those thousands of workers out in Oklahoma, who made all the smart bombs for the military, lost little sleep when one of their products killed a bunch of innocent civilians in Afghanistan or some other place. To them, it meant nothing but job security – another bomb had to be replaced.

A lab mistake led to another tongue-lashing. "What's wrong with you lately? You'd better shape up if you want to keep this job," he was told. Not only would he never be promoted, his position was now in jeopardy.

He called Anne DuBois.

Two months after the meeting in Virginia, Raful Shomali joined Nur, Alexander, and Shariff at Sharusman Manufacturing.

Anne's role was in the U.S. and she would stay in Washington, at least for a while.

CHAPTER 6

The compound was perfect for their work. On the inside, considerable amount of shrubbery grew all around the fence, and several large trees were scattered throughout the otherwise bare area. The ground was mostly dirt, with uneven gravel paths leading from building to building. Except for the guards and the workers who had built the infrastructure, no one ever approached the area. It was a development lab and a facility to accommodate expanded production when needed, and no one second-guessed its purpose.

The three structures stood along the back of the compound. On the left was Building 1, where the research laboratory was set up and where Alexander and Raful lived. Except for a rare trip to Manila or the countryside, the two men spent all their time in this building. As a precaution, it had been decided that, as foreigners, they should not roam around. When not working, they would sleep, read, or watch the TV hooked to a satellite dish behind the building. Nur, who had rented an apartment less than two miles away, brought in groceries and other necessities.

On the right was Building 3, similar to Building 1 and facing it. One set of double doors and two windows faced the center of the compound. Inside was a large room where packaging and sealing machinery, similar to that on the main factory floor, had already been installed. The equipment was still idle and the building remained unoccupied. Its purpose was ostensibly to fill expected production growth, although the real purpose was far more sinister. There were two additional small rooms to the side of the assembly area, which were empty.

Building 2 stood between the others and at a right angle to both. The main entrance led to a foyer where four doors connected to four separate rooms laid out in an inverted U-shape. Each contained a toilet, a sink, a shower, and a floor drain in one corner. A plastic shower curtain prevented water from splashing into the room but provided little privacy. Each door had an external padlock and a slot through which small items could be delivered into the room without opening the door. A staircase led to the attic where one-way mirrors allowed a peak from above into the individual rooms. All windows were nailed shut with wooden boards and sealed from the inside with sticky tape.

Personal protection was a priority. The four scientists and the three guards that secured the compound around the clock had been vaccinated against smallpox. But, assuming that any of the new strands were resistant to the common vaccine, there was no telling what might happen if they were exposed. They took extreme precautions with body protection, breathing gear, and decontamination of tools and clothing. The guards were just not allowed near any of the buildings.

***

The four scientists made an excellent team, complementing one another well in backgrounds and expertise. Furthermore, the molecular biology techniques were straightforward for researchers with their experience. Although complex, genetic engineering was a routine, well-documented, cut-and-paste process to manipulate the genetic sequence of an organism. Using special enzymes as scissors, scientists could cut a gene from one organism and paste it into a piece of viral DNA. Then, with slightly more elaborate methods but still using commercially available biochemical agents, they could get this modified piece of DNA to replace the corresponding segment in the target virus. It was tedious and skillful work, but someone with patience and the proper training could accomplish it.

Alexander and Nur were responsible for the genetic engineering of *Variola*. Raful concentrated on the isolation, purification, and testing of the various engineered strains. Shariff provided the equipment, tools, and literature research through his access to the university network. He also used his department's biological facilities to conduct key testing of the most promising strains.

The emphasis was on repeating the Australian mousepox experiment. Nur had suggested it and the others had quickly concurred. As reported in trade journals, Australian scientists, in an attempt to control rodent population, had taken mousepox, a relatively benign mouse virus, and inserted a foreign gene into its genetic sequence, hoping that the altered virus would render the infected mice infertile.

Instead, they obtained a virus so infectious and deadly that it killed every exposed mouse. The foreign gene in the mousepox DNA allowed the virus to synthesize interleukin 4 – IL4 – a chemical compound acting as a messenger in the immune system and, therefore, of huge importance in the defense of living organisms against foreign invaders. With the new gene, the virus could bypass the mouse's defenses and became lethal.

"We can do with smallpox what the Australians did with mousepox," Nur explained. "We insert the human IL4 gene in its genetic sequence and see what we get."

"How complicated will that be?" Shariff asked. Of the four, he had the least practical experience.

"It's time-consuming but not difficult," Alexander answered. "I worked with IL4 at Vektor. We inserted the gene in a number of viruses, including *Vaccinia*. We never tried it on *Variola major*, but I expect it won't be very different."

Vaccinia was the virus used in standard smallpox vaccines, and Alexander's experience was directly applicable here. Shariff obtained the required genetic material and lab kits. A number of labs in the U.S. and Europe were ready to supply them, and he easily got what he needed.

Using the proper precautions and following standard processes, they were able to insert the human IL4 gene into various locations in the virus genome sequence. Isolation and purification of the assorted recombinant strains was a monotonous and lengthy task where Shomali's experience and skill made all the difference. Finally, the different strains were tested for stability, replication, survival in a variety of media, resistance to known antiviral drugs, and a host of other characteristics.

The work was moving along smoothly when the U.S. and British forces invaded Iraq. Nur went berserk.

"That's it," he exclaimed. "I don't want to wait any longer. Forget all this work. Let's just release the virus and stop the bullies."

"Patience, my friend," Shariff answered. "If we move before we're ready, they'll win."

"I just can't take it," Nur insisted. "What a bunch of hypocrites! They had decided long ago that they would go after Saddam. Yet, they went through the whole U.N. inspection charade only to gain time to deploy their troops and to spy and weaken the Iraqis. Once they were ready, they simply replaced international law with the law of the jungle – the strongest do whatever they want."

"You're right, but that's another reason why we should stick to our plan," Shariff replied. "They may win this battle, but the war is far from over."

Nur kept seething, but channeled his rage into a renewed dedication to their work. After several months, they had two specimens that appeared particularly stable and resistant in lab tests and mimicked well the Australian mousepox genetic sequence. They were ready to start human testing.

As anticipated, developing a vaccine proved much more complex. After a number of unsuccessful attempts, they decided it couldn't be done within an acceptable timeframe and stopped trying. The events around the world demanded immediate action, and they were almost ready to join the war.

"By the way," Shariff told Nur. "Even in the jungle, long-term survival is not for the strongest, but for the fittest. We'll prove it once again."

***

Preliminary test plans had been elaborated in advance, but agreement was not easy. While Managadze proposed an extensive test program using as many as forty subjects, Shomali and Ahmad were opposed to the use of innocent individuals as guinea pigs.

"Killing a bunch of unsuspecting people to test this virus isn't what I signed up for," Raful stated.

"What do you think will happen when the virus is released into the population? Will it be any different?" Alexander retorted.

He was right, of course. Shomali had joined them out of anger and had not fully considered all the implications of the mission. Intellectually, he knew what would happen, but now reality was setting in and he was struggling with his emotions. Getting to know someone who would very likely die to test their samples was beyond anything he was prepared for.

But what was the alternative? They simply couldn't develop a new bug and let it loose without knowing how it would behave. It would be a recipe for disaster. The last thing they needed was to go through all this trouble and then release a dud. They didn't have the time or the means for elaborate non-human testing, and there was no way of determining pathogenic behavior without testing on real individuals.

Eventually, they agreed on a plan that required a relatively small quantity of test subjects. The objectives were clear – they hoped to have a recombinant *Variola* strain resistant to the existing smallpox vaccine. Ideally, the new version would be at least as contagious, at least as virulent, and with a similar incubation period. If both samples failed, they would simply go ahead with the original *Variola major*.

The lack of a vaccine would not derail their plans, but it would make the logistics much more cumbersome, not to mention risky in a very personal way.

***

The first of the women arrived one night in Shariff's closed van. Recruiting them was awkward because he had never used the services of a prostitute and didn't know how to approach one. But, as it turned out, they approached him, and he had only to drive through the streets where they hung out.

"Hi baby, want to have some fun?" a brunette asked. She was petite, thin, maybe in her early thirties although it was hard to tell with all the make-up and the poor street lighting.

"Hop in," he answered. She opened the passenger door and sat next to him. He took off and she directed him to an area of town where he could park without being disturbed.

"Look, I'm not here to have fun as you put it. I have a proposition for you," he told her as he stopped the van.

She moved closer to him, seductively. "What a shame. You have the perfect car for it. Are you sure you don't want some pussy? Don't I make you horny?" She opened her blouse letting her small breasts hang free as she walked her fingers from his knee toward his crotch.

"I'm sure, and you can stop it," he said sharply, removing her hand.

"Fuck! You're wasting my time. Look, I need to earn a living and don't have time to chat. Take me back," she demanded as she re-buttoned her blouse.

"As I said, I have a proposition and you'll be well compensated if you're interested."

The woman looked at him suspiciously. "What kind of kinky stuff do you want me to do?"

Shariff went into his prepared story. "I'm part of a medical team studying infectious diseases, primarily in your profession. We want to find out what diseases are out there, how many people carry them, and how they propagate. We're recruiting a few women like you and are willing to pay. Are you interested?"

"So what are you, a doctor?"

"No, more like a lab technician," he said, laughing nervously.

"And what do I have to do?"

"Come with me and spend some time in our lab. You'll be tested and monitored for a few weeks."

"A few weeks?" she said, uncertain. "And you're willing to pay me for all the missed income?"

"That's right. You tell me how much and I'll pay. I'll even give you one week in advance."

"And that's all I have to do? Be tested in your lab?" she asked, both curious and doubtful.

"That's about all," he lied. There would be much more to it. There was an excellent chance she would never return if he took her now. "We'll also give you a vaccine or two and keep you for observation to see how you react," he added, trying to clean his conscience by adding the half-truth.

"And you'll pay me the equivalent of what I make in the streets, and I won't have to screw anybody or do any crazy stuff?"

"That's correct. You'll even get three free meals. Unless you actually enjoy what you're doing, it's a great deal."

She didn't answer immediately, just looked at him. He could see that she was tempted by the offer. But there was another detail he needed to check out before deciding to take her.

"Listen," he went on, "this is one of the best offers you'll ever get. Just say yes, and we'll stop at your house to tell your family or friends, and we're on our way."

"Oh, that won't be necessary. I live with three other women, but we all come and go as we please. We don't get alarmed if someone doesn't show up for a while."

That was exactly what he wanted to hear. Even though a missing prostitute was not a high priority with the Manila police, it was wise not to take any unnecessary chances. He had already gotten to this stage with two other women but ended up rejecting them. They would be missed, and he didn't want to run the risk.

They agreed on a figure, and he learned her name.

"Consuelo, can you move into the back of the van?" he said. "I don't want anyone to see me running around with a hooker. They may get the wrong idea."

She did so reluctantly, and they were off. He closed the curtain behind the front seats, leaving Consuelo guessing as to their destination. Forty-five minutes later, he stopped at the compound and led her into one of the rooms in Building 2. A table, a chair, a small TV, and a folding bed had been setup for her.

Another woman arrived the following night and was lodged in the room next to Consuelo's. Dolores was heavier, round-faced, had short legs and knobby knees, and probably relied on her ample bosom to attract clients. Like Consuelo, she was locked in her room from the time she arrived. This led to complaints and a stream of profanities but, at this point, she had no choice but to accept her confinement.

Both women were vaccinated on their first day using the

standard smallpox vaccine. They were provided with a number of magazines to keep them entertained and told to just relax.

One week later, two more women arrived. Juanita looked very young, perhaps less than twenty years old. She was also petite, thin, very dark, and very pretty, probably a runaway. Rosa was tall and looked to be the oldest. She had been a dancer before becoming a stripper in a club and eventually a prostitute. Each occupied one of the vacant rooms in Building 2.

All four women were then injected with experimental virus samples. Consuelo and Juanita received sample labeled VJ while Dolores and Rosa received sample VQ. These were the laboratory labels of the two most promising strains developed. The science was simplistic, but it was the best they could do given their present conditions and the reluctance to use too many human test subjects. They had four scenarios: two different virus strains, each with and without the smallpox vaccine. Each would have a statistical data set of exactly one, but it was better than nothing.

"We don't need statistical models correct to the sixth decimal place," Raful had told his colleagues while discussing the testing sequence. "All we want is some idea of the behavior of the new strains."

The women were then monitored for symptoms, and most contact with them was through the opening in their door. Alexander and Nur were the interfaces. If they needed to enter one of the rooms, they would do so in full protective biological gear. They would then follow thorough decontamination procedures when they left the rooms. Any disposable equipment or tools would be burned.

Raful refused to even see the women.

For the first week after exposure, the women felt normal. They spent their time watching TV, reading, or sleeping. They wanted to leave their room and walk outside, but that was not permitted. They were paid for the week as promised, which pacified them a little – this was steady income without being humiliated, and the food was edible. They could survive being isolated for a few weeks.

On the ninth day, Rosa started complaining of headaches, nausea, and chills. She was given Tylenol and told to relax, and she was monitored carefully. By day eleven, she was crying in pain, had developed a rash, and tiny red spots appeared over most of her body. The spots became blisters filled with pus, which kept spreading over large areas of skin. Within days, she became unable to speak and would only grunt.

Two weeks after exposure to the virus, Rosa was still the only woman showing clear signs of smallpox infection. The other three, who could hear her groans but could not see her, were frightened but remained healthy.

"Looks like VJ is a dud," Alexander said. "I expected to see some symptoms by now."

"It's a limited sample and we don't know the incubation period. Maybe it's still early," Nur replied.

He was correct. By day fifteen, Consuelo developed a low-grade fever, followed the next day by Juanita. They were also nauseated, and Juanita complained of fatigue. On the third day after it appeared, the fever spiked and a rash covered most of their bodies. Very few blisters developed but their skin became purple and painful, and Consuelo began bleeding severely from the rectum, mouth, and nose. She lost her ability to speak, breathing became difficult, her lungs filled with fluid and, six days after the symptoms had begun, she died of asphyxiation.

Juanita wasn't faring much better. Like Consuelo, the rash had turned into dark skin but the mucous tissue around her mouth, eyes, anus, and genitalia were completely raw. There was blood in her stool and urine. Her breathing was forced and with an audible wheezing. The sores around all her body orifices bled profusely. Her eyes appeared filled with blood and she became blind. She died a few hours after Consuelo.

"I need to know what the virus did to the internal organs of these women," Alexander told Nur.

"We don't have a pathologist," Nur answered.

"How difficult can it be to do a post-mortem examination?"

"You're not serious, are you?"

Alexander's unemotional approach to the project had already astounded Raful and Shariff, but now even Nur was surprised.

"The women are dead, aren't they?" Managadze replied. "It's not like I'm going to hurt them, or that they'll object. I can certainly cut them open and take a peak."

Nur didn't argue. They put on their biological gear and went into Consuelo's room carrying a body bag. She was lying on her cot in a contorted position, and her blue shorts and yellow T-shirt were stained with blood. She was already cold and stiff. Her eyes were red and open, and dry blood was smeared all over her virus-mangled face, further distorted by her final death struggle. Alexander got closer and forced her lower jaw to open her mouth. Coagulated blood hid much of the physical damage, but it was quite apparent that the membranes of the nose, mouth, and throat were raw and had been hemorrhaging.

They placed the bag on the linoleum floor and carefully moved Consuelo's body into it, laying her on her back. They zipped it up just enough to cover the face and moved the bag from the floor to the cot in order to make the work easier. Alexander exposed the soft portion of the belly, from chest to pubic area.

He hesitated. He was not sure how to proceed. He tried to remember a movie or a book that would give him a clue but couldn't. What difference does it make, anyway? he thought. He picked up a scalpel, looked at Nur through his facemask and shrugged as if to say, "I don't know what I am doing, but it doesn't matter."

He made an incision starting at the sternum and proceeding along the edge of the rib cage, down to the left hipbone. He made a second incision along the right side. Then he pulled the triangular piece of skin, fat, and muscle and folded it inside out over the pelvis. A sickening odor overcame them despite the protective helmets, and Nur gagged. They cut and examined the main organs in the abdominal cavity. They didn't have to search hard, and they certainly didn't need a pathologist's trained eye. The amount of hemorrhaging was astounding – blood was everywhere. The intestines and stomach appeared to be the worst, but hemorrhagic spots could be seen in the kidneys, liver, spleen, ovaries, and lungs. The virus had overwhelmed the body's defenses, and Consuelo never had a chance.

For the first time, both men were frightened – this was a truly nasty bug. They removed tissue samples for analysis, pulled the belly flap back over the abdominal opening, and sealed the bag.

"Do you still want to autopsy Juanita?" Nur asked before removing his protective clothing.

"No need," Alexandre answered, shaking his head. "Consuelo was vaccinated and that didn't stop the virus. I'm sure Juanita isn't any better."

Meanwhile, Rosa's pus-filled pustules became hard and within a few days they turned into scabs that covered most of her body. Her eyes were still shut because of the wounds, but she was recovering. She never lost consciousness and slowly regained her ability to speak. Eventually the scabs fell off, leaving a profusion of scars.

During the entire time, Dolores was terrified, crying, cursing, and burying her head in the pillow to avoid hearing her neighbors' screams. But she never developed any symptoms, even after five weeks.

This was very good news for the project, almost as good as they could expect. Although the data was not statistically significant, they had learned a lot.

On the one hand, sample VQ appeared to behave very much like the un-engineered *Variola* virus. Dolores, who had received the smallpox vaccine before being exposed, never developed the disease while Rosa, who had not been vaccinated, showed symptoms that were undistinguishable from a standard smallpox infection.

On the other hand, sample VJ proved to be a most pathogenic virus and was clearly resistant to the standard smallpox vaccine – you didn't need more than one example to demonstrate that the vaccine didn't work. Also, the strain appeared to have a long incubation period, over two weeks in both cases, which was ideal for the distribution schedule they envisioned. More importantly, the strain had killed both test subjects.

The two victims were buried in a deep grave in the woods behind the compound, while Dolores and Rosa were paid but kept in their rooms. Understandably, Rosa was very upset after recovering. The scars, especially on her face, rendered her very unattractive and effectively ended her ability to earn a living in her line of work. Her whole skin was pitted after the scabs fell off, and she was suicidal for days after seeing her disfigured face in a mirror.

"I can't release Rosa looking like that," Shariff told the others. "Her appearance will raise questions."

"The last thing we need is someone poking around here," Nur agreed.

"There's something else we can do with them," Raful said. "It's a hunch, but easy to try. It's possible that exposure to one smallpox virus strain will provide immunity against a different strain."

Shariff told the surviving women that they would stay a while longer. Since they had no choice, they had to accept. Alexander exposed the women to the VJ virus strain, and they waited.

Ten days after exposure, Dolores developed aches in her back and joints and a low-grade fever. Her mouth and throat were sore, her eyes and genitals itched, and a red rash appeared on her cheeks and chest. She became hysterical, convinced that she would die or end up hideous like Rosa. She smashed her TV against a wall, banged her head on the door, and refused to eat, all the while cursing the men. They gave her painkillers to minimize the discomfort but after five days all symptoms had vanished. The scientists observed her for another two weeks, and she remained perfectly healthy.

Rosa never developed any symptoms from the VJ virus.

The men were euphoric. It appeared that they had the smallpox virus they wanted: a genetically engineered, highly-virulent biological agent resistant to the only known smallpox vaccine. From a sample of two, it also now appeared that exposure to the VQ virus provided some immunity against the nastier VJ strain. They had, in reality, a two-step vaccine. They did not know what the survival statistics would be, and they were certainly not in a position to develop a simple immunization procedure, but there was a chance that they could protect themselves before the release of the pathogen.

"So, can we try it?" Alexander asked. He knew it would be a huge leap of faith with the limited data they had.

"Yes, but we could end up dead," Raful answered. "I want to see additional data before I expose myself to a lethal bug."

"I agree," Nur added. "It will add several weeks to our schedule, but we need more information before we play Russian roulette with our lives. Shariff, can you get two more girls?"

"Sure, I am becoming an expert at it. A regular pimp."

"It's not like we're going to harm them now if the process works as we think," Nur said. "We may even be saving their lives."

"We should get two men and two women," Raful interjected. "We also want to validate that the virus is sexually transmitted. We can move on to the next phase of our test plan. The results will answer some of the questions."

"How am I going to get the men?" Shariff asked, scratching his head.

"The same way you get the women," Nur replied. "There are plenty of them in the streets of Manila. You don't need to look very hard."

A day later, they had two new women whom they moved into the rooms vacated by Juanita and Consuelo. The rooms had been fully scrubbed and disinfected. Two men arrived shortly after. Rosa and Dolores had been moved to Building 3, and their rooms had been disinfected to house the men. Both were male prostitutes in their late twenties, picked up in the same fashion as the women. All were given the smallpox vaccine, followed by the VQ shot five days later. Some experienced varying degrees of discomfort, but all recovered quickly.

After three weeks, the two women were injected with the VJ strain. Then, one of the men and one of the women were brought together and paid to have unprotected sex during the first week after the women's exposure to VJ. The other pair was paid to do the same during the second week. By the end, both women had begun feeling some of the symptoms of the disease.

The men, who had not been actively exposed to the VJ strain, were monitored very closely. The first started complaining of nausea and back pain thirteen days after the first encounter. The second man never complained.

"It's very interesting," Alexander said. "The virus is being transmitted sexually, even during the incubation period."

"A lot of people are going to be infected before anyone suspects anything," Shariff answered, clearly pleased.

"How do you explain the lack of symptoms by the second guy?" Nur asked.

"Either he wasn't infected or just didn't show it," Alexander answered. "But it doesn't matter. One out of two is good enough." The others agreed.

"By the way, how are your lab tests?" Nur asked Raful.

As they were testing the viruses on the live subjects, Raful was performing detailed stability studies on the VJ strain. Shariff had purchased a number of gels and biological media that, while passing for regular condom lubrication, were expected to preserve the virus alive at room temperature for a minimum of eight weeks, the interval required to package, deliver, and distribute the product.

"Quite well," Raful said. "I've already decided on a couple of lubricants that look very promising. I am now testing them on the condoms to ensure that the lubrication won't affect the integrity of the latex."

"How does it look?" Nur insisted.

"So far so good," Raful answered. "I've now packaged and sealed dozens of condoms in the chosen media, and I've aged them at temperatures between 0 and 45 degrees centigrade. I've also sealed and aged the VJ strain in the same media. As of now, there's no sign of degradation of the condoms, and the virus remains alive."

In the meantime, Alexander had set up a development bioreactor in the lab. The needed virus quantity was much too large for growing in standard cell culture media. The bioreactor was a small unit designed for antibody manufacturing, but adapted for virus production. It was adequate for their needs. Also, the equipment in Building 3 was made operational, and Shariff and Nur, both familiar with the manufacturing process, worked with Rosa and Dolores to complete the production set up and to train them in the use of the equipment.

By the time the last four individuals had completed the vaccine test, Raful reached a decision on the lubricating media.

"What do you think?" he asked Shariff after reviewing the data.

"I agree with you," Shariff replied. "The media does not appear to deteriorate the latex condom, is very similar to regular lubricants in viscosity, wetting, and touch, and preserves well the VJ strain. How long has the aging gone on?

"Six weeks now," Raful answered. "Other samples are still being aged to determine how long the virus will survive."

One more test was needed and, to make room for new subjects, the four latest test individuals, all healthy, were paid and returned to the Manila streets. They had not been mistreated, their symptoms had been mild, the pay and the food had been good, and there was little danger that they would complain about their experiences. They didn't know it, but they were now better prepared than anyone else on the planet to weather the coming upheaval.

Four new prostitutes were brought in, again two men and two women. As before, they were given the *Vaccinia* shot, followed five days later by the VQ virus. After three weeks, they were paired up and asked to have heterosexual intercourse using condoms that had been aged for nine weeks after being sealed with the VJ infected media. Lab tests indicated that the virus was still alive and healthy in the chosen lubricant. Within sixteen days, three of the four subjects demonstrated the mild symptoms now expected after contact with the virus.

"I think we're done," Alexander said. "VJ is clearly transmitted the way we expected."

"And the VQ vaccine provides adequate immunity," Nur added.

"I agree," Shariff answered. "The numbers are not large, but we've had ten people survive exposure to VJ after the VQ vaccine. It's good enough for me." The others nodded.

"So, are we ready for the big leap?" Shariff asked.

"I'm ready for the VQ shot, if that's what you're asking," Alexander replied.

"Not just the VQ," Shariff answered. "For the next two months, we'll be working with the VJ strain. I propose that we expose ourselves now and get it over with."

"Why take the risk?" Alexander asked. "If we take the proper precautions, we don't need to get exposure."

"We have much work to do," Shariff insisted. "We'll be working in production mode, and we may become infected despite the precautions. If we do it now, we can work unencumbered by biological suits and decontamination procedures. It will save us time, and I think the risk is relatively low."

The others accepted the suggestion with a great deal of trepidation. The four scientists, already vaccinated against the standard smallpox, exposed themselves to the VQ strain and later, to the VJ virus, while remaining confined to the compound to avoid infecting anyone on the outside. Shariff and Nur staggered their sessions to maintain the management of the factory and the contact with customers and distributors.

Of the four, only Raful suffered a major reaction. Two weeks after the VJ shot, he developed severe pains, had difficulty breathing, vomited frequently, and became dehydrated. His skin turned red and painful to the touch, and his eyes became blood-shot. He recovered within days, but the experience heightened his anxiety about what they were about to do to millions of unsuspecting people.

CHAPTER 7

Anne DuBois was suddenly very busy. The e-mail from Shariff indicated that they would be ready for the final rollout of *SharusMan*, the company's own brand, in six to eight weeks.

Sharusman Manufacturing Company had started operation in Manila with a generic condom available in three styles – regular, ribbed, and ultra-thin – all non-scented, all with a silicone-based lubricant and reservoir tip, none with spermicide. Hector Garcia had proved to be a dynamic and dedicated employee with a knack for understanding the business and excellent interpersonal skills. In a country with significant opposition to modern methods of contraception, he had been able to develop well-targeted marketing campaigns without offending sensibilities, while maintaining Sharusman's relative anonymity outside of its market.

Pricing was the key to the product appeal. Large profit was not a priority, and Shariff dictated the policy.

"It's a market entry strategy," he told Hector, explaining the aggressive pricing.

Unaware of the cost structure of the company, Hector never raised any questions. Within one year, the company had been number two in condom sales volume in the country. Three months later, it became number one and Sharusman was breaking even.

Six months after the domestic launch, Shariff and Anne had devised a plan to expand internationally.

"The targets are North America, Western Europe, and Japan," Shariff said during one of the many phone conferences between the two.

"How about China, India, or Brazil? These countries have large populations and huge potential markets."

"They also have very low labor costs. Exporting there is a money-losing proposition. We're not trying to turn a big profit, but we also don't have the funds to operate at a large loss."

"How are we going to distribute the final product into those populations?"

"We'll have to think of a different plan."

Anne was the official international director of marketing and sales, and she would manage the European and American operations. Shariff appointed Hector to manage the Japanese market.

Anne had succeeded in placing their condoms with several large retailers in the U.S. and Canada. Sales were picking up but still small, not surprising considering the stiff competition. The same was true in Europe. Though sales remained sluggish, a number of retailers had picked up the product, which was now selling in England, France, Spain, Holland, and Italy and showed slow but steady growth from month to month. Given the low international overhead, Sharusman was covering its international expenses – not exactly a profitable endeavor, and not the kind of operation you wanted if you were in the business of making money. But all they wanted was a presence.

Sharusman had steadily increased monthly output since beginning operation and was now producing in excess of sixty thousand condoms daily to satisfy its domestic and export markets. Production had gone from one to two shifts, then overtime was added to the second shift. It was now operating at near peak capacity, with the factory running in three shifts six days a week. To further increase capacity, expansion would be needed. This was not part of management's plans, as they were nearing their over-all objective. They could, of course, use the equipment in Building 3, but that setup had a very specific purpose that had nothing to do with increasing production.

***

"4LifeSake" had been conceived by Anne after the World Summit on Sustainable Development in South Africa. Although already fully involved with Sharusman, she couldn't stay away from the Summit and had traveled to Johannesburg with several environmentalist friends. There, she participated in a number of demonstrations and loudly proclaimed her shame at being an American because of U.S. opposition to important environmental and population proposals, many of which ended up rejected or watered down due to American pressure.

"I've found a solution," she told Shariff on the phone after returning to the U.S. "I know how to place the condoms in the countries where we don't have business."

"Great! Tell me about it."

"In Johannesburg, I became aware of the huge number of anti-AIDS activists all over the world. I made contact with representatives from several leading groups and a few social marketing agencies. That's when the idea occurred to me. I think it'll work."

"What's your idea?"

"These groups distribute free condoms to teenagers and the poor, and among commercial sex workers and their clients. They depend on support from a variety of organizations, such as UNICEF or the World Bank, and often seek donations from individuals or the private industry."

"And we can be one of their benefactors," Shariff interrupted, already excited. "That's brilliant!"

"I thought you'd like it," she answered, pleased.

"Like it? I love it."

"We can set up a formal plan to donate a portion of our production to these agencies. The gifts will be perceived as social awareness, and I'm sure they'll be well received."

Shariff proceeded to set the plan in motion. With Anne's help, he drafted the "4LifeSake" mission statement, then sent a message to the employees explaining what it was and how it would work. He assigned Hector, who knew nothing of the program's sinister purpose, to work with Anne to implement it.

During the previous year, Sharusman had given away at least ten percent of its production as part of its "4LifeSake" program. The free condoms were donated to social organizations active in HIV/AIDS education and prevention. These groups worked with government agencies and, at times, with the private sector to educate the populations at risk of contracting sexually-transmitted diseases.

Anne put Hector in touch with the Philippine affiliates of a large international agency dedicated to population control and AIDS prevention in a number of countries around the world. They were only too happy to get additional support.

Ironically, in order to supply them, the company had to tighten the manufacturing specifications and increase the number of standard production tests. This was required by the agency to fight the reputation for poor quality of its donated condoms. Sharusman was forced to add tests for size tolerances, hole reduction, tensile strength, burst resistance, lubricant quality, package integrity, and time/temperature aging. It was doubly ironic that these tighter controls made it easier to penetrate the foreign markets by facilitating compliance with ISO and ASTM standards mandated by U.S., European, and Japanese regulations.

Gradually, the "4LifeSake" program absorbed an ever-larger share of the factory's output and was now approaching eighteen percent, at Shariff's insistence. Hector was somewhat surprised at his boss's magnanimity, but he was well paid and did as he was told.

With the increased donations, Shariff requested that the agency distribute his condoms not only in the Philippines but also in other markets where it operated, such as India, China, Indonesia, Brazil, and Mexico. In exchange, he promised even larger contributions and offered to pay shipping costs. Over time, he made direct contact with the agency's representatives in the various countries.

Over a four-month period, ten thousand condoms were delivered from the Philippines to each of twenty-one different countries in Asia, Africa, and Latin America. Shariff handled those deliveries personally. Anne followed up with e-mails and phone calls to each country representative to obtain information on delivery intervals, customs delays, and eventual distribution timeline. The product, delivered by commercial courier, typically reached its destination within three days of the promised delivery date. The in-country logistics varied, but most samples were distributed within ten days of reception.

Concurrently, Anne DuBois developed similar relationships in the U.S. and Europe. She contacted a number of non-government organizations providing HIV education and testing and delivering contraceptives and health care. As usual, Anne explained the company's generosity as part of its social responsibility in the countries where it did business and as a marketing tool to generate name recognition. "Being a good-citizen is good business," she would tell her contacts. She provided all required product test and reliability information, and most organizations were glad to receive and distribute the donated product.

In one year, more than one million condoms were given away in over forty countries. "4LifeSake" was a complete success as reflected by the volume of thank-you messages received from all over the world and the multiple requests for additional donations.

***

Finally, everything was ready for the production of *SharusMan*. Not that there was much to get ready for from the factory perspective. *SharusMan* was identical to the generic condom except for the packaging: new name, new labeling, and new package colors. Otherwise, there was no difference, and the production line was in full swing from day one.

The real changes were taking place at the compound behind the factory. Now that development was completed, most of the equipment had been removed and the lab had been converted into a lubricant preparation and application facility. Dolores, Rosa, and the last four prostitutes had been trained as production workers under Nur's supervision. Everyone was immune to the virus and there was no need for special precautions, other than making sure no one left the compound.

Starting with the fourth week of *SharusMan* production, about one third of all condoms were removed from the factory floor and taken to the compound for foiling. Foiling was the last stage of production. It consisted of thorough lubrication of the latex condoms and the wrapping and sealing of the individual condoms into aluminum-based foil. Because foiling was one of the bottlenecks in the production sequence, this change was perceived by the factory foremen as a way to alleviate capacity constraints and increase production volume.

The process sequence at the compound was identical to the factory process, with two important differences. First, the lubrication used in Building 1 was a biological medium impregnated with the *Variola major* VJ strain. Continuing tests indicated that the virus remained viable ten weeks after packaging. Second, Building 3 was set up with a dipping tank and an extra drying chamber. After sealing, the finished product was immersed in an alcohol-based chemical to kill any virus on the exterior surface of the aluminum foil, and then thoroughly dried. As in the factory, random samples were vacuum tested to verify package integrity.

The finished product was packaged into boxes of twenty-four dozen condoms, and thirty-six boxes were packaged into a carton. It took seven weeks to produce eighty cartons.

The first thirty-three cartons were sent to Anne, fifteen to her office in Washington and eighteen to her London apartment, which also served as the European office. She had prepared all the labels and contacted the various social marketing groups informing them that they could count on another free delivery. She prepared a letter to go with every shipment:

From: Anne DuBois
Intl Director, Marketing & Sales
Sharusman Manufacturing Co.

Dear Friends,

It is with pleasure that Sharusman Manufacturing Company is again providing you gratis over 10,000 of the finest condoms on the market to support your social program. We cannot think of a better way to introduce our new 'SharusMan' brand than to show our commitment to the health of the communities where we operate and to the well-being of those who can most benefit from our product.

'SharusMan' is being produced commercially, and we attach all relevant physical and reliability data. You'll find that the product meets or exceeds all required standards. Please accept this offering as a token of our social responsibility.

Sincerely,

Anne DuBois

Shariff drafted similar letters to go with the cartons still in

Manila. Most were in English, but several were translated into the languages of the countries where they were to be delivered.

Anne prepared a second letter for the retailers already selling their products:

From: Anne DuBois
Intl Director, Marketing & Sales
Sharusman Manufacturing Co.

Dear Customer,

As part of our promotion to introduce our new 'SharusMan' brand, we are making available, free of charge, the attached samples for distribution at your points-of-service. While you obviously decide how POS promotions are run in your business, we suggest that you give away one free sample for every condom purchase at your store, whether your customer buys our product or not.

We are truly excited about the positive reaction our new brand has received in the marketplace and look forward to a long and mutually-beneficial relationship. We are confident that once the users try our new condoms they will want to continue using 'SharusMan.'

If you have any questions, don't hesitate to contact me.

Sincerely,

Anne DuBois
Sharusman Manufacturing Company

Shariff had the letter translated into Japanese under Hector's signature.

"Our presence in Japan is minuscule," Anne commented. "I'm concerned it won't have the impact we want."

"There is no time to worry about market share now," Shariff replied.

"We should at least send a package to one of the social agencies in Tokyo. It will ensure rapid distribution."

"I can do that, but the important thing is to get the eighty cartons out and distributed simultaneously. There's one thing we can't afford at this point – that a few condoms get accidentally opened or used too early. The bulk of the initial distribution must take place within one to two weeks."

He knew that some of the condoms would probably be delayed somewhere or even never distributed, but there would be plenty of samples to produce the desired outcome. To improve the odds, Shariff and Anne devised a careful delivery scheduled based on the distribution data collected from the previous shipments.

"Do you suppose some overzealous customs official will decide to inspect a carton and rip open one of the condoms?" Shariff asked.

"I guess it could happen, but it isn't very likely. It's more probable that some will be stolen," she replied.

"It would be too obvious," Shariff said after thinking about it. "Each destination receives only one carton, and each carton is fully packed. Removing a box will be noticed immediately.

"Well, we just can't account for everything," he continued. "We have at least a week, maybe two, from exposure to the first symptoms, then maybe another week before someone figures out what's happening. It will take a major blunder for the project to fail now."

"So we go ahead as planned," Anne said. "Each agency receives one full carton and each retail store receives one box."

"Correct."

"When can we start?"

"As soon as you're ready."

"I'm ready. I just need to print out a few more letters."

"Let's do it, then. I have Nur to help me. We can get this thing rolling tomorrow." It was mid-morning in Washington, but because of the difference in time zones, it was already late in Manila.

"Okay, D-day is February third. The goods should be delivered in time for Valentine's Day," she joked.

"And you have a ton of Valentine's presents for your compatriots," Shariff replied. Valentine's Day was not something that anyone cared about in the Philippines. Another U.S. invention to sell cards, and candy, and flowers, and crap, he thought. But maybe that would change soon.

Over the next four days, Nur and Shariff loaded boxes into the van and took them to an international courier's office in Manila for shipping. They could have done it all in one day, but the schedule called for a staggered shipment. In the meantime, Anne flew to London to take care of the European deliveries and then returned to the U.S. to complete the task.

The production at the compound was over. Shariff paid the six prostitutes, explained that their services were no longer needed, and returned them to Manila. Rosa, with her badly pitted face and scarred lips and eyes, invited continuous stares. At least she's still alive and doesn't have to worry about what's coming, Shariff told his nagging conscience. Her earnings of the last six months, without any expenses, had been substantially higher than those of the average Filipino worker. She would be okay, even if she could no longer earn a living at her previous profession.

Raful and Alexander cleaned out all vestiges of their activity at the compound. The production equipment was left but thoroughly sanitized to remove any virus contamination.

Alexander received his final payment and decided to go back home. His mercenary income was not huge, but he had managed to save it all, plus the payment for the *Variola* specimen – enough for a comfortable retirement in Georgia.

Raful also decided to go home. He would rent an apartment somewhere in Florida, near a beach, for the rest of the winter, and he would watch the outcome of their work. He was not proud of what he had done, but what could he do about it now? "What's done, is done," he mumbled as he prepared to leave.

Once the shipments were completed, Shariff informed Hector that he was taking a vacation and leaving him in charge. The foremen knew the routine, all he needed was a forecast. And Dr. Usman, who had petitioned the university not to teach during the current semester, left with Nur to join MIIGro friends in the southern Filipino city of Zamboanga.

None of the men said goodbye to the others.

In Washington, Anne DuBois contacted all the agencies and retailers scheduled to receive the packages to get one last status report on deliveries. Reassured that things were working according to plan, she drove to Dulles International Airport and boarded a flight for the first leg of her trip out of the United States.

CHAPTER 8

The temperature had dropped below twenty degrees in Chicago, and the wind was adding meaning to the city's nickname. The Winnebago left the south side shelter and wandered through the frigid streets, its radio blasting a rap tune.

"Anyone out in this cold must be either nuts or desperate," a fuzzy-faced young driver said to his two companions.

"Or both," replied a man sitting in the back. He was tall, in his mid-thirties, with intense brown eyes dominating a face partly covered by a scraggly beard, a sociologist who had been volunteering for this one night a week for several years. On the floor at his feet was a shopping bag full of AIDS/HIV literature, safe-sex brochures, lubricants, and condoms.

"Slow down, Mark," a woman in the passenger seat told

the driver. "Look ahead, in front of that store window on the right. Let's see if they want to come in. Talk to them, Bruce."

The man in the back opened the side window as the car came to a stop next to two women shivering on the sidewalk, one wearing a gray overcoat open to show a miniskirt, the other with a fake fur coat slung over a low-cut blouse.

"You girls want a place to warm-up a bit?" Bruce asked. The miniskirt started to walk away, but the other girl was tempted.

"Come on in," Bruce insisted. "We have hot coffee if you want, and we won't hold you if you don't want to." He opened the side door, and the fur coat came in and sat down. The miniskirt stopped, hesitated for a few seconds, then also stepped in. Bruce poured two cups of coffee, and no one spoke while the shivering women took a sip and warmed their hands on the paper cups.

"Do you gals have a place to stay?" Bruce asked. "You're gonna freeze out there."

"We have to make a living, okay?" the miniskirt answered, sharply.

"Yeah, we have a place to crash a few blocks away. We'll head that way later," the fur coat replied, more politely.

"Do you have any of these?" Bruce asked, pointing to the items in the bag.

"I can use some," the polite girl answered.

Bruce DuBois gave each of them lubricants and a handful of the new condoms they had just received. He also gave them a couple of brochures, insisting that they read them. After a few minutes, the girls left with a coffee refill and a reminder to use protection.

"Let's keep moving, Mark," the woman in the passenger side urged.

Mark McCann drove slowly forward. The tall, skinny young man was a sociology grad student at Northwestern University who, like Bruce, volunteered his time one night a week. The experience was invaluable field research for his master's thesis. He lived off-campus with his girlfriend, Meiling Wong, an international student from Taiwan.

For the next six hours, the three people in the Winnebago roamed the streets looking for other prostitutes, homeless people, and runaways, providing some warmth and hot coffee, offering to take them to the shelter for the night, and distributing condoms and brochures.

A drunken teenager took several condoms and proceeded to rip them open and throw them back into the car.

"Stop it," Bruce yelled. One of the lubricated condoms hit him right on the cheek. He picked the open condoms off the floor, threw them in the wastebasket, then cleaned his fingers and beard with a paper towel.

"I can't wait for next week," he said. "I've had enough of the cold, and this job sometimes gets on my nerves."

"Going somewhere?" Mark asked.

"Brazil," Bruce replied. "A Brazilian friend invited me to the Carnival."

"Wow! I understand it's a blast," Mark replied. "I'm going to New Orleans for Mardi Gras. We can compare stories when we come back."

By the end of their shift, they had taken twenty-two people to the shelter and had given away over three thousand condoms.

Before he left for the night, Mark picked up three of the left-over condoms and stuck them in his pocket.

***

Giulia Cardinali had a good marriage and a wonderful family. Her husband of nine years, Aldo, a systems engineer with a telecommunications company in Rome, was a sensitive and funny man. They had two beautiful daughters they both adored, but Giulia knew that Aldo would love to have a son.

"Why don't we have another child?" she floated the question one evening in bed.

"You've got to be joking!" was his immediate reply.

"No, I'm not. We're still young."

Aldo lifted himself on one elbow and looked at his wife to make sure she was serious.

"And we make beautiful babies," she added jokingly.

"No one in Italy has more than two kids. It's financial suicide," he said as he lay back down.

Giulia didn't press the issue but asked her obstetrician about it on her next visit.

"No, there's no problem from a health perspective," the doctor told her. "You're what, thirty-six years old?" he asked, looking at the birth date on her folder.

She nodded.

"You're on the pill, correct?" She nodded again. "I suggest you stay off the pill for a couple of months if you want to get pregnant. It'll give your body a chance to get back to normal. After that, it's up to you."

Giulia now needed to convince her husband. "Aldo, are you sure you don't want a little boy?"

"Nobody can guarantee it'll be a boy."

"And if it's another girl, is that so bad? I know kids are expensive, but we can afford it, can't we?"

"Our family will think we've lost our marbles."

"We do it for us, not for them, and they'll love the baby once he arrives." She wrapped her arms around his neck and placed a gentle kiss on his lips. Aldo pulled her closer and held on for a while.

That night, Giulia put her birth control pills away without taking one. A few days later, she noticed the contraceptive area in a store window and went inside. She didn't want to get pregnant right away to comply with her doctor's suggestion. When she purchased a small package of condoms, the store clerk added an extra one for free, a different brand that was running a promotion.

That evening, after putting the girls to bed, Giulia slipped on her sexiest negligee while Aldo relaxed in front of the TV.

"Look what I got," she said as she sat on his lap and pulled the condoms from behind her back. They both had a good laugh. They had never used a condom before, as she had always either been on the pill or trying to get pregnant. She kissed her husband, slowly opened his shirt and ran the tip of her tongue down his chest to his navel. She undid his belt, unzipped his pants, and sent her fingers gliding over his inflating bulge.

Their lovemaking had become predictable over the years. They knew each other intimately, what pleased and displeased them, and they enjoyed each other in a way that was physically satisfying and emotionally fulfilling. There was no need to perform. Their sex was traditional, and neither felt the urge to be innovative in bed or follow the tricks and contortions often suggested in movies and on TV.

But Giulia was being innovative tonight, perhaps because the condoms were a novelty. She grabbed the single one, ripped it open, and with a sly smirk, she slowly slipped it down her husband's erected organ. She removed her panties, gently pushed Aldo down on the sofa, and unhurriedly lowered herself onto him.

***

Renato Nascimento drove his motorcycle up Augusta Street, dodging pedestrians, cars, and other motorcyclists. He had an urgent delivery for a guest at a hotel several blocks away. With thousands of other motorcyclists, he played a vital role in the business life of this huge city where cars often moved slower than pedestrians. They delivered packages, letters, and documents all over São Paulo.

It was 7:00 P.M., and the ladies of the night were already lining the street in their high heels, short skirts, and tight see-through tops. As the night advanced, the skirts would move up and the tops would move lower – that was the nature of the business.

Suddenly, there was commotion on the sidewalk. "My purse! Someone please help!" a street woman yelled, frantically pointing at a man running away.

The car traffic was at a standstill, and the pedestrians were just standing by. On impulse, Renato accelerated his bike and sped around the next corner after the thief. Surprised, the man threw the purse into the middle of the street, ran down an alley, and quickly disappeared behind a closing door. Renato stopped, picked up the purse, and turned around to return it to its owner.

"Thank you," she said as she checked the purse, visibly relieved and grateful.

"You owe me one," he said with a smile and a wink.

"That can be arranged," she replied, erasing his smile.

"I don't mind, really," she added, noticing his embarrassment. "You recovered my money and my keys, the least I can do is show my appreciation."

Renato scratched his head, wondering what to do. Not that he was afraid of sex – he had been doing it since he was fourteen – but he didn't need the services of a hooker. Many girls in his neighborhood were so ready and willing that paying for sex was unnecessary. However, she was offering it for free, it would be interesting to find out what a professional could do. And she was not that bad looking: well-shaped legs, round butt, small tits, pretty brown face, just the way he liked a woman.

"I have a delivery to make so I'm in a bit of a rush. But it's just up the street. If I come back in twenty minutes, is the offer still good?"

"Sure, if I'm still here," she answered. "I won't turn down business waiting for you."

"Fair enough." He revved up the motorbike and sped away. When he reached the hotel, he gave the receptionist the package and asked him to sign off for it. He would normally go up to the guest's room to make the delivery himself and get the tip, but today he had a woman waiting, and he was already horny with expectation.

She was still there. "So where do we do this? I don't have a car," he said.

"Come with me."

He followed her down the street and around a corner. He

locked the bike to an iron window bar and went up a flight of dark, narrow stairs into a small room with dirty walls, a washbasin, and a cot. To his surprise, the bed was made and clean.

"You're my first job today," she said, catching his look.

She put her purse down on the bed and teasingly started to strip while rubbing her partially naked body against Renato's. Then she undressed him. Slowly and expertly, she ran her lips and fingers over the sensitive portions of his body, caressing, rubbing, squeezing, biting, and extracting pleasure moans from him.

Renato was fully aroused. She opened her purse and pulled out a condom she had gotten the night before from a health worker. She put the condom on him but he barely noticed. She lay in bed and pulled him over her. As he penetrated her, a rush came over him, and he was done faster than he ever remembered.

***

A leaflet had been delivered door-to-door around the Tokyo arena and inserted in some of the major newspapers. "We apologize in advance for the traffic delays and noise surrounding the arena this evening. We are very sorry for any disruption the concert may cause to those living or working in the area."

The British rock band meant a full house, and Koki Nakamura had been lucky to get four tickets for him and his friends. His parents were not thrilled, but his father remembered how much fun it had been some twenty-five years ago when he had seen that same rock group perform. He relented.

Koki walked the fourteen blocks from his home to the arena. As he got close, the traffic was backed up and people were walking shoulder to shoulder on the sidewalks. The evening was cold and most everyone was bundled in thick jackets, hats, gloves, and scarves. He found his friends at the designated location and walked toward the entrance.

"Condoms, free condoms here," a young man shouted, his face red from the cold.

"Protect yourself from AIDS, use a condom," a young woman yelled standing next to him, while doing her best to avoid being trampled over.

Even though Japan had a relatively low incidence of HIV/AIDS and an almost negligible rate of teen pregnancy, it also had the lowest AIDS awareness among industrialized nations and significant taboos about open sex discussions. AIDS and teen pregnancy were on the rise, prompting a number of civic groups and government agencies to initiate programs aimed at changing attitudes toward sex education and promoting prevention.

Koki accepted a packet from the woman's extended arm and stuffed it into his coat pocket. Later, he threw away the literature and kept the condoms.

Inside the arena, the fans were as loud and rowdy as rock 'n roll fans anywhere. The excitement and noise increased as the band moved on to its more popular songs, and young women charged forward to throw panties, bras, and flowers onto the stage – teenage girls hysterical over sexagenarians who could be their grandparents and sang decades-old tunes.

As the frenzy increased, Koki pulled out one of the condoms, broke the wrapping foil, brought it to his mouth, and proceeded to blow it up like a balloon. He knotted the opening and punched it over the audience. Others joined in hitting the inflated condom from section to section until someone punctured it some forty yards away.

He took another condom, stretched it, and inflated it to an incredible size.

"Go, go, go," the young crowd shouted.

The latex expanded to the applause of those around him who tapped the cylindrical shape until it burst with a bang, scattering bits of condom over faces and clothing.

***

She took another look at herself in the full-length mirror, then took a lipstick from her purse and retouched her lips. As she returned it to the purse, again she noticed the foiled package and smiled. "Just in case things go well," she mumbled.

That's if I still remember how it's done, she thought next.

Sarah Wilson had not been intimate with a man since her husband had suddenly left her for some floozy from his office. She never saw it coming. As far as she was concerned, they were happy together, even talking about starting a family after four years of marriage. And then he was gone. She had been devastated, and it had taken her several years to get her confidence back and be able to go out on a date again.

Making friends had never been easy, maybe because she had always been afraid to get hurt. During her last year in junior high, she had been forced to move out of her home and away from her best friend. She had cried for weeks. Since then, she had never made friends as close as she had been with Anne DuBois. She still had nightmares about men in white protective suits stealing anything that was precious to her.

Her ex-husband had asked her out during her first week at Rutgers, and she never dated anyone else until they married four years later. When he abandoned her, she simply decided that men were scum.

Then she met Todd at a company picnic. They were paired up by chance for some silly game intended to get everyone moving and ended up talking the rest of the afternoon. He was easy to be with, and she found herself enjoying his phone calls. When he asked her out, first for lunch, then for a show, and eventually for dinner, she eagerly accepted.

Todd was not what you would call a hunk. A good six inches shorter than her former husband and some twenty pounds overweight, he had the most charming smile and a demeanor that made her feel comfortable. He never pressured her, even apologizing for taking so much of her time after an unusually long dinner. He never tried so much as to kiss her lips, even though she sensed he wanted to. He would give her a peck on the cheek, and that was that.

I'll have to go to bat if I want to get to first base, she told herself with a smile, thinking how ironic that she had fallen for someone even shyer than her.

While picking up a prescription at her local pharmacy, she passed right by the condom display and a thought stopped her. If anything ever happens, we'll need protection, won't we? She looked around somewhat embarrassed, quickly picked up one with the 'Get one free with a six-pack' promotion, and paid for it without looking at the cashier. Once home, Sarah took the free condom and slipped it into her purse, hiding it under her make-up, wallet, and cell phone, in case someone peeked in.

***

Moshe Sheps was a pimp and an entrepreneur. He ran several brothels in Tel Aviv filled with beautiful women, most of them blond, as was the preference of Palestinians and Israelis alike. It was a very profitable business. Each woman cost him between ten and twenty thousand dollars, but she would earn him that money back in about one month. He now operated five places with a total of forty-nine women.

Elena Alexeevna had been lured from Russia with the promise of making in a month what would take her two years at home. Upon arriving in Israel, she became a virtual slave – her passport was taken away, and she was paraded naked in front of brothel owners and sold to Moshe, the highest bidder. She was housed in an apartment with eight other women and forced to turn ten to fifteen tricks daily for about thirty dollars each. She was allowed to keep only her tips.

After four months of being locked in with the other women, not speaking the language and never being allowed out of the apartment alone, Elena was desperate. She asked for help from one of her customers who spoke some Russian. He was the son of immigrant Russian Jews, but he was also a policeman getting a freebee from Moshe. She was beaten in front of the other women, and her daily quota was increased.

Shimon Salomon was a social worker with a private organization working in the slums of Tel Aviv and Jaffa where a melting pot of misery existed in the midst of sewage and mosquitoes. There, Moroccans, Egyptians, Russians, Arabs of various nationalities, even Jews lived in decaying apartments. Women often drifted into prostitution, and the organization provided education and contraceptives to prevent the spread of AIDS and reduce unwanted pregnancies.

Shimon had a profitable hobby on the side providing Moshe with a number of services. Through his friends in law enforcement, he would learn of women scheduled for deportation, typically after brothel raids. Often, these women preferred the life of a sex slave in Israel to the miserable conditions back home, and Shimon would channel them back to Moshe's business. Or he would find attractive prospects among the desolation of the slums and would "rescue" them for Moshe. Or he would pass along a tip about a scheduled raid, for which he received a substantial payment. More importantly, Moshe would make his ladies available to satisfy Shimon's bizarre sexual desires.

The two men met at a small café near one of Moshe's places. They had been doing business for several years but still needed to be careful, so they arrived separately and sat near the back.

"We've just received something that may interest you," Shimon said after the usual pleasantries.

"Oh?"

"A company is introducing a new line of contraceptives and sent us over ten thousand complimentary condoms to generate name recognition. They expect us to distribute them in the streets for free."

"And if you don't?" Moshe asked, guessing what was coming.

"If we don't, too bad," Shimon laughed. "No one else in the organization knows of this."

"Are you sure?"

"Positive. I've been the only contact with the director of

marketing, and the package was sent to my attention. These are quality products. If you want them, it's an easy deal."

"Sure. Bring them over. You can even try on the new product if you want," Moshe replied with a wink.

"I'll try it on Elena. She's a beauty."

CHAPTER 9

She had not yet come down from the clouds where she had been for the last ten days. Todd had responded just the way she had dreamt it, and she was now going around as if in a fairytale. I'm acting like a teenager, she thought. The emotions were strong, and real, and sweet, and if it were a dream she didn't want to wake up.

Sarah had picked Todd up in front of his apartment, and they had enjoyed dinner at a Mexican restaurant.

"Aren't you going to invite me in for a night cap?" she had asked on the way back, surprising him. He hadn't expected the question, certainly not on a Sunday night.

She had parked and once inside, she had approached him slowly, held his face with her hands, and kissed his lips. Todd had been stunned. She was doing what he had wanted to do for some time but had not found the courage. And this was not just a peck. Softly but forcefully, she had wrapped her arms around his neck, pressed her body against his, and kissed his mouth with lips waiting for a response.

His body had responded as if hit by a thunderbolt. He had led her to the bedroom, their clothes had come off, and it had been after two in the morning when Sarah finally left his apartment.

She had stayed awake until almost dawn, too excited for sleep. Todd was only the second man she had ever been intimate with, and it had been much more fulfilling than she remembered. He was much more sensitive and caring than her former husband had ever been. He seemed to genuinely care about her, her pleasure, her satisfaction, her happiness, her well-being. She was sure now that she loved him.

She decided to call in sick that morning. Her co-workers already knew of her relationship, and she would probably give away the events of the previous night. But a huge bouquet of flowers was delivered to her desk, and she had to tolerate the knowing smiles when she arrived the next day. She decided she didn't care.

The following weekend, they drove to Atlantic City and Todd continued to woo her. They were like two honeymooners exploring each other, and he seemed to worry more about her feelings than himself. She felt loved, and pampered, and special.

Sarah was looking forward to the next weekend with Todd, yet her stomach was queasy by Wednesday evening. "Maybe something I ate," she told him. "Nothing that a good night sleep won't cure."

However, the next day she was running a fever. Not wanting to call in sick again, she got up and went to work. By early afternoon, her supervisor sent her home. It was obvious that she was ill. She called her doctor who prescribed some antibiotics and told her to rest, but she didn't improve. By Friday evening, the pain was overwhelming. She was having difficulty speaking and couldn't keep anything in her stomach.

Instead of driving to New York City for the weekend as planned, Todd took Sarah Wilson to Morris General Hospital in Morristown, New Jersey.

***

I can't wait to get home, Aldo Cardinali thought as he sat in the gate area of Miami International Airport while waiting for a connecting flight to Rome. He hated business trips, and this one had been worse than usual.

He enjoyed leisure travel with his wife and daughters. Since their wedding, they had traveled abroad every year for two weeks and had visited almost every country in Europe. His wife had also accompanied him on business trips to the U.S., Argentina, and Venezuela. It was hard to admit, but he felt a little lost without Giulia. Outside of the work place, he rarely thought of himself separate from his family. First and foremost, he was a husband and a father, and he liked it. Although he had a circle of friends whose company he enjoyed, his best friend was Giulia.

He had been away for an entire week of technical meetings on behalf of his employer's new investment in Chile. He was tired. It had taken nearly a whole day to fly from Rome to Santiago with a stop in Miami, and the entire weekend to recover from the seven-hour time difference, plus he had worked twelve-hour days every day of the week.

"They don't pay me enough for this crap," he told himself. At least he was going home.

Aldo had another two hours to kill. He pulled his laptop from the carrying case, turned it on, and tried to work on a report he needed to deliver on Monday, but he couldn't concentrate. He felt hot and his body ached, and the painkillers he had brought were in his checked luggage.

I am getting a cold, he thought. He gave up on the report, closed the laptop, and went looking for a place where he could buy something to take. He found it, but it was already closed for the night. In broken English, he asked the clerk in the coffee shop where he could buy some Tylenol and was directed to the main terminal. Because he was connecting on an international flight, he was confined to the gate area and couldn't get there.

"I have some," a woman sitting at the counter said as she looked through her purse.

"Thank you so much," Aldo replied, accepting two white tablets. He bought a bottle of water and swallowed the pills.

The plane took off one hour behind schedule. Aldo got only worse as the flight progressed. He tried to sleep but failed to find a comfortable position in his narrow coach seat. A few lucky passengers had empty seats next to them and could stretch out, but Aldo was not so lucky tonight. His entire body ached, he was sweating even though the passengers next to him were wrapping themselves in blankets, and he felt nauseated.

"Honey, you look terrible," Giulia said as she hugged him at the Rome airport on Saturday morning.

"I feel worse than I look, I'm sure," he answered. "I didn't sleep a wink since yesterday morning."

"You can sleep all day if you want," she replied. She took over the luggage cart and headed toward the terminal exit.

But he couldn't rest, even in his own bed. His temperature

was very high and his face was flushed. The pain in his joints was excruciating when he tried to move. Although he had not eaten in almost twenty-four hours, he vomited as soon as he swallowed a spoonful of soup. On Saturday evening, Giulia called their family doctor. He was not available, so she drove Aldo to the emergency room at the hospital.

***

Mark McCann and Meiling Wong were playing hooky from school. They needed a break from the cold and the books, and were flying to New Orleans for Mardi Gras. They would stay with a friend who had already graduated from Northwestern and was now working in Louisiana's largest city.

They had never been to New Orleans and were looking forward to the next four days.

"I'm not showing my boobs to anyone just to get some silly beads," Meiling told Mark as they drove to O'Hare Airport. She had heard about the wild Mardi Gras events in the French Quarter, and how some women exposed their breasts in public to get cheap glass beads from the men.

"You won't have to," he laughed. "Besides, there is nothing for you to show," he added as he jumped to avoid a punch in the face. Good thing she was driving.

She knew, the second she mentioned her boobs, that she had set herself up for a wisecrack from him. They both had an excellent sense of humor and often made fun of each other's shortcomings. Neither got offended because neither meant it. With Meiling, it was her Chinese accent, her small stature, her tiny breasts, or anything Mark could find to pick on. With Mark, it was the fuzz that passed for a beard, his big nose and floppy ears, his bowlegs. They were not a handsome couple, but they could laugh with and at each other and truly enjoyed each other's company.

"New Orleans isn't just Mardi Gras," he said when he stopped laughing. "From what I hear, it's a great city to visit year round. I want to taste the Cajun food, listen to the blues, appreciate the European architecture and what remains of French culture, lose fifty bucks at the casino, and take a paddleboat ride on the Mississippi."

"You can't do all that in four days," she countered.

"Yes, I can. I have it all figured out," he said. "That's if I can get rid of this stupid cold."

For more than a week, Mark had been battling the flu, which was now down to a nasty cough, but it felt like the cold was returning. His body was achy and his stomach unsettled.

"I still don't know if it's a good idea for us to go. What if you get worse again?" she asked.

"I won't. I've taken enough cold remedy and vitamin C to keep a horse healthy for a year. The warm southern weather will help." He didn't add that he would hate to lose the money he had paid for the non-refundable tickets.

But he was wrong. He coughed during the entire flight, and the aches only got worse. The following day, he was running a high fever and could barely talk. Meiling also appeared to have caught the bug from him, and she was shivering.

By late afternoon, their friend drove them to an emergency clinic, hoping that a doctor would prescribe something to salvage their mini-vacation. When the doctor examined Mark, he noticed signs of bleeding in his throat and nose and burst blood vessels around his eyes. He concluded that this was no ordinary cold and made immediate arrangements for Mark to be transported to the hospital.

***

Life for Elena Alexeevna remained unchanged – she would be paraded along with other available girls before prospective customers, would serve whomever was sent her way, would do whatever the customer wanted, no matter how perverted or degrading, and would do it with a smile as if she enjoyed it all, or she would be slapped around by Moshe or his assistants.

Once her shift was over, usually around four or five in the morning, she would lie in the same bed where she had entertained her customers and cry herself to sleep.

Because they were revenue-generating commodities, Moshe took good physical care of his women. Condoms, lubricants, skin-care items, pain-relief medications, and over-the-counter drugs were readily available. All women had routine health checks for VD and HIV, and the latest clean bill of health for each girl was available for clients' inspection, should they request it.

"Well-fed, well-groomed, well-maintained mules, that's what we are," Elena would lament to her colleagues. They agreed, but most were now resigned to their way of life. They worried about what would happen to them once they were no longer desirable, but there wasn't much they could do about it. All they could do was save their tips in a sad attempt to build a meager nest egg.

On a Wednesday morning, Elena woke up feeling sore all over, with a bad headache and an upset stomach. Staying in bed was not an option and would only invite a whipping. She kept popping pain pills into her mouth throughout the day and carried on her assigned duties with clenched teeth and a fake smile. By the end of her shift, the pills were no longer relieving her pain. She went to bed without a complaint, but sleep was impossible.

On Thursday, her fever had risen, she was vomiting and shivering, and it was obvious that she would not be able to work. Her condition worsened over the next two days, with Moshe yelling at her to stop faking it even though it was apparent she wasn't.

After two other women started complaining of pains and aches, Moshe called the doctor who routinely treated them. When he arrived, Elena could not speak and suffered from vaginal and anal bleeding.

"You need to send her to the hospital," the doctor told Moshe. "She's very sick, and I don't have a clue as to what it is."

"This bitch is going to cost me more money. What a lousy acquisition," Moshe yelled.

"That's your business, but she needs immediate medical attention that I can't provide," the doctor answered. "Besides, you have other women with similar symptoms. Everyone will end up sick if you don't get them out of here."

***

Renato was returning to his *favela*, a large slum on a hillside overlooking Ipanema beach. He had left five years earlier after a fight with his father, but he missed his family, his old friends, and the carefree lifestyle that could not be found in São Paulo. He splurged on a plane ticket and was flying home to Rio, just in time for the big event.

"First time to the Carnival?" he asked the man sitting next to him. The man nodded, somewhat awkwardly. "You're in for a good time," Renato added.

"Stay away from the organized parties," he continued.

"They're intended to separate the foreigners and the rich from their money, but they're not genuine."

"What do you suggest?" the man asked in a thick foreign accent.

Renato was a little embarrassed. He had mistaken the man for a Brazilian. The beard and unruly hair hid the pale facial skin, and Renato had not noticed that the nose and hands had not seen much sun lately.

"American?" he asked, guessing the accent.

The man nodded and extended him a hand. "My name is Bruce," he said.

"How did you learn to speak Portuguese?" Renato asked while shaking his hand.

"I came to Brazil several years ago on a trip and ended up staying six months."

"You will have fun." Renato said, speaking more slowly and completely. "I guess Americans like the organized *samba* parades and the events arranged by the hotels. But try one of the street parties. Those are authentic and never stop."

He was correct. Carnival was a major festivity that built excitement over several weeks and culminated in a frenzy during the five days that ended with Fat Tuesday. Some block parties featured the floats and costumes everyone associated with Rio de Janeiro but mostly, they were semi-spontaneous events with drums beating an electrifying rhythm, plenty of drinking, streets teeming with people dancing and singing, and a sexual overcharge that provided an escape from lives of poverty.

"There, that's where I grew up," Renato pointed out the airplane window to a cliff where small, unfinished houses appeared to pile on one another in an effort to cling to the rock. The plane passed unnervingly close to one of the many hills of Rio on its approach to the airport. Beyond Renato's cliff was the mountain where the large statue of Christ stood with extended arms, ready to embrace Rio. Before landing, the plane headed out over the water then veered slowly around as if to show off the beauty of the many beaches, hills, and neighborhoods of the spectacular city.

At the airport, someone was waiting for Bruce, and Renato looked for a bus.

"Oh, my baby!" his mother screamed when she spotted him walking up the hill from the bus stop. His younger brother had been waiting and trailed him carrying his bag.

"It's great to be home. How's dad?" Renato said, trying to recover from his mother's suffocating hug.

"Drunk, as usual," she answered with a shrug. He nodded. It had been one of the reasons he had left home. The lack of opportunities for the poor and uneducated pushed many over the edge, and he did not want to end up a drunk and a loser. São Paulo was not much better, but at least he didn't have to face his father's abuse. He would see him later. Right now, he planned to enjoy the big party.

"I've got a miserable backache," he said. "Must be from that cramped airplane seat. Mom, do you have something I can take?"

"Let me see." She went into the tiny kitchen and returned with two aspirin, which he swallowed with a cup of water.

"I'm going to see Thais," he said as he put the cup down and walked out to find his former girlfriend. By late afternoon, he was already with his old friends. There were parties everywhere tonight, and they were going to attend as many as they could before they got too smashed. There were also lots of women more available and willing than usual. The heat, the music, the drums, the suggestive clothing, the provocative dancing, the touching and grabbing, all created an atmosphere that kept the young men horny all night.

Renato came home after daybreak and went to sleep. When he woke up around noon, he was running a fever and his entire body ached, but he could not give in to the pain, not in the middle of Carnival. He found his mother's aspirin, swallowed four, and went back to town to replicate the previous day.

On Saturday, he could hardly get up. At first, he thought it was an unusually bad hangover – after all, he had not abused his body this much for a long time. His eyes were bloodshot and the pain in his head and muscles was excruciating. When he urinated, he noticed a reddish stream and decided he needed to curtail his sexual activities for the next few days.

By mid afternoon, he was worse. His urine was redder and his nose was bleeding. The skin on his face and chest was painful to the touch, and his eyes were now bloody. The fever had not subsided and he became concerned, mostly because he would be unable to go out tonight and enjoy the party.

On Sunday morning, Renato was in very bad shape. The throbbing in his head was worse than any hangover he had ever experienced. Every orifice in his body was now bleeding and he couldn't speak. He could no longer focus the pain because it was everywhere.

"Wake up, son. We must take your brother to the

hospital." Renato's brother was sound asleep, hung over after another Carnival night, but his mother's alarmed tone quickly cured his headache. He fetched a taxi and took his brother to the hospital.

They waited in the emergency area for several hours, partly because he had no insurance and partly because the doctors on duty were overwhelmed with stabbings and accidents from the night before. It was always like this during Carnival. People drank too much and got into fights, or boyfriends became jealous of their women enjoying themselves and stuck a knife into some poor bastard who had pinched them.

While they were waiting, a bearded man was brought in. He was shivering and vomited shortly after sitting down. Despite the pain, Renato recognized the American from the airplane.

When Renato's turn finally arrived, Dr. Claudia Senna was puzzled. The patient was obviously very sick, but the symptoms were not like anything she had ever seen. She ordered blood and urine tests, started him on antibiotics just in case, and gave him a painkiller shot.

"Come take a look at a young man admitted a while ago," she told her colleague, Dr. Ricardo Teixeira.

"What do you think?" she asked after giving Teixeira time to examine the patient.

He scratched his head. With all the visible blood, there had to be extensive internal hemorrhaging, but he had no clue as to what could be causing it. Senna could see that he was also at a loss.

"Where does he live?"

"His family lives here, but he was in São Paulo until Thursday," she said.

"Whatever is eating at him must have arrived with him."

"I think you're right. According to his family, he was already complaining when he arrived."

When the American was admitted, Dr. Senna was baffled and worried. "Same symptoms," she said. "If this is some contagious bug, it's a nasty one."

"How long have you been in Rio?" she asked Bruce.

"Three days."

"Where are you from?"

"Chicago."

"How long have you been feeling sick?" she asked next.

"Since I arrived."

"Did you come directly from Chicago, or did you stop somewhere?" Teixeira asked.

"I changed planes in São Paulo."

The doctors looked at each other. "Maybe we should find out if anyone in São Paulo has seen anything like this," Dr. Senna said.

CHAPTER 10

"Frank, it's for you," Doreen DuBois said as she came into the living room with the portable phone. She shrugged at his raised eyebrows to indicate she didn't know who was calling.

Because of the TV, Dr. Frank DuBois had not heard the phone. He had spent most of Sunday afternoon in a recliner chair with his feet up and a couple of technical journals on his lap, his attention going back and forth between the papers and the Nets game. The point-guard had just missed his fourth straight shot from the line. "Why can't they learn to shoot free throws?" he asked his wife as if she cared.

"Hello," he said as he took the phone and muted the TV.

"Dr. DuBois, sorry to disturb you at home. This is Dr. Joseph Skarzinski at Morris General Hospital. We have a very sick patient here and we're very concerned. We can use your help."

In addition to his teaching and research at the University of

Medicine and Dentistry of New Jersey, DuBois was an advisor to the New Jersey Department of Health and was affiliated with Morris General in Morristown. He often provided expertise to his colleagues on issues of contagious diseases and microbiology, his field at UMDNJ. Dr. Skarzinski, an internist, routinely relied on his help.

"Can you tell me more?" DuBois asked.

"We have a young woman with severe toxemia, hematemesis, and vaginal bleeding. Apparently it started three or four days ago with aches and nausea, then she developed a fever and has gotten progressively worse."

"Is she conscious?"

"Yes, but in a lot of pain. She can't even talk."

"What about the patient's lifestyle?"

"Nothing unusual that we know of," Skarzinski answered. "Professional woman, steady boyfriend."

"Any traveling or unusual hobbies?"

"She hasn't left the state in several weeks. Nothing stands out."

"There are many reasons for bleeding," DuBois tried to reassure his colleague.

"True, but we're most concerned this may be contagious. The woman's boyfriend has been here with her since she was admitted Friday night and is now complaining of the same symptoms she experienced earlier."

That was information Dr. DuBois did not want to hear. "I'll be there in thirty minutes," he said.

***

Monday morning steadily became very hectic for the hospital administrator at Morris General. First, there was the call from Frank DuBois when she was still in the shower. Then the one from the CDC as she walked into her office. After receiving the message from Dr. Venkatraman, and armed with DuBois's preliminary results, she sprang into action. First, she ordered her staff to ensure that all isolation and protective precautions were being followed, and a note was sent to every physician and emergency response person at the hospital informing them of the potential outbreak. Then she went to the phone.

Most disease reporting was still done by mail, but this was not the kind of reporting that could be delayed. Although she was still waiting for final confirmation of smallpox, she would rather be accused of crying wolf than reproached for not moving fast enough. All relevant local agencies and response organizations were contacted. Calls were placed to the Morris County Health Department, all hospitals in northern New Jersey, the clinical laboratories doing diagnostics testing, the N.J. Department of Health, the local and state police, the Morristown Mayor's office, the N.J. Office of Emergency Management, and the N.J. FBI.

By 11 A.M., UMDNJ reported that all tests done on the specimens submitted the night before continued to support the diagnosis of the *Variola* virus. The New Jersey Governor, informed of the situation and aware of the disaster in the making, immediately took charge. He called the Governors of New York, Delaware, and Pennsylvania to warn them. He engaged the NJOEM to coordinate all control and prevention procedures throughout the state, including medical and law enforcement activity. He also called the CDC Director to request immediate availability of smallpox vaccines for all New Jersey health and emergency response teams, as well as CDC personnel to assist with epidemiological investigation, surveillance, and isolation protocols. Then he rushed to Morristown.

Following September 11, the CDC had revised its guidelines for bioterrorism emergency response, including a detailed *Interim Smallpox Response Plan and Guidelines* document, which spelled out the responsibilities and actions of the state and local public health agencies.

One concern was the limited amount of training and drilling by the different professionals and volunteers – it was difficult to practice for something that had never happened before, and health officials clung to the false hope that renewed security and intelligence efforts would prevent a major episode from taking place. Still, enough people were familiar with the document and understood the required activity.

The emergency response started in earnest. Until proven otherwise, the outbreak was assumed to be smallpox. Given his early role in identifying the disease, Dr. DuBois was asked to work with the NJOEM director to coordinate the effort.

"How many vaccine doses do we need to protect the emergency teams?" the Governor asked.

"At least a quarter million," DuBois answered. "Only a handful of doctors and nurses have been vaccinated, and we need to include all medical and law enforcement personnel."

"Should we mandate the vaccination of the general population?"

"Yes, if the outbreak becomes widespread."

"Can we do it?"

"We can, if we get the vaccine and avoid panic."

"I'll take care of the vaccine," the Governor said. "In the meantime, I want all available isolation facilities in the state at the disposal of the emergency team." These were special rooms with negative air pressure and ultra fine HEPA filters to confine the virus.

"They already are," DuBois replied. "In addition, we've established a quarantine center in Morristown at the General Washington Hotel. Others are on standby in Newark, Jersey City, and Atlantic City, should they be required."

"Let's hope we're over-reacting. Are you getting the support you need?"

"I think so," DuBois answered. "We've identified staffers to manage these centers, and the CDC is dispatching specialized personnel to provide emergency refresher training on breathing apparatus, protective gear, decontamination procedures, and vaccine distribution and delivery."

"How are we informing the public?"

"We're printing guidelines for surveillance, contact identification and tracing, isolation strategies, and general procedures and protocols. All will be distributed as quickly as we can. We've also created a website where all relevant information will be available online."

The Governor nodded.

The emergency team established a command center with connections to all appropriate state and national agencies, major state hospitals, and the quarantine centers. The New Jersey Institute of Technology had developed a state-of-the-art, internet-based Health Alert Network that connected New Jersey's Health Department with over one hundred local health offices. A rapid telefax system was then used to link these local departments with community police, fire, and medical response agencies.

"This network was developed in part with federal money, specifically to provide reliable communications in case of a bioterrorism event," DuBois told the Governor.

"Let's hope it's money well spent," the Governor replied. He then picked up the phone and called David Reiss again to request an allocation of six million vaccine doses from one of the National Pharmaceutical Stockpile storage sites to the N.J. Department of Health. He was not taking any chances. If smallpox were confirmed, he wanted everyone in the state vaccinated.

***

Sarah and Todd were moved into the isolation room at Morris General. Dr. Skarzinski, several health workers, and other patients who had contact with them in the emergency room were the first to move to the quarantine center in Morristown. They were also scheduled to receive the first vaccines.

"Vaccination within three or four days of exposure provides effective protection against smallpox," Dr. Skarzinski explained to those with him.

Next, they needed to retrace Sarah's and Todd's steps over the last few days and identify anyone who might have come into close contact with them, particularly after the onset of symptoms. Sarah was now too sick to help. Todd, in excruciating pain and throwing up blood, had difficulty concentrating but was able to answer questions from police and epidemiologists in full protective gear. The investigators visited their offices, questioned their managers and co-workers, and ordered thirty-two people into the quarantine center.

State epidemiologists started an investigation aimed at identifying the source of the virus. Right now, their only clue was that Sarah and Todd must have been exposed to the virus together, rather than infecting each other.

"A person exposed to smallpox is not infectious until the onset of symptoms," Dr. DuBois explained to them. "Symptoms require at least seven to ten days of incubation. More typically, it's twelve to fifteen days. The patients' symptoms appeared almost simultaneously, there has to be a common source."

With that, the investigators concentrated on the couple's activities and the places they had visited over the previous three weeks. There was the weekend in Atlantic City, but that was too close to the onset of Sarah's symptoms. Nothing else about their whereabouts or behavior raised any red flags.

***

Shortly after noon, news correspondent Cecilia Chapman received a message in New York City. After a number of follow-up phone calls, the young, attractive brunette and her news crew rushed to New Jersey. At Morris General Hospital, it was apparent that the staff was following unusual procedures. Masks were being issued to all patients showing up at the emergency area, people were being interrogated as they arrived, and anyone with unexplained fever or malaise was immediately escorted to a separate waiting room. Cecilia was barred from entering the hospital but, from an unidentified nurse, she was able to gather that a contagious virus might be loose in the state.

By mid-afternoon, a network anchorwoman suddenly appeared on TV screens. "We interrupt our regularly-scheduled afternoon programming to bring you this breaking story from

New Jersey. Cecilia Chapman is standing by at a hospital in Morristown. Cecilia?"

The image shifted. "We have learned of a potentially serious virus outbreak in New Jersey," Cecilia said. "Sources at Morris General Hospital tell us that two seriously ill patients have been moved into isolation, and that a highly contagious and dangerous disease may be spreading through the population. We are told that the New Jersey Governor is here to personally supervise the emergency response. No one from the hospital has agreed to talk to us on camera, and our calls to the New Jersey Health Department have so far remained unanswered, but the activity here is anything but normal."

The camera moved from the reporter to an ambulance arriving. The medics were donning facemasks as they carried a patient into the emergency area – not unusual, but not routine either. "We'll bring you more details as they become available. Now back to you at the studio."

That afternoon, the Governor called a press conference from the General Washington Hotel. Reporters from all major networks and print media were swarming to Morristown on rumors of an outbreak, particularly now that similar news stories were coming in from Rome and Rio de Janeiro. The Governor wanted to avoid sensationalism and provide useful public information instead. He gravely read his prepared statement.

"We have a potentially severe health issue in New Jersey. On Friday night, a woman was admitted to Morris General Hospital with unusual symptoms. She got progressively worse through the weekend and by Sunday, her male companion was exhibiting similar health problems. This morning, the staff at the hospital, with the support of the University of Medicine and Dentistry of New Jersey and the New Jersey Department of Health, concluded that the patients were infected with a dangerous and contagious virus. Even though we're still awaiting final confirmation, we're treating the situation as an outbreak of smallpox, a highly infectious and potentially fatal disease."

The Governor looked at the assembled reporters and continued. "I have declared a state of emergency that primarily impacts the procedures to be followed at health clinics and hospitals throughout the state. It also includes a mandatory quarantine for anyone found to have been in close contact with an infected patient. As we learn more over the next few days, new measures may be implemented.

"All civilians must follow the instructions of the police, fire, and emergency service personnel. Everyone's cooperation will be crucial to avoid a disaster. We ask anyone who develops unexplained fever, aches, nausea, or skin rashes to avoid contact with others and immediately report to the nearest hospital emergency room or call the emergency squad."

The Governor paused and stared straight into the cameras. "It's important for people to stay calm, go on with their regular routines, and follow instructions. There's no reason for panic. We have mobilized all appropriate local, county, and state resources to combat this outbreak and are getting the support of federal health agencies.

"We are making available to the public information that people can use to protect themselves. This information can be obtained at your police and fire stations, schools, most doctors' offices, and via a website that has been set up." He gave the web address and most TV stations flashed it on the screen. "We have people and plans to safeguard your health and that of your friends and family. With your help, we will overcome this challenge," he said in conclusion.

"There are rumors that this is a terrorist act. What do you know about that?" Cecilia Chapman shouted as soon as it looked like the Governor was finished.

He had expected the question.

"Our priority right now is to prevent an epidemic that can have devastating consequences," he answered. "How the smallpox virus got loose, if indeed it is smallpox, is unknown, and I won't speculate. Part of the work ahead is to determine how these people were infected, but the main effort right now is surveillance and confinement of the virus and treatment of the sick. That's what I want everyone to focus on."

The Governor paused and looked around the room. "We must not panic," he said. Then he added with a pointed finger, "And we must refrain from inducing panic. I am specifically requesting your help, ladies and gentlemen of the press." He left the podium to exit the pressroom.

"Is there going to be a massive vaccination effort?" the thin brunette was heard again above the reporters' loud questions.

The Governor decided to answer. "If smallpox is confirmed, all those at risk will be vaccinated. I won't go into details, but the priority will be given to emergency personnel and those in quarantine. We have a plan of action that will work, and I am pleased to see how the various emergency teams, from Red Cross volunteers to federal agencies, are already coming together. However, we can only guess at what's ahead. I say again, let's stay calm, get the pertinent information, and follow proper procedures. If we all act responsibly and with civility, we'll get through this unscathed. Thank you."

***

The Secretary of Homeland Security was due to update the President again in twenty minutes and the news had not gotten any better. There could be no doubt now that this was a concerted terrorist release of a biological weapon. Although various labs around the world were still working to confirm the virus, the analysis already done in New Jersey, Israel, Paris, and Rio de Janeiro, plus the latest reports from New Orleans and Tokyo, were enough to call a worldwide emergency.

This would be Russ Stone's challenge of a lifetime. His department, set up by the President in the aftermath of September 11, still had to be tested. There had been considerable bickering and turf games during the planning phase, but the President had prevailed – the nation could not afford lack of coordination if a major emergency were to arise. Now Stone had to prove that the President's confidence was warranted. Of course, the department's primary mission – to reduce America's vulnerability and prevent terrorist attacks within the U.S. borders – had already failed.

He wasn't going to dwell on that; it was spilled milk. No one honestly expected terrorism never to strike again. The main task at hand was to minimize the damage, contain the bug, and prevent a nightmare. During their earlier meeting, the President had made it clear that Stone would have *carte blanche* to obtain all required resources and synchronize all activity. The President himself would clear any roadblocks, should they appear.

Right now, it was important to get the CDC and FEMA organized and implement the emergency plans they had developed for just such an event. A smallpox outbreak was one of the possibilities they had contemplated and prepared for – at least they didn't have to waste time thinking about how to proceed. They had a known enemy and all they had to do was to mobilize the required resources and implement well-thought-out plans. The big question was the extent of the attack. They now had six occurrences in five different countries. One had to imagine that, given the long lead-time for symptoms and the possibility that some patients might not be immediately recognized, the magnitude of the problem would not be understood for several days.

Meanwhile, David Reiss had ended a two-hour meeting with his staff, going over the mobilization of personnel and readiness status for his agency. He felt that his organization was as ready as it would ever be. According to his notes, all the different teams were prepared:

- The CDC laboratory was already working on the analysis of the specimens received from New Jersey and New Orleans. Three more samples were on their way from Brazil, Japan, and Israel. There was a priority rating on all ongoing projects that would determine the work to be halted in order to accommodate emergency work. The lab team would also perform genetic testing on the virus to determine if any mutation or deliberate re-engineering had taken place.

- The vaccination team was fully engaged. Vaccine deliveries had been authorized and teams had been dispatched to New Jersey, Louisiana, and Illinois. They would provide instruction and assist medical agencies in defining immunization strategy, establishing vaccination locations, and monitoring the administration of the vaccine.

- Another team had been assigned the responsibility for quarantine, surveillance, and contact identification and tracing. This team would assist local agencies in the implementation of protocols for isolation of known cases, surveillance in areas where cases had not yet been detected, and vaccination and monitoring of victim contacts. Several members were already in New Jersey, and others were on their way to New Orleans and Chicago.

- An epidemiological group would work with FBI personnel to identify sources of infection and provide a central coordination point for regional epidemiological efforts.

- Finally, a coordination team was available to serve as a liaison with other federal agencies, identify and provide expertise to local emergency groups, and coordinate the CDC response with the various local and national health authorities.

Venkatraman knocked at Reiss's door to give him an update. As he left, the CDC Director picked up the phone and dialed Russ Stone's emergency line.

"Russ," he said when Stone picked up, "Louisiana and Illinois have now declared a state of emergency. No cases have been detected in Illinois, but given that the infected couple in New Orleans and the American in Rio de Janeiro arrived from Chicago, the Governor is taking no chances and is alerting all local and state agencies."

"You don't think he is over-reacting, do you?" Stone asked.

"Not at all," Reiss replied. "I think we should do it at a national level. I know that all governors and state health departments have already been warned, but we should enforce preventive action everywhere. If this turns out to be widespread, that's the right thing to do. If not, let's think of it as a worthwhile drill."

"Do you think we're really ready for something like smallpox?" Stone was looking for reassurance from someone whose life had been spent chasing nasty microbes.

"I hope so, Russ. We're following existing guidelines, and the local authorities are taking this seriously and getting personally involved. We're prepared here at the CDC."

"Hopefully the public won't panic."

"You're right about that," Reiss said. "And there's something else that has me worried."

"What's that?"

"Every case detected so far appears to be hemorrhagic smallpox, a very virulent form of the disease. It's over ninety percent deadly. Could be that the more common variety has not yet been detected because of its milder symptoms, but either way I'm very concerned."

"Can you elaborate?"

"Well, if this is hemorrhagic smallpox, almost everyone who develops symptoms will die, which will add to the panic. On the other hand, if we're only detecting the most severe cases, then we have a lot of contagious people out there right now infecting a lot of others. Either way, it's bad news."

"You're giving me the kind of information I need for the President," Stone replied. "He wants to go on national TV tonight and has asked for recommendations on what to say and do at a national level. I need your help."

***

The smallpox outbreak was the lead news at all networks by 6 P.M. The Governor of New Jersey had confirmed the early rumors, and the CDC labs had verified that the virus was indeed smallpox. The Governor's press conference was re-broadcast nationally. By then, the press had also confirmed the international cases, and reporters were already camped out in front of a New Orleans hospital after a tip was received at a local TV station.

The reporters were failing to follow the N.J. Governor's request to avoid sensationalistic headlines and comments. Despite the broadcast of useful information on smallpox, most of it prepared by the CDC, each network already had its own medical expert providing commentary and advice, in some cases offering 'what if' scenarios with the limited information available. All networks were already calling it a global act of biological warfare and speculating about the terrorist groups and rogue nations with the capability to do such a thing. Several programs mentioned a number of ways in which a bioweapon could be released, and some were speculating about retaliatory action by the nations affected. Others were scrambling to read the publicly available guidelines from federal agencies, trying to figure out what preventive action the federal government would take in addition to the steps already implemented in New Jersey.

After his meeting with Russ Stone, where they were joined by Paul Fiorelli, Director of the FBI, the President talked on the phone with the Prime Ministers of Japan, Israel, and Italy and the President of Brazil. He also called the Secretary General of the United Nations, who was traveling in the Middle East, and updated him on his discussions with the various world leaders. The President urged him to drop everything and focus on the new threat, as it was probable that other nations would soon discover new cases. The Secretary General had already talked with the World Health Organization's Director and would be traveling to Geneva the following morning. WHO was making an assessment of the resources needed to support member nations and was getting ready to coordinate a worldwide containment response.

The President faced the cameras at 8 P.M. Eastern Time. All networks interrupted their regular programs to carry his message. International news networks were carrying it live all over the world, even though Europe, Africa, and most of Asia were asleep. They would wake up to the rebroadcast, which would run non-stop with additional related information.

The President entered the pressroom with an attitude of authority and confidence. Russ Stone was by his side as he started his address to the nation. As the leader of the most resourceful nation on earth, the President knew that he was also addressing the world.

"My fellow Americans, our nation is again under attack. More precisely, the world is under attack by a virus named *Variola major* that causes smallpox in those infected. At home, we have confirmed cases of the disease in Louisiana and New Jersey. Abroad, the outbreak has been detected in Japan, Italy, Israel, and Brazil.

"Our information indicates that this could not have been accidental. We are dealing with a deliberate, coordinated, and global terrorist activity. We still don't know who masterminded this despicable act, but we'll track down the cowards who did it.

"Meanwhile, our priority is to control the virus and minimize any damage to our economies and societies. All local police, fire, and medical emergency response teams are being mobilized nationwide, and in some cases they are already deployed. They are the first line of defense. The coordination of the domestic response will be the responsibility of Homeland Security."

The President looked over to the department's secretary and proceeded. "Russ Stone has my complete support to mobilize whatever resources are necessary and to implement whatever emergency measures will be required to contain the disease, minimize casualties, and maintain order. The FBI, the CDC, Health and Human Services, the Department of Defense, FEMA, and all required federal resources will be coordinated through his department."

The President paused to clear his throat. The reporters scribbled furiously on their notepads. "Starting immediately, all air travel passengers will be checked for symptoms of the disease and won't be allowed to board if any are detected. Airport security will work with health authorities to implement screening procedures. Also, all inbound flights from countries where the virus has been detected will be stopped until we have a better understanding of the situation. Obviously, we are ready to reciprocate with any country that requests it. In addition, by executive order, we're making it a criminal offense for anyone with obvious symptoms to cross state lines or deliberately come into physical contact with others, including family members. It is also a criminal offense for anyone to refuse isolation or quarantine when health officials deem it necessary. Finally, I'm mobilizing the National Guard to assist local law enforcement in carrying out these orders. Other measures will be implemented as appropriate."

The President paused again, and lowered his voice. "My fellow Americans, make no mistake. The current outbreak has the potential to create havoc and devastation if we let it. My urgent message to you this evening is threefold.

"First, stay calm. Hysteria can't affect our thinking or our behavior, or interfere with the duties of emergency personnel.

"Second, be informed. Information on the virus, its symptoms, and its spreading mechanism will be available nationwide. Find out how to prevent infection and what to do if you or anyone around you becomes symptomatic. Containment is the number one job ahead of us.

"Third, follow instructions. Your local, state, and federal emergency response teams are already in place where the virus has been confirmed. We have trained personnel to implement the procedures developed for this kind of emergency. With your help, we will win this battle.

"God bless the United States of America."

"Mr. President, how widespread do you think this outbreak is?" a reporter shouted.

"I don't have an answer for you at this time. The experts tell me that the victims already identified must have been exposed to the virus approximately two weeks ago. But we have no idea as to what the delivery agent might have been, or how many more people may have been exposed. We have epidemiologists from the CDC and health agencies monitoring the situation. They'll try to answer some of those questions."

"Do you think Al-Qaeda is behind this?" another reporter yelled.

The President did not hide his annoyance. "As I said, we don't know at this point, and it isn't our main concern. Containment is our priority." He pointed to a raised hand.

"Mr. President, we obviously have an international incident and need to pay attention to how other nations respond to the outbreak." The statement was from a senior White House reporter from one of the networks. "How are we going to ensure that inactivity, or lack of expertise and resources elsewhere in the world, won't defeat what we do at home?"

"It's one of the key issues we are tackling," the President replied, squinting at the reporters. "I have already contacted several world leaders, and our federal teams are working closely with the World Health Organization and foreign labs and agencies to ensure a concerted global effort. The air travel restriction I announced is one defensive measure. Others will be put into effect as required, but helping other countries help themselves and cooperation with global organizations is the best policy." He pointed to a female reporter for the next question.

"Mr. President, how do you think the stock market will react tomorrow morning?"

The markets had closed before anyone on Wall Street had taken the rumors too seriously, but market indicators already showed that it would be a bad opening in the morning.

"I hope that cool heads prevail," the President answered. "We'll do everything we can to protect our economy. A coordinated response to this outbreak should contain the disease in a timely fashion and keep any disruption to a minimum. Remember what happened following September 11. After an initial dive, the market recovered nicely. Our economy is strong, and there is every reason to keep investing in our future."

With that, the President waved to the reporters and left the room.

CHAPTER 11

"Eight more cases," Fiorelli informed Stone as he returned from the press conference.

He frowned. "Where?"

"One more in New Jersey, two in New York, three in Chicago, one in San Francisco, and one in Dallas."

"Damn it."

Russ Stone was a large man, stern and stoic, who usually concealed his emotions well. He had accepted the Homeland Security position with the confidence of someone who could not contemplate defeat. But now he was in the driver's seat of a wagon that appeared to be accelerating out of control, and he was starting to wonder if he could validate the President's trust.

"That's not all," Fiorelli added. "Abroad, the Pasteur Institute is studying two cases in Holland and one in France, and the Brazilian President is addressing his nation after new cases were detected in São Paulo."

"It confirms our worst fears, doesn't it?" Stone asked, not needing an answer.

"The situation will get ugly quickly, Russ," Fiorelli said. "In New Jersey, people are already swarming to emergency rooms complaining of every conceivable symptom, and the medical personnel are getting swamped. I'm sure the same will happen all over the country."

"Are all those people sick?"

"No, but the early symptoms are so similar to regular flu that people are becoming alarmed. We also have reports of some faking it, hoping to get priority on the vaccination schedule."

Stone stared at the FBI director, shaking his head. "If people start to panic, God help us."

"There is no panic yet, but screening everyone is time consuming and the waiting rooms are full. Shouting matches and insults have already broken out."

"Are the police prepared if the situation escalates?"

"Yes and no," Fiorelli answered. "We have adequate resources for now. The problem is that the emergency teams are afraid of interacting with potential patients without the proper precautions, and a number of local departments still lack basic equipment, like breathing apparatus and protective gear. FEMA is working with the state emergency agencies to plug the holes."

As the evening progressed, other cases were diagnosed and the number of contacts in the quarantine centers increased quickly. Dr. DuBois called the CDC late in the evening.

"The guidelines for quarantine are inadequate," he said.

"How's that?" Dr. Venkatraman asked.

"Right now we have two types of facilities," he explained. "The isolation rooms for people known to be infected or showing acute symptoms of the disease, and the quarantine centers for those who had contact with contagious patients but not showing any symptoms. That's not enough."

"What else do you need?"

"A separate containment center for anyone with prodromal symptoms, like pain, fever, nausea, or fatigue, but still no rash or bleeding."

"Why don't you put them in isolation? You can move them into quarantine if it proves to be a false positive."

"For two reasons. First, we don't have enough isolation units. But more importantly, those patients refuse to be placed with the contagious group."

"The patients don't have a choice," Venkatraman replied, his voice denoting some exasperation. "The President was very clear. If they don't follow the recommendations of the emergency teams they can be arrested."

DuBois laughed at the remark. "It's a hollow threat," he said. "The last thing law enforcement wants is to arrest individuals with symptoms of smallpox. Where are they gonna put them?"

The Office of Emergency Management decided to split the quarantine centers into 'contact' and 'suspect' quarantine. The 'suspect' individuals would be transferred to the hospital isolation rooms if their symptoms worsened.

Local law enforcement officers wearing HEPA-filter breathing apparatus supervised the quarantine centers, while volunteer medical personnel became responsible for monitoring all quarantined persons. For each, there was a file containing relevant physical data, plus information on date, place, and circumstances of contact, person contacted, and symptoms if any. The promise of priority for vaccination minimized the resistance to quarantine and kept the centers fairly calm.

***

Vaccination started on Tuesday morning when the first batches became available. Priority was given to quarantined persons, medical personnel in emergency rooms, emergency volunteers assigned to transport and care of victims, lab technicians working in the collection or testing of specimens, nurses performing the vaccination, and epidemiologists and law enforcement personnel interviewing contacts and staffing the quarantine sites.

Mass vaccination centers were setup at the quarantine hotels and major hospitals. Each received the allocated vaccine doses, special bifurcated needles, forms for tracking and control, and at least one trained medical technician. Other technicians, mostly volunteers, were assigned to each location and were vaccinated and trained. The training was straightforward for anyone with emergency medical experience.

"The 'ring' vaccination concept will be used," a technician explained to Cecilia Chapman on camera. "Each verified case will be encircled with a buffer of vaccinated people. It's the method utilized decades ago to eradicate naturally occurring smallpox."

"How safe is the vaccine?"

"It's considered relatively safe, but adverse reactions can occur," the technician answered. "Particularly at risk are individuals with immunosuppressive disorders such as HIV/AIDS or leukemia, persons with a history of eczema or heart disease, and pregnant women. We have a recommendation not to vaccinate anyone at risk."

Except for the need to control non-priority individuals demanding vaccination, the centers ran smoothly. The emergency response planning of the last two years was paying off.

The same could not be said about emergency rooms. TV networks and radio stations ran frequent special news bulletins.

"By mid-day today, there were eighty-five individuals in isolation in New Jersey hospitals," Dr. DuBois told Cecilia in another interview. "Many saw a physician during the weekend, some as early as last Thursday, but their symptoms were misdiagnosed as the flu, an allergy, food poisoning, or even adult chickenpox."

"What happened to those patients?" Cecilia asked.

"They returned when their situation worsened. Emergency room personnel are now aware of the smallpox outbreak and are finally making the right diagnosis."

"We see increasing confusing at emergency areas in northern New Jersey. What is NJOEM doing to help this situation?"

"Hospitals with room to spare have set up two separate emergency areas, one for suspected smallpox patients, another for non-infectious cases, like accident victims, heart trouble, or strokes. However, smaller hospitals and clinics don't have that luxury, and some waiting rooms are indeed overflowing with a mixture of patients. We're taking steps to ensure that all emergency areas have separate facilities and asking law enforcement for help to maintain order."

Throughout the state, businesses were taking precautions but attempting to run as usual. Business trips were cancelled and employees already away were called back. Larger companies were making arrangements to get their medical department workers vaccinated and distributing smallpox prevention information to all employees. The topic of conversation in the hallways and cafeterias was the same. People were concerned, but there was no alarm.

Understandably, there was considerably more worry in the places where confirmed cases worked. Epidemiologists showed up to interrogated the victims' colleagues. Employees wearing surgical masks and gloves disinfected the desks, tools, keyboards, telephone receivers, elevator buttons, and anything the victims might have touched. Co-workers were often asked to go into quarantine. Cecilia Chapman followed a surveillance team to an office where a case had been found.

"This is unreal," a woman was saying, shaking her head in disbelief.

"I can't just go with you and leave my family. I need to pick up my children from school," another woman, crying and trying to pull away, told the volunteer dragging her into a waiting van.

"I have pets at home. Who's going to feed them?" a young man asked the police officer leading him away.

"You'll be able to call a friend or a family member," he was told.

"No, I won't," the man answered, "The dog will bite anyone who tries to come in without me there."

"You'll think of something," the officer replied.

"Ma'm?" Cecilia asked an older woman being led away from the building, "Do you know why you're going into quarantine?"

The woman was visibly shaken. "I sat next to a man who came down with the disease. Now they think I'm infected."

Quarantine was a major disruption in people's lives. But the fear of exposure, the promise of vaccination, the understanding of the situation, or the threats of prison were prevailing.

***

Dr. DuBois returned to Morris General. He put on the protective mask and special clothing and went into the isolation room. Twelve patients had been admitted and only two beds remained empty. Many of the victims moaned despite the painkillers being administered intravenously.

Sarah's situation was critical. She could not speak and was drifting in and out of consciousness. There were lesions in her throat, mouth, and lips, and her skin displayed blotches that had turned almost black, along with clusters of large open sores. Her eyelids were raw wounds that kept her eyes shut.

Todd was struggling. His bleeding was heavy and coming from every orifice in his body. He was having difficulty breathing because of the blood accumulating in his lungs. The initial rash had turned into huge, confluent lesions. He let out a groan when the doctor touched his skin.

DuBois shook his head. "He's not gonna make it," he told Dr. Skarzinski, who had returned from quarantine after being vaccinated and was now in charge of the isolation patients.

The doctors looked at the other patients. All had obvious smallpox symptoms at different stages of progression. All had sores and bleeding, most were conscious and in pain, and several shivered uncontrollably. At least three were as ill as Sarah and Todd. DuBois shook his head again and they left the isolation room.

"How's the quarantine center?" DuBois asked as they shed the biological suits.

"Becoming less organized," Skarzinski replied. "Once vaccinated, people don't want to stay."

"How're the emergency teams keeping them in?"

"They aren't. They're releasing anyone who's vaccinated and wants to leave. People will remain quarantined, but at home."

"They'll never keep track of them."

"They're trying. All those released have to provide an address and a landline phone number and are expected to stay confined to their own homes and away from family members. They also have to answer the phone if called by a surveillance worker. They receive written instruction on house quarantine procedures, including how to check their vaccine reaction."

Dr. DuBois shook his head, but said nothing.

"The main problem is the lack of epidemiologists and surveillance personnel," Skarzinski continued. "Someone has to investigate, report on suspected cases, and track family, co-workers, and other contacts. So many cases are being identified that the available resources are already swamped."

***

New Jersey was dealing with the outbreak better than many other states. There were now over twelve hundred isolation cases throughout the country and the numbers were increasing quickly. All state and federal agencies were bracing themselves for an emergency that appeared more frightening by the minute. Russ Stone was in the middle of the storm, and holes in his ship were popping up everywhere.

"Dallas ran out of space in their isolation facilities," he told

Reiss on the phone, his voice betraying some alarm. "We're bringing in mobile isolation units provided by the Army, but it's just a stop-gap measure. These units don't have the capacity we'll need. Other cities will follow if this keeps up. How can we house all the infectious patients without exposing the entire population to the freaking virus?"

"We're preparing alternative facilities," Reiss replied.

"Like what?" Stone asked anxiously. "If the press gets a hold of this they'll eat us alive."

"We have a plan. We're looking into using clean rooms, like the ones for integrated circuit manufacturing, and turning them into isolation areas."

"Aren't those positive-pressure rooms? We need the opposite."

"That's correct. But they have all the filters and physical isolation required. By installing vacuum equipment and reversing the filtering units, we'll have adequate facilities."

There was a moment of silence, with Stone absorbing the information.

"How long until they're ready?" he asked.

"I don't know yet."

"Damn it, Dave, that's not good enough," Stone barked impatiently. "I need to know when we can place patients in those facilities?"

"Maybe as early as tomorrow. We already have engineers at various sites working on converting the rooms. Equipment is being disconnected and moved. Hospital beds and supplies, protective gear, and decontamination solutions are being brought in, and emergency personnel are being readied. If everything goes right, the first unit will be operational in Dallas tomorrow afternoon."

Stone sighed in relief. This particular problem appeared to have a solution, at least temporarily, and there were clean rooms all over the country, weren't there?

"Remember," Reiss continued, "to appropriately treat these patients, they should be in a critical care unit. This obviously won't be the case. But our priority is to isolate them to avoid spreading the disease, don't you agree?"

Stone didn't answer right away. Reiss added, "Look, given the numbers, even in the hospital all we can do is monitor them, prevent dehydration, and alleviate their pain."

"I guess it'll be okay. We really don't have much of a choice, do we?" Stone replied.

***

Wall Street was having a rough day. The markets, following what had already happened overnight in Asia and Europe, opened sharply lower. Led by travel and tourism stocks, the markets never stopped diving. During the first three hours of trading, the Nasdaq lost thirteen percent of its value, and the Dow Jones Industrial Average lost 500 points before trading was halted.

***

The news from abroad wasn't any better. Large numbers of smallpox cases continued to be reported in every continent.

"This is getting out of hand, David," Emile Gastineau told the head of the CDC on the phone. "It's not just the number of cases, it's how widespread they are. How are we going to control this virus?"

"It's the nightmare we talked about but never really expected," Reiss replied.

"The virus has now been detected in about half of the European countries. In Amsterdam, we have over forty cases. In Madrid, about thirty, and thirty-five in Rome. I fear that these numbers may increase tenfold over the next seventy-two hours. Europe is simply not ready for this, and WHO won't be able to provide the assistance required to quell such an outbreak."

Reiss had to agree. As stressed as the U.S. emergency response was becoming, no other country was close to having the medical facilities, the communications networks, or the coordinated emergency procedures and personnel the United States had. The September 11 terrorist attacks had forced the government and emergency departments to prepare for other such events, including a biological attack.

For the last two years, the CDC had been getting ready for the worst. Whether it would pay off remained to be seen, but at least they had the basics. However, most other countries had not felt the urgency, as they didn't perceive themselves as obvious targets of terrorism. A lot of what they had in terms of documentation, plans, and protocols had been borrowed from the CDC, but this didn't help when it came to personnel and facilities.

"The situation is already very difficult," Gastineau continued. "Our emergency teams are not trained to deal with an epidemic of this magnitude. We don't have enough HEPA respirators and protective gear. Our police and fire departments aren't used to responding to medical situations requiring tact and caring. Hospitals are already operating under stress because of a very high incidence of influenza."

"How's your vaccine supply?" Reiss interrupted, fearing the answer.

"If we do it right, we have enough to protect the doctors and emergency room personnel," Gastineau answered with a sigh. "Depending on the numbers, we may have enough for the quarantined contacts, but it's going to be tricky. What we have is not evenly distributed. We can't force countries to give up their stock, and it's unlikely that anyone will share."

"That's a recipe for disaster," Reiss said. "We can't control this virus if it isn't properly confined everywhere."

"You're right. Unfortunately, politics will play a role and no one will give away something they desperately need."

Reiss was well aware of it. As CDC Director, he controlled more vaccine doses than the rest of the world combined, and he didn't expect to be allowed to give any away even if it were the right decision to stop the virus. The U.S. government's priority was to protect its own people.

"And we're not even addressing what's happening outside of Europe or North America," Gastineau continued. "Most countries don't have a prayer – no facilities, no personnel, no processes, no communication, no vaccines. WHO could help if it were a country or two, but we are looking at dozens. In Brazil, the city of São Paulo alone is reporting more than two hundred cases."

On that sad note they hung up. Both had their hands full at home and it would take all their energy and resources, as well as luck, to kill the killer. But the problem was global. Although they could do little about it right now, they could not forget it.

CHAPTER 12

On Friday morning, the fifth day of the epidemic, Reiss flew to Washington for meetings with senior emergency personnel and policy makers and headed directly for Russ Stone's office.

"Thanks for coming up," Stone said, rising to greet him. "How was the trip?"

"Fine," Reiss answered while removing his heavy coat. It was a cold morning in the nation's capital, and a fine drizzle was coating everything with a layer of ice and making walking and driving very treacherous. Luckily, the traffic out of the airport had been light. "I've never seen a plane so empty out of Atlanta."

"And the airlines have already cancelled half of their flights. I fear some won't last," Stone said, sitting back down behind his desk and motioning to Reiss to take a seat. He went right to the main issue in his mind. "Do we have any idea yet as to how the virus might have been spread?"

"No, Russ, we don't," Reiss admitted. "As you know, we're working closely with the FBI, CIA, NSA, and international agencies to find the delivery mechanism, but so far, nothing."

"Until we do, we won't know who the perpetrators were. The President keeps asking. He wants to go after somebody."

Reiss knew it. The Secretary of Defense kept calling him with the same question. "We need to find the sources of the outbreak before we can guess who did this. Everybody wants to blame someone, but we must keep in mind that the first cases didn't appear until two weeks or so after the deed, and whoever did it isn't bragging."

"Any clues that may help us, anything we can give the President?" Stone asked.

"We're beginning to see a pattern, and it looks like we were probably wrong initially. The data is as interesting for those who aren't getting sick, as it is for those who are."

"How's that?"

"For instance, there are no cases of children under twelve anywhere in the world. There are also no women over the age of sixty, although we do have a handful of men. Initially, we thought that the virus might have been transmitted by aerosol spray in crowded places, like shopping malls, trade shows, or conference centers. But then we would expect a random distribution of patients, including children and older folks."

"Conference centers and trade shows don't necessarily have a lot of kids or senior citizens," Russ Stone replied.

"True, but there would have been a few with an aerosol release. With so many places throughout the world, we would have seen at least some. Two other clues are also very interesting. We still don't know where they'll lead, but they're definitely significant. First, is the huge number of infected prostitutes in some cities. In Israel, forty-two contracted the virus, all from the same five brothels in Tel Aviv. There are dozens of such places in that city, yet no other prostitute became ill. There are almost five hundred confirmed cases there and except for the hookers, there are only sixteen females. All the others are men, and many admitted being clients of the women. We're working with the Israeli authorities hoping to find a smoking gun. That is the one place where we can focus on a set of individuals and locations."

"Do you think there's a sexual transmission component in this nightmare?" Stone asked, surprised.

"Again, we don't know yet, but the second clue could be as important," Reiss replied. "There's a large number of couples coming down with the disease together. Of course, it's no surprise to see people who live together being infected by the same agent, but it's odd that other family members have shown no symptoms. We also have a few infected couples who had casual sex only once within the incubation period, with no other interaction before or after. We still can't explain it."

"So when do you think we'll know how this was done?" Secretary Stone asked, somewhat impatiently. It was always the first question the President asked when they met, and the country wanted some kind of explanation. Equally important, he wanted to be the one informing the press, and not the other way around. If the media learned the facts before he did, it would be another blow to his department.

But Reiss, although confident that the investigation was on the right track, was concerned about providing a date. Infected patients were showing up every minute and what they saw might be only part of the story. There could be more than one delivery process, and to commit to a definite answer was ill advised. Besides, why didn't Stone ask Paul Fiorelli? The CDC was overwhelmed just fighting the spread of the epidemic. Finding out who and how was the role of the FBI.

"Again, I can't say with certainty. If we're lucky, we may know before the weekend is over." Now he had given Stone something he could take to the President.

Stone jotted something down on a pad. "Smallpox cases throughout the country already exceed twenty-five thousand," he said without looking up. "Do you think we're seeing the worst of it?"

"If it was a sudden release, then we may be seeing the bulk of the infections, and the vaccine will now prevent uncontrolled spreading. But we don't know that yet."

Stone got up and walked to a large map on the wall where he had tried to keep track of the smallpox cases by sticking pins into the locations where they occurred. He had given up when some areas became covered with pins, places like the New York metro area, Chicago, Los Angeles, Dallas, and Miami, but the map showed a clear pattern.

"We know that the cases are clustered around the largest metropolitan areas. Isn't that some kind of clue?"

"That's to be expected in a deliberate release. We still need to find out how it was done."

"We'll be in trouble if this gets much worse," Stone said, now looking intently at Reiss. "The disaster response teams are overwhelmed. The makeshift isolation areas are housing the bulk of the victims because the ones in the hospitals are full. And the DMATs are proving ineffective. We need new ideas to fight this disaster."

FEMA had tried to mobilize the disaster medical assistance teams to aid the local medical staffs in providing emergency care. But DMAT teams consisted mostly of voluntary doctors and nurses who were now desperately needed at their own facilities.

"There are other big holes in the process," Reiss replied. "For every confirmed case, we should have ten to thirty contacts vaccinated and quarantined, but we are nowhere near that. The tracking teams are unable to follow up with the interviews of so many contacts. Also, in-house quarantine monitoring has become sporadic or even ignored."

"Why don't the local police departments do it?"

"That was the intention. They were informed of all quarantined persons in their area and asked to check in on individuals not answering the phone or suspected of breaking the rules. But the magnitude of the disaster has stretched all available resources."

Stone shook his head. Reiss didn't add that many quarantined individuals, now vaccinated and feeling fine, decided that they were no danger to others or to themselves. Thinking themselves immune, they were going about their own routines.

***

Rio de Janeiro did not appear to have been directly targeted by the terrorists, whoever they were, and the lives of its eight million inhabitants were still proceeding close to normal. A number of businesses were experiencing difficulty because of the commercial collapse in São Paulo, and the hotels and resorts were nearly empty. But every year, there was a letdown after the carnival folly, so this was not unusual. Those who could afford it were starting to accumulate non-perishable foods at home and planning what to do if things got out of hand, but there was no panic.

Rio had seen only twenty-one initial smallpox cases, all outsiders arriving for the carnival from Buenos Aires, São Paulo, and cities in Europe and the U.S. If there were more, they had left town before the onset of symptoms, and travel restrictions had apparently prevented others from arriving. All such patients had been placed in isolation at the few facilities with the ability to house highly contagious patients.

"How do you expect us to treat these patients without a vaccine?" Dr. Claudia Senna yelled on the phone at a health department official in Brasilia. She was the chief physician in charge of the isolation facilities and many in her staff were calling in sick for fear of the virus.

"I can't give you what I don't have."

"But that's suicide. A minor mistake can mean death."

"You have biological suits and decontamination procedures. You must make sure your staff is trained."

Dr. Senna decided not to force any doctor or nurse to treat the smallpox patients for the time being. She asked for volunteers.

"Rather be a living coward than a dead hero," one doctor said, an attitude shared by many.

Still, an adequate group of selfless, some would say insane, professionals had agreed to work with her.

Medical and government personnel were well aware that the virus would not spare the city and that a second wave of patients would soon turn up. Health officials had tracked over two hundred contacts, but there had certainly been many more in the madness of Carnival. The contacts had been quarantined. Many were from out of town and had to be taken forcefully – they did not relish the idea of having the big party ruined for them and even worse, not being able to go back home when the Carnival was over.

But quarantine was just that: enforced isolation of those suspected of exposure to the virus. There was no vaccination or medication to prevent the disease from developing. City officials were extremely concerned and had no idea how to handle the crisis.

***

Worldwide, the numbers reached over one hundred thousand, but it was feared that many victims were not being counted. Despite the ongoing coverage wherever there was a TV antenna or a radio, many people would not seek medical help until their condition was critical. To make matters worse, most cities in Third World countries did not have adequate facilities or personnel to tend to the needs of the sick. A major epidemic was something they could not handle, and once the first cases were diagnosed, panic immediately set in. Without vaccines, many nurses, technicians, even doctors refused to treat symptomatic patients. Others failed to show up to work, ambulances drivers refused to pick up suspected patients, and voluntary personnel disappeared.

Brawls broke out in emergency rooms, with victims' families demanding attention but no staff or facilities to provide it. Patients with non-virus related problems blocked hospital entrances to anyone suspected of being contagious. TV broadcast unrest stories and gruesome images from around the world. A screaming mob was clubbing a symptomatic woman in front of a Caracas hospital. In Bangkok, a bloody-nosed man made his way through an emergency room at gunpoint, yelling for a doctor. And in Cairo, a bewildered man ran through an open-air quarantine center, screaming and spitting on other patients and health workers, until a security guard shot him.

Emile Gastineau tracked Reiss down in Washington and was told that the CDC Director could not be interrupted, but he insisted.

"This better be important, Emile, to justify pulling me from a meeting with Fiorelli," Reiss said as he picked up the phone.

"Sorry about that. He can wait. What I have to tell you is more important," the head of the Pasteur Institute replied. "As you know, our lab has been dissecting the virus and studying its genetic structure around the clock, and we came across frightening information. The virus, although a strain of *Variola major*, was genetically altered."

Reiss was stunned. "Are you sure?" He was also wondering how the French had arrived at that information before his own labs. If it were true, it would be a bit embarrassing for the CDC, but there was no room for wounded egos in the middle of a crisis.

"David, I wouldn't be calling you if I weren't sure," Emile said with a hint of resentment. "Our scientists were able to identify a segment of the virus gene sequence that is totally foreign."

"Any idea of what it encodes?"

"Our analysis indicates that it is the human IL4 gene."

Reiss run his fingers through his curly, salt-and-pepper hair as he considered what he had just heard. His stomach was suddenly in a knot.

"Shit!" he exclaimed. "The Australian experiment replicated in smallpox."

"Bingo!"

"It confirms what we already suspected. This isn't your average smallpox. Virtually all cases are either the flat-type or the hemorrhagic-type."

"That appears to be true all over."

There was a brief silence. Both men knew that these two types of smallpox, also known as black pox, were extremely deadly, with fatality rates above ninety percent.

"We'd better have enough body bags," Gastineau finally said.

"Damn! That study should never have been released," Reiss exclaimed, referring to the report published by the Australian researchers who had initially introduced the IL4 into the mousepox. "We're adding weapons to the terrorists' arsenal."

"True, but nothing we can do about it now." The French doctor had had time to absorb the news and was less emotional. "What's important is the meaning of this information."

"It means we don't know squat." Reiss took a deep breath and added, "We must assume that whoever created this mess chose this strain because it's worse in some way than the standard virus."

"It induces black pox almost exclusively. That's bad enough!"

"But we don't know how it spreads, how to treat it, or how to control it. Everything we know about *Variola major* may not apply here."

"My main fear," the Frenchman said, "is that the vaccine won't work. If that's the case, we should all be running and hiding in a cave somewhere."

"Good Lord, do you know what that would mean? We could lose half of our emergency teams in two weeks."

Reiss was shaking. During his twenty-four years at the CDC, he had chased deadly pathogens in remote areas and crowded slums of every continent, and he had seen close calls before. He thought he could handle any news with cold-blooded professionalism. But he had never faced a threat manufactured by some twisted human mind, or a deadly virus running amuck in every corner of the globe.

"We need to keep this from the press for as long as we can," Gastineau said. "We're already past the breakpoint in Europe. A rumor would create such hysteria that it would be impossible to recover. We need to feed this information very carefully to the appropriate emergency leaders and have a coordinated plan."

They decided to talk again in a few hours and hung up. The CDC Director went back to his meeting with renewed urgency.

"We've got a break," the FBI Director said as Reiss got back. His eyes were sparkling and he was almost radiant. Fiorelli rarely succeeded in hiding his emotions, an ironic trait given his position, and his hands spoke louder than his voice when he got excited. "I just received a report from Israeli intelligence."

Reiss stood in front of Fiorelli's desk waiting for him to explain.

"They've found the method of distribution, at least in their country." He paused, looking at Reiss. "Are you ready? Infected condoms!"

Reiss said nothing as he digested the new information and tried to figure out if it matched the outbreak pattern or the type of individuals being exposed.

Fiorelli continued. "The Israeli investigators went through the affected brothels with a fine tooth comb and examined every piece of evidence. They interviewed every woman still able to speak. Their pimp is also sick, you know."

Reiss didn't know and didn't care. He gave Fiorelli an inquisitive look.

"He's near death and they couldn't talk to him. But when asked if they could remember any unusual event from two or three weeks ago or if anything had changed in their workplace, one of the women mentioned a new kind of condom. Apparently, they didn't like the lubrication because the new condoms caused friction burns," he said with a grin.

"It fits, you know," Reiss interrupted. He was no longer listening to the details but thinking about how virus-laced condoms could spread the disease. "All those prostitutes, all those couples, even those cases where there was only a casual encounter. They all used condoms, and the condom infected both partners."

"Exactly!" Fiorelli replied, slapping his desk. "The Israelis were able to obtain some of the condoms still in the women's apartments and found that the lubricants used are actually preservation media for the virus."

"Do they know where the condoms came from?"

Fiorelli looked through some notes on his desk. "It's a brand called *SharusMan* manufactured by a company in the Philippines. They still don't know how the condoms got to Israel because the company has no retail or distribution there. Our investigators here have already started to question victims about the condoms, and some have recognized the name and admitted using them. We've asked the Filipino authorities to investigate and are getting a team ready to fly to Manila." He was visibly pleased to have positive news.

"Our field scientists must join the group," Reiss said. "We must figure out what they did and how they did it, and whether they developed any vaccine. Anything we can find out will help."

"Of course, but why would they develop another vaccine?" Fiorelli asked, puzzled.

"Well, that's part of what I just learned." Reiss paced the room, too agitated to sit still. "The call I just received was from Paris. The Pasteur Institute has determined that the virus was genetically engineered, and it's not clear whether it'll behave like normal smallpox."

"What does that mean?"

"It means that it was probably modified to behave differently from the original virus. One danger is that this recombinant strain is resistant to the standard vaccine."

The FBI Director deflated right in front of Reiss. Every senior person in his agency, everyone in Homeland Security, lawmakers, military leaders, the executive branch including the President, the emergency response teams, all had been vaccinated and presumed protected. What if they weren't? His thoughts were the same as Reiss's minutes earlier and he turned white as ghost.

"We've got to pass this information upward," he finally said, dejectedly. "We must tell Stone right away. And we need a recommendation for the DoD and the President. If you're right, it'll turn this nightmare into . . . I don't even want to think about it."

***

Dr. Frank DuBois was frazzled. He was working eighteen-hour days between his responsibilities in the emergency team and lending a hand in the care of the isolation patients. He would go home around midnight, crash for a few hours, and be out the door again by 6 A.M.

"Did Bruce call?" he asked Doreen.

"Not since before he left."

"When was he coming back?"

"Should've been yesterday, but I think all flights from Brazil have been cancelled."

Frank had forgotten about that. "More reason for him to call. The phones still work."

They were both worried about their son. He was a free spirit who cared deeply about people but nothing about status or personal wealth. After graduating from the University of Chicago with a degree in sociology, he had accepted a position as an adjunct professor at the school. He volunteered for three or four different social activities and was often going somewhere to give a hand to a special cause. He had learned enough Portuguese to get by and had already used it in Angola, in Mozambique, and several times in Brazil with Habitat for Humanity.

But he had always found a way to call his parents with a quick "everything's fine." He knew of their angst regarding his sister and didn't want to add to it.

"How do you think he's gonna come back?" Doreen asked.

Frank shrugged. "As long as he's okay . . ." And he left for work.

Both he and Doreen had been vaccinated and were probably protected. Nonetheless, he was very careful. In spite of his expertise with viruses, or maybe because of it, he always had a sense of uneasiness when dealing with pathogenic micro-organisms. "Exposure to a virus by a vaccinated person is like being shot while wearing a bullet-proof vest," he would tell his wife. "What if they shoot you in the head?" He religiously checked his breathing equipment and protective gear before he donned them and would follow methodically all decontamination procedures.

At Morris General, the vaccination program was on its fourth day. There were a lot of tired nurses and assistants, but the work was proceeding without major incidents. Since their arrival, the National Guard had been doing a good job of supporting local law enforcement in coordinating the crowds. They also supported the transportation and distribution of food, medication, equipment, decontaminants, and other items to quarantine centers and off-hospital isolation sites.

By mid-afternoon, DuBois entered the hospital through a side entrance and headed toward the isolation room. He put on the protective gear and went in.

"Two patients have died," Dr. Skarzinski told him.

"They didn't last long."

"Internal bleeding," Skarzinski explained.

Dr. DuBois nodded. Given all the madness going on, no one was responding to blood drives, and the blood supply was at critically low levels even for regular surgery and transfusions.

Replacing the blood loss in the hemorrhaging patients, who had a low probability of survival anyway, wasn't an option. More than a few patients would just bleed to death.

One of the deceased was Sarah's boyfriend. Todd had been taken away only a few minutes earlier.

"How are you doing, Sarah?" DuBois asked gently. She was clearly recovering. All bleeding had stopped and she was alert. One of her eyes was still closed, but she could see with the other. Her voice was hoarse and speaking was painful, but she could say a few words. She had never developed the pus-filled pustules typical of smallpox. Instead, clusters of blisters coalesced all over her body forming large legions, while the rest of her skin turned dark purple. The pain was bearable only because of the painkillers pumped into her. Large scabs were now starting to form, indicating that the worst was probably over.

She had been crying. Although very weak, she had seen Todd being removed in a body bag. They had not talked for days. When she had recovered enough to look for him, he had been too ill to say or do anything. Now he was gone, and she was alone again.

"Okay," she whispered, her lips moving without sound.

"You're gonna be fine," Dr. DuBois said. "The worst is already behind you."

Sarah responded with only a sad smile.

She had recognized the doctor the night he had showed up by her hospital bed. As a child, she had spent many days and nights at his home. She still remembered fondly the play dates with Anne and often wondered what had happened to her. Anne's father would play silly games with them and crack jokes about their gap-teeth and school crushes. When they were small, he was always the one who read them a bedside story and tucked them in when she slept over.

Sarah had been too sick to say hello, and it was clear that Dr. DuBois had not recognized her, but it had been comforting to see him there. The protective coats and face masks around her brought up nightmares from long ago when similarly dressed men had destroyed her home and stolen a cherished friendship. His familiar face helped scare the demons away. She had been glad to feel his presence every day throughout her ordeal, a soothing memory of happier times.

The patient's smile must have stirred Dr. DuBois's memory. He stared at the name on the patient's file, then again at the blotched face on the pillow. Sarah Wilson. He tried to place the name, then the face. Then he had it.

"Little Sarah?" he asked.

She attempted to smile again and nodded.

"Sarah, how wonderful to see you," he said with a smile of his own hidden behind the mask. "I'm so sorry we met again under such horrific conditions. I hadn't recognized you until just now. My God, it's been so long! When was the last time I saw you?" he asked, then answered his own question. "It must have been Anne's high school graduation party."

Sarah nodded again. After her family's move from Basking Ridge, she and Anne had rarely seen each other, but they talked on the phone and went to each other's birthday parties. The last time they had seen each other had been at their respective high school graduations. By then, it was apparent that they had different interests, and they drifted apart. Anne went on to Ohio State while Sarah stayed closer to home and attended

Rutgers University. Communication between them simply stopped.

Since then, Sarah had been kicked around by fate. Her mother had died during her college sophomore year after a battle with colon cancer. Her father had been killed by a drunk driver four years later, two months shy of her wedding day. She wanted children, but just as she was ready to start a family, her husband had betrayed her. She reverted to her maiden name trying to forget his deceit and concentrated on her work. It took years, and chance, but she had met Todd. After much indecision, she had allowed herself to bring another man into her life and to trust again, to be happy again, and to love again. But now fate had intervened once more. Why am I being spared? she asked herself.

Dr. DuBois must have read her thoughts. "I'm so sorry about your friend," he said. "He was very sick, and it was almost better that he went quickly."

She sobbed, but her eyes were dry because tears could not exit the damaged tear ducts. The doctor saw her pain and wanted to hug her as he used to when she and Anne were twelve. But he couldn't because of her condition and his suit, so he gently placed his gloved hand on hers.

"You're gonna be okay," he said again. "I'll come back tomorrow. Hang in there and don't let despair get the best of you. Everything will turn out all right."

He forced a smile and turned away. He wanted to believe his own words, but looking around the room and aware of the turmoil outside, he knew that everything would *not* be all right, at least not anytime soon. It would be a long time before life returned to normal.

CHAPTER 13

The events of the week had turned Cecilia Chapman into a star. Pretty and elegant without being glamorous, she had caught the attention of American TV audiences by being the first to break the news of the epidemic and by her factual yet compassionate reporting over the previous five days.

This was the chance she had dreamed of since college. While as concerned and frightened as anyone by the spread of the deadly virus, she would not let this opportunity pass her by. It was unfortunate that big breaks for reporters often meant some kind of tragedy. Typically it was a war or a disaster in some far-away place. This one just happened to be at home. She was taking to heart the New Jersey Governor's challenge and doing her best to present the facts as she saw them, be as informative as possible, and avoid melodrama.

The network news director quickly realized the audience's

response to Cecilia and gave her the anchor post for all epidemic-related stories. Her 'Outbreak News Bulletin,' running almost non-stop with continuous updates like the all-news networks, became the program of choice for Americans to get the latest on the disease. Cecilia invaded the American living rooms and stayed there – an informative, honest, and soothing voice in the midst of the developing calamity.

On Saturday morning, Cecilia was hard pressed to find any reassuring news to relate to American audiences. The main stories were grim and frightening. The NYSE had lost thirty-one percent of its value during the week despite the multiple trading stoppages imposed after particularly steep drops. Nasdaq had ended the week down fifty-two percent, the lowest level in more than two decades.

Hospitals around the country were ordered to discharge all non-smallpox patients except those in life-threatening situations or too sick to move. A number of the emergency workers vaccinated during the week were starting to exhibit malaise, low-grade fever, and other mild side effects, and some were calling in sick and adding to the stress in emergency response.

Service industries were laying off people in record numbers. Many restaurants had closed their doors, some as a precaution and others for lack of customers. Supermarkets had run out of canned foods and other durables days ago, and looting incidents had occurred in various cities as law enforcement shifted their priority from patrolling the streets to helping fight the disease.

Most school districts in the affected cities had cancelled all classes indefinitely. A number of businesses had also closed their doors temporarily by the end of the week, as their just-in-time inventory, production, and delivery processes were affected by disruptions in air transportation.

All of this before any smallpox related deaths were officially reported. That had changed overnight. Cecilia would open her Saturday morning bulletin by announcing three deaths in New Jersey, the first fatalities in the country, but a sprinkle of death announcements was trickling in from around the world.

"This is the beginning of a grim reality with this epidemic," an unidentified source at the CDC said. "We think the death rate will be much higher than normal." If normal for smallpox was thirty percent or so, what did that mean? Cecilia decided not to broadcast the statement – reality was alarming enough without speculation. But she included comments from several doctors working with victims around the country.

"The severity of the symptoms tells me that many more will succumb to the virus," Dr. Joseph Skarzinski stated, after announcing the deaths at Morris General Hospital.

***

The U.S. investigative team would not arrive in Manila for another six hours, but the Filipino authorities, with the support of local WHO delegates and U.S. intelligence already in country, all in full biological gear, rushed to the Sharusman Manufacturing Company plant and seized it. Although more than one thousand cases of smallpox had been reported in the Philippines, they quickly determined that none of the company's employees had been infected, even though they had not used protective clothing. Either they had not been exposed or had been vaccinated.

Hector Garcia was bewildered. For three weeks now, he

had been trying to run the business, but Shariff had left without a contact number and with only limited instructions as to what to do in case of an emergency. His right-hand man, Ahmad, had also left, and neither had bothered to contact him to find out if he needed help. A number of pricing issues, delivery complaints, and supplier quality problems had come up that he simply could not handle alone. He desperately needed them back but didn't even know when they were returning.

And now these people in the space suits, some heavily armed, were stopping everything and taking over. They were asking all kinds of questions, and he had no idea what they were looking for. Hector deemed it unwise to complain, so he cooperated and answered their questions honestly and as thoroughly as he could. All the employees were kept at the facility and interrogated. The foremen at the other shifts were called in and also questioned.

The back lot facility and whatever had taken place inside its buildings quickly became the focus of the investigation. No one, including Hector, had any knowledge of what had happened there.

"Honestly, I don't know. I've never been there," Hector repeated over and over again. "My job is sales and marketing. I deal with customers, I don't spend much time at the factory, and I have no idea of what took place at the compound. I was told it was a development lab."

The three compound guards, who had been laid off by Shariff before he left, were located and brought in. They told what they knew, which wasn't much.

"There were four people here," one explained. "Dr. Usman, Mr. Ahmad, and two others who lived in Building 1."

"Who were they?" a Filipino investigator asked.

"I just assumed they were researchers," the man answered. "They kept to themselves and rarely said hello. I thought it was because they were foreigners."

"Did you know their names or nationalities?"

The guard shook his head. "They were white and spoke only English among them."

"One was called Alex, or Alexander," another guard interjected. "I heard Dr. Usman call his name when I helped them carry in some lab equipment. I thought the other one had Middle Eastern features, but I never heard his name."

"What did they do all day?"

"Dr. Usman and Mr. Ahmad came and went all the time. The other two worked, slept, and watched TV, as far as I know. If they left the buildings, it was to smoke a cigarette or sit for a while and enjoy some fresh air. They stayed near the buildings and never came close to the entrance to the compound. I only saw them leaving a few times, usually on a Sunday with Dr. Usman."

"Did anyone else ever come in?"

"Yes, for the last four or five months," the third guard replied. "Several people arrived in Dr. Usman's van, usually in the middle of the night."

"In the middle of the night?" a Filipino investigator asked, surprised.

The guard nodded. "I thought it was odd, but what the boss does is none of my business. He said that they would be bringing in factory people to accommodate production growth. I thought it was part of it."

"What did these people do?"

"I really don't know. They stayed inside all the time and I never saw them outside the buildings. For the last couple of months, I know they were working because a lot of work-in-progress was brought over from the main factory for completion here."

The investigators exchanged looks. Here was an important clue. There were two production lines and most of the company's production was probably safe, possibly everything completed in the main factory facility. It also explained why none of the unprotected workers had contracted the virus. Whatever evil had happened here, it had been at this back lot facility, and the people responsible had disappeared three weeks ago.

They asked to see the production records. Over a period of roughly two months, almost one million condoms, non-lubricated and unpackaged, had been taken from the factory production line for completion at the compound.

"What happened to the people who worked here?" one investigator asked the guards.

They shook their heads. "Maybe they were let go, like us."

"How about the product finished at the compound?" they asked Hector.

He looked baffled and shrugged. Then he remembered something. He had received a few letters from people he didn't know, thanking him and his company for a generous gift that he knew nothing about. He had been so busy that he had not given the letters a second thought, but now . . .

"I received a few letters that I don't understand," he said.

***

Director Fiorelli had enough information to piece together part of the puzzle. Investigators in Manila had called a phone number found in a letter received from an anti-AIDS organization in Tokyo. A follow-up uncovered courier records for packages shipped out by Shariff Usman of Sharusman Manufacturing. In the meantime, following the thread of information from the letters received by Hector Garcia, Fiorelli's team had searched Anne DuBois's Washington office while British intelligence went through her London apartment.

The rumor of infected condoms transmitting the virus was spread by a number of websites. It had leaked in Israel, but the Internet was abuzz with all kinds of wacky news, theories, and suppositions. The press had not picked it up yet. Investigators had quietly purchased *SharusMan* condoms in a number of cities and found that most were clean, until they tested the promotional samples. The letters stored on Anne's computer hard-drive tied it all together.

"Any ties to any terrorist group we know about?" Stone asked.

Paul Fiorelli shook his head. "Not yet. We have three names and we are gathering as much information as we can. There are at least two others and sooner or later, we'll know who they are. But that's all."

"Motive?"

Fiorelli shook his head again. "We know who, what, where, and how. We'll eventually find out why."

"I must brief the President," Stone said. "He wants to address the nation."

***

"For the first time in this generation, armed troops are patrolling our cities and replacing local law enforcement in quelling civil disturbances," Cecilia Chapman told America. "This action, even if requested by several governors and mayors, is surprising given that the administration has remained silent on the subject. The presidential press conference scheduled for noon in Washington is expected to shed light on these developments and to update the nation on the spread of the disease and the status of the terrorist investigation."

In the early morning, military personnel had left Army bases around the country and headed to the metro areas most affected by the outbreak. The National Guard had been supporting the local teams since early in the week, primarily focusing on patrolling and helping at emergency areas and quarantine centers, tracking and guarding individuals under home quarantine, and containing small-scale violence.

However, the situation was becoming ever more volatile, and it was apparent that a heavy-handed approach might be required at any time. It was actually surprising that more violence had not already erupted. Nerves were tattered, people feared for themselves and their families, lifestyles were being altered without normalcy in sight, and patience was wearing thin.

As announced, the President addressed the nation at noon, Eastern Time. His demeanor as he came into the pressroom was somber. He seemed to have aged since his address on Monday and appeared haggard. He walked to the podium with Fiorelli and Stone right behind him.

"My fellow Americans," he said in a tired voice. "First, let me thank each and every one of you for your civility, your cooperation with the emergency teams, and your forbearance in response to the difficult events of this past week. I also want to commend the thousands of men and women working tirelessly to control the epidemic. It will take an extraordinary effort from all to conquer this invisible enemy, but we are a strong and selfless people, and we will prevail."

The President looked straight into the camera and took a deep breath. It was obvious that the preamble was a feeble attempt to rally the people – even he had doubts about the outcome.

"Over the past week, the world has seen the onset of a tragedy as sudden, as cruel, as widespread, and as unpredictable as any event in human history. A pandemic of global proportions has been unleashed by a small group of terrorists whose intentions we are still trying to determine."

The President paused, looked briefly at the reporters, and then proceeded. "This is what we know at this time: a small international group, including at least two Americans and operating in the Philippines under the cover of a legitimate business, somehow obtained a sample of *Variola major*, the virus that causes smallpox in humans. They had the expertise to genetically modify the virus and maintain it alive outside the lab for an extended period of time. They concealed it in a medium used as a lubricant in birth-control devices."

He paused again and cleared his throat. "Under the false pretense of social responsibility, they donated hundreds of thousands of condoms to be distributed by anti-AIDS teams in some fifty countries around the world. Many were also distributed for free in Europe and North America under the guise of a marketing promotion. Thousands of people were exposed in every continent."

The President seemed to be getting angry as he spoke. "We have an emergency like nothing we've ever experienced before, and we can expect many casualties. There's nothing more urgent for us right now than to unite in the fight to eradicate this virus. Because contagious diseases know no borders, our federal agencies are working closely with their counterparts in other nations and with international health and humanitarian organizations. We must inventory all available resources worldwide and allocate them where they'll make the most impact."

The President took a deep breath again and assumed an attitude of authority as he continued. "The enemy is tiny and invisible but make no mistake, this is one of the toughest challenges our nation, indeed the world, has ever faced. Earlier today, after consulting with the Secretary of Defense, the Joint Chiefs of Staff, the Secretary of Homeland Security, the Attorney General, the Director of the FBI, and with the approval of the congressional leadership, I declared martial law throughout the country. I've ordered all branches of the military to be ready for deployment at home should the extent of the calamity warrant it, and I've ordered all reserve units to report to active duty. Several Army units have already been deployed to assist law enforcement personnel where requested by the local authorities. I expect others to follow."

Tiny beads of perspiration appeared in the President's forehead that shone under the lights. He went on. "Starting immediately, all non-essential air and inter-state travel is prohibited. Individual states may implement additional limitations on intra-state travel. All conventions and trade shows will be postponed and all sporting events cancelled.

Schools, including colleges and universities, will be closed. All home quarantines will be stopped and all victim contacts must report to designated centers.

"Testing centers will be set up at state lines to check for symptoms of the disease. Persons traveling on essential business will be tested, and the measures already implemented at the airports will continue. Businesses with more than twenty-five employees are ordered to check their workers daily for symptoms. All religious leaders must do the same before every service. Indoor shopping malls are required to implement similar measures or they will be closed. Finally, smallpox victims who die will be cremated before the remains are returned to their families.

"To avoid a meltdown of our financial markets, trading at all major stock exchanges will be stopped until the epidemic is under control. In an international agreement reached this morning, most major foreign exchanges will also halt trading indefinitely."

The President paused again and looked into the camera. "My fellow Americans, the challenge ahead is Herculean, and we'll need everyone's collaboration to get through. The first line of defense, including local police, firefighters, medical professionals, and voluntary organizations, add up to over two million emergency workers already deployed nationwide. They are supported by personnel from all appropriate federal agencies and by the National Guard. The bulk of our military forces is now available to plug holes in law enforcement, logistics, coordination, and anywhere they can be of assistance. Let's keep the calm and cooperate with those in charge. With your effort and God's help, we'll overcome this ordeal. God bless us all."

Atypically, the press was silent for a few seconds after the President's speech. Following his momentous message, any question might sound stupid. He used the opportunity to exit the room, leaving Paul Fiorelli and Russ Stone to answer questions.

"Director Fiorelli," a network correspondent started, "What do we know about the culprits in this bioattack?"

"We know it was a very small group, perhaps no more than five individuals. We have the identity of three of them."

Fiorelli pulled a sheet of paper from his coat pocket and read from it. "One is Shariff Usman, a professor of biology in the Philippines and the owner of a contraceptive manufacturing company. His company produced and distributed the infected condoms. He is a Filipino Moslem and an outspoken defender of the Filipino Islamic minorities. Another is Nur Ahmad, an American Moslem of Filipino descent, until two years ago a PhD student at Johns Hopkins University. The third is Anne DuBois, also an American. She's an environmental activist and a former member of a radical environmental group. We're still trying to determine the identity of the others."

"Do we know where they are presently?" the reporter insisted.

"No, since we learned their identities only a few hours ago. We know they disappeared three weeks ago and have had time to move about and hide without arousing suspicion. If they assumed different names, they could be hard to find."

"Do you think they had help from an organized terrorist group?" a female White House correspondent asked.

"Again, it's too soon to tell," Paul Fiorelli replied. "It's possible that they were sympathizers of some extremist group, but that's just speculation. They certainly needed financing, and it's not clear if their business generated sufficient profits to cover their activities. We're working with the Filipino authorities to answer those and other questions."

"Mr. Fiorelli, how did they get a hold of the virus in the first place?" the woman insisted.

"We don't know that."

"The President stated that they had modified the virus. What does that mean?" The question was shouted from the back of the room.

Fiorelli looked at the head of Homeland Security. "The honest answer is we don't know," Stone answered. "We suspect that the virus will demonstrate some behavior that is different from the standard smallpox. What we do know is that the infected patients exhibit a form of the disease called black smallpox, a more virulent version. What other surprises may be ahead for us, we'll need to wait and see."

"Can you elaborate on the President's statement about allocating resources globally where they have the most impact?" The question was from a correspondent with a foreign news agency.

"Resources and expertise around the world are not evenly distributed," Russ Stone explained. "Yet, if a nation does not control the virus within its borders, it will spill over and ultimately affect its neighbors. Part of our challenge is to ensure that every region of the world deals as effectively as possible with the pandemic so that societies and economies can go back to normal."

"Can you give an example?" the foreign correspondent insisted.

"Vaccine is an example. I know this is difficult to sell to the American people, but we are already evaluating the possibility of allocating some of our vaccine supply to countries that have none. This may mean that we don't have enough to inoculate our entire population, but it will allow the immunization of critical medical personnel in other countries and avoid a total exodus of doctors and nurses."

"Mr. Secretary, will the domestic deployment of military forces be under your control?" another reporter shouted.

"Coordination between military activity and that of other federal emergency teams will be through the Department of Homeland Security. My main function is to ensure a concerted response effort. Will I be giving orders to the Joint Chiefs or the Secretary of Defense? Of course not. They are in charge of the military forces. We all have one goal, and we'll work together to accomplish it."

Another question came from the floor, but Stone raised his open hand and continued, "Let me add one more point. Smallpox is now the problem all of us must solve. It's a national security problem. It's an international affairs problem. It's a civil liberties problem. It's an economic problem. Obviously, it's a health services problem. As such, it demands the full attention of everyone in government, especially the President. No meaningful decision will be made without the President's evaluation and agreement. As commander-in-chief, he's in full command of all aspects of this war."

***

Rio de Janeiro had to prepare for the onslaught in a hurry. When the news of infected condoms broke, social volunteers were dismayed to discover that they had been distributing

SharusMan condoms in Leblon, Ipanema, Copacabana, and other neighborhoods for nearly two weeks. Their city had been directly targeted, except that their carton had arrived later than most.

"We must identify alternate isolation and quarantine facilities immediately," Dr. Senna said at a meeting with health officials. "We can expect thousands of infected patients over the next few days, and our hospitals have only a handful of isolation beds."

"We don't know if these condoms are infected," an official replied. "Maybe it won't be that bad."

Dr. Senna exploded. She was a gentle woman, at times overly sensitive with the suffering of her patients, but she couldn't tolerate incompetence. "Where the hell have you been lately? Under a rock? Look at what's happening in São Paulo – it will happen here if we don't do a better job."

The news arriving from São Paulo was indeed frightening. All order and civility had broken down and the Brazilian government had already sent in the army. Many inhabitants were fleeing and arriving in Rio with horror stories.

"We need to find places that are somewhat isolated from the residential areas," Dr. Senna continued. "They'll be easier to manage and present less risk to the population."

"And where do we find isolated places in a crowded city," the official replied, defiantly.

"Are we here to identify solutions or to expose roadblocks?" Senna asked, exasperated. "I don't know where to find them. You tell me!"

"We'll work on that," another official replied, more conciliatory. "We'll look at the stadiums, hotels, churches, and other large structures. We'll come up with something."

"You do that, and do it quickly," she answered. "And make sure you notify the population about the condoms. Get the TV stations to show pictures, and send volunteers through the same streets to warn the pimps, the prostitutes, the teenagers, and anyone who might have received them."

Dr. Senna returned to the hospital. As she arrived, workers were carrying away another body bag.

"That's number eight," Dr. Ricardo Teixeira said.

"How are the others?" she asked.

He shook his head. "Only the American shows any signs of recovery."

She donned her protective suit and went in. A nauseating smell of blood and antiseptics filled the room. Several patients were moaning and a few were unconscious. All had extensive lesions and signs of bleeding on their faces and bodies. Renato, her first smallpox patient, was gasping and wouldn't last long.

She spotted Bruce DuBois. He appeared much more alert than previously and was following her with his eyes.

"Oi, Bruce," she said and smiled.

"Am I gonna die?" he asked in English, barely audible. He was somewhat aware of his surroundings. He could hear the cries and see the disfiguring wounds of the patients around him, and he certainly could feel his own pain.

She thought of her own son and wondered how he was doing. After the death of her husband in a freak sailing accident some twelve years ago, Ronaldo had been her life and emotional anchor. He had chosen to follow on his mother's footsteps and was now completing his medical degree in London.

She missed him and worried about him. They spoke on the

phone frequently, and she knew that the virus was creating havoc in London just like everywhere else. The fact that Ronaldo had been vaccinated gave her some peace of mind.

Dr. Senna examined Bruce thoroughly. His face was covered with wounds, but scabs were starting to form under his beard. The bleeding had stopped and his lungs sounded clear. She shook her head and smiled again. "No, you are coming around. It will take a while, but you will be fine." She had an accent, but her English was perfect. "Just rest and do not worry about a thing."

CHAPTER 14

Winter began the month of March with a vengeance. On Monday morning, one week after the public announcement of the outbreak, Chicago and St. Louis experienced below-zero temperatures while the entire northeast, from Virginia to Maine, was paralyzed by one to two feet of fresh snow.

Dr. DuBois left his home after spending an hour shoveling his driveway. As he cautiously drove on the slippery roads, children were out enjoying the snow. The kids understood that there was a danger out there and that people could die. Some had nightmares when the lights went out at night, but during the day, the disease was no scarier than the big bad wolf. When they woke up to a sunny sky and lots of fresh snow on a Monday without school, they just went out and had fun. What could a little virus do to them?

Some parents had joined the children in the snow-covered yards and streets. Many businesses were closed either because of the martial law restrictions or due to disruptions in regular commerce. Employees were calling in sick or using vacation days, and close to half of the population was temporarily out of work.

It had been a difficult and emotionally wrenching weekend for Frank DuBois. He had been at the hospital on Saturday when a hysterical Doreen paged him. Without warning, their daughter's name had been broadcast by the Director of the FBI on national TV as one of the persons responsible for the epidemic. Frank had rushed home to try to understand what was going on and console his wife.

He was bewildered. Could Annie have done what they accused her of doing? Could the sweet child he had rocked to sleep, burped, and taught to ride a bike really be associated with a group of international terrorists? There had to be a mistake, maybe it was a different person. But how many environmentalists were named Anne DuBois? Frank didn't know what to think. Maybe she had done it – he had not seen her or talked to her in ten years. He no longer knew his daughter. She never called, not even for Christmas or birthdays. He had tracked her in Washington a few years earlier, but she had never returned his letters or phone calls and when they went to visit she was gone.

He remembered the old Annie with love and cherished memories, and he longed to see her and hug her again. But in his heart, she had died the day she stormed out of the house screaming insults. The new Anne was someone that he no longer recognized. He didn't know why or how she had changed, but this young woman was not the child he had raised.

But now she was back to haunt them. Doreen was

inconsolable, hurt and crying at first, then enraged and cursing her daughter when the pain momentarily subsided. A few friends had called wanting to express their support, but Doreen had been in no mood to talk to anyone.

Things were about to get worse.

The first TV news van showed up by late Saturday afternoon. Others followed and by nightfall, every New Jersey and New York TV, newspaper, and radio station had a news crew camped in front of the DuBois home. They parked on the lawn leaving huge tire tracks on the soggy ground, jumped on the bushes next to the house, invaded the backyard, and set equipment up on the deck. They knocked on doors, shouted their names, and focused their lenses on the inside of the house through the curtains. After obtaining the DuBoises' home and cell phone numbers, they kept calling until the phones were disconnected.

Dr. DuBois managed to contact a friend at the police department, and a police squad ordered the reporters to the curb. But the cops were mostly ignored. Powerful lights illuminated the exterior of their house forcing the couple to close all window curtains and blinds. They kept the lights off and hid in their bedroom. Doreen lay in bed, crying.

Frank turned on a small TV in the bedroom. It was showing a picture of a *SharusMan* condom. "Anyone having used one of these," the network expert was explaining, "should report to one of the quarantine centers immediately and inform the emergency personnel. Don't panic if you used it. It doesn't mean that you are infected because not all condoms were contaminated. But you need to take the proper precautions to protect yourself and those around you.

"Also," the expert went on as the camera again focused on an intact condom, "if you have any of these around the bedroom or in your purse, turn them over to the local police or to an emergency worker. Don't be afraid, they're not contagious until the wrapping foil is ripped open. And for God's sake, don't use them."

The camera shot changed to Cecilia Chapman.

"On a related story, we have obtained a photo of Anne DuBois, one of the Americans suspected of unleashing the deadly smallpox virus," Cecilia said as Anne's pretty dark eyes and brownish blond hair appeared on a corner of the screen above her right shoulder. Someone from the network had obtained a copy of the high school yearbook from Anne's senior year. "She was raised in Basking Ridge in suburban New Jersey where her parents still reside," Cecilia continued. A live feed appeared from the DuBois front yard.

A field reporter had his back to the house. "Yes, Cecilia, we are in front of the DuBois home in this affluent New Jersey suburb," the reporter said. "We know that Anne's parents are inside, but they have refused to appear or make any statements for our cameras. We have also learned from neighbors that the DuBoises have been estranged from their daughter since her college years. They are both college graduates and respected members of their professions and community. Coincidentally, Anne's father has played an important role in the coordination of the emergency response team in New Jersey."

As the reporter spoke, the network showed Frank's face captured during an interview earlier in the week. The image then shifted to a taped clip of the same reporter interviewing a young woman who held a small child.

"I knew Anne well," the woman was saying. "We were in high school together and we lived on the same street, but we weren't really friends. I don't think she had any close friends. She was polite and had good grades, but she had all these crazy ideas about saving the earth. She was going to prove that pollution was killing the planet."

"Anything to indicate she would resort to violence or terrorism?" the reporter asked.

"Not really. As I said, she was a bit weird when it came to environmental issues. She was outspoken about global warming and thought that the use of all chemicals should be stopped, but there was nothing to indicate that she would go crazy. I feel sorry for her parents. They are really nice people and don't deserve this."

Frank turned the TV off. He hurt, but he didn't need pity. His stomach was rumbling, but he wouldn't venture into the kitchen where the cameras could see him. He lay down next to his wife and tried to sleep.

On Sunday morning, the reporters were at it again. Some had camped in front of his home all night. Frank went downstairs to the kitchen, picked up some milk and cereal, and returned to the bedroom.

"How long are they gonna stay there?" Doreen asked. "You'd think nothing else of importance is happening in the world." Frank wondered the same thing.

Mercifully, by late morning the snow started to fall, heavy and wet. The reporters decided to leave and were all gone by the time three inches of snow had accumulated on the ground. They had not returned thanks to the storm.

Bruce had not called yet, and they worried about him too.

"Do you think he's okay?" Doreen asked for the hundredth time.

"He's a grown man. He's fine," Frank answered without conviction.

"Why doesn't he call? It's not like him."

"The epidemic is global, maybe things are chaotic in Brazil. Or maybe he called when the phone was disconnected."

"I wonder if he knows about his sister."

"It's possible. Bad news travel fast."

"I just wish he'd call," Doreen said with a sigh.

***

It was around eleven when Dr. DuBois finally made it to the hospital. Doreen stayed home, unable to face her co-workers, but for him work was a distraction that kept his mind from dwelling on the situation. Besides, he was needed.

Activity at the hospital was slower than it had been in a week. Some medical staff were calling in sick with post-vaccine malaise and others were having a hard time getting to the hospital because of the snow. Of course, patients were experiencing the same difficulty. Vaccination of all emergency personnel throughout the state had been completed and the vaccine was now available for the general population, but impassable roads were winning over the fear of the virus.

Sarah Wilson smiled when she saw him. He guessed it was a smile because the scabs around her lips and eyelids and the sores under her nose and on her cheeks made it painful for her to move any of her facial muscles.

"How are you today?" he asked as he approached her bed. She gave him a thumbs up. "You're coming around just fine," he said as he examined her. "All we need is time for these sores to completely close and the wounds to heal. You'll have to stay here until the scabs fall off or you may contaminate someone else. It'll probably be another three weeks, but you'll be going home alive."

Since Todd's death, Sarah had seen another nine people taken away in body bags. None of the patients around her seemed to be recovering. As bad as she felt, she had to consider herself lucky.

Around the country, only a few confirmed cases showed any signs of recovery. The death rate was as high as feared, and the deaths were coming on rather quickly, usually from excessive bleeding, asphyxiation due to blood in the lungs, or heart failure.

Dr. Skarzinski was surprised to see his colleague at the hospital.

"I saw the news," he said. "I don't know what to say. I'm very sorry."

"Let's not talk about it," DuBois answered, waving off the topic. "How are we with isolation beds?"

Skarzinski got the hint. The subject was too painful and was better left alone.

"All existing sites are full, and we're seeking new locations," he answered. "We keep getting a steady stream of new patients."

"It'll be that way for a while, I suspect," DuBois said. "People acquired the condoms over a period of weeks; some were used immediately, but others were kept for days or weeks before they were needed. Even after the disease broke, people were still using the infected condoms without knowing that they were committing suicide two at a time."

"Hopefully, everyone heard the news by now and got rid of them," Skarzinski replied.

Dr. DuBois spent the rest of his day visiting the isolation centers around Morristown and Newark. The situation was desperate everywhere. Except for fluids and painkillers, there was nothing more the medical staff could do for the victims. He felt indescribable frustration but kept going, as if seeing the misery and feeling the pain would dull his own anguish.

At one of the units, in two side-by-side beds, a couple was holding hands. Dr. DuBois went over to them. The man was too sick to speak and didn't even notice him. The woman shook her head when she saw him, and a silent tear rolled down her cheek. She had seen the expression on the doctor's face and understood the prognosis. "At least we'll go together," she said with some difficulty. "I just don't know who'll take care of my children."

He felt helpless, and useless, and turned away to hide his eyes. At that moment, in that place, Frank DuBois cursed the daughter he had loved and, for the first time in many years, he broke down and cried.

***

Frank returned home early, emotionally drained. Doreen had asked him not to be late in case the reporters returned. Besides, since she had refused to leave the house, he needed to stop at the supermarket.

Some supermarket shelves had been restocked, but the previous abundance was no longer available. Canned goods had flown off the shelves faster than the clerks could replenish them. Batteries, pastas, rice, sugar, flour, sodas, cooking oil, potato chips, anything that could be stored for any length of time had been purchased in record quantities. The store had only a limited number of goods in inventory, and most items would be unavailable for some time. The just-in-time manufacturing and inventory system did not allow for quick changes in demand. No one would starve, at least not right away, but the selection was narrow. Most scarce were perishables. The variety and quantity of fruits, vegetables, and fish were very limited, and what existed was not very fresh.

Frank bought what he needed and headed for home. Doreen's suspicions were well founded. It was already dark, but as he turned into his street he saw the news van parked by the curb. It was cold and the reporters were inside the van, expecting someone to come out of the house. He pressed his garage-door opener just in time for the door to be fully retracted as he drove in. He pressed the remote again, even before the car was completely inside. They might have taken a shot of the car, but the door closed before they could get to him. Having missed a perfect opportunity, the news team left.

"They were here all afternoon," Doreen said.

Frank turned the TV on. Secretary Stone was being interviewed live.

"We are pleased with the way businesses and individuals have tried to abide by the President's mandates under martial law. Screening at churches and malls during the weekend proceeded uneventfully. At state border crossings, the National Guard has taken over. We have seen some traffic delays but in general, traffic has been very light."

"Any problems with the elimination of home quarantine?" the interviewer asked.

"That has been the most difficult to implement. People

have lives and families, and it's a major disruption. Others simply refuse to have their freedom restricted. Consequently, many people didn't bother to report to the quarantine centers. Health volunteers, with the help of law enforcement, had to go looking for them."

"Why did the President eliminate home quarantine?"

"Because it wasn't serving its purpose. People were disregarding the rules and making it impossible to contain the virus. The magnitude of the problem doesn't give us the luxury of being flexible. We must ensure that infected people don't go around spreading the disease."

"Mr. Secretary, there have been reports of violence between the health workers and some quarantine patients who refuse to be taken to the centers. How widespread is the problem?"

Stone rubbed his chin and shifted in his chair. "It hasn't been as smooth as we'd like it," he conceded. "We've had people hiding in the house when they were tracked down. Others went out the backdoor as the emergency team went in the front. A number of individuals had to be taken forcefully and we even had some episodes of people threatening the health workers. Quite a number remain unaccounted for. It's a problem we have to deal with, and we're taking steps so that it doesn't happen again."

"How are you going to accomplish that?"

"First, all new contacts will be quarantined as soon as they are identified. There won't be an opportunity for people to go home and decide that they don't want to be taken away from their families. Second, we're increasing security at the centers. We don't want to treat people as prisoners, but we can't afford unlimited fairness or tolerance because the cost may be too high. We're under martial law for a reason. Some liberties will need to be restricted temporarily. The price of unlimited freedom is unaffordable."

After the interview, Cecilia Chapman came on with a new "Outbreak News Bulletin." The number of smallpox deaths nationwide was now over one thousand, and confirmed cases in isolation exceeded eighty thousand. Footage showed victims' families grieving, small children now orphans, and police dragging screaming individuals to quarantine centers.

The network had uncovered quite a bit of information on Anne DuBois, her activities, and her whereabouts for the last decade. They had background on her involvement with the environmental extremist groups and showed pictures of her apartment and her office in Washington. They also had information on her parents' professional activities. They ended the segment with an image of Frank's car going into the garage. The DuBoises watched, incredulous, learning more about their daughter in five minutes than they had in ten years.

Reporters had also gathered considerable information on Nur Ahmad. They had stationed themselves in front of his family's apartment in Seattle as they had done in New Jersey. But in this case, they managed to ambush Nur's parents as they returned home.

"Mr. Ahmad," a reporter shouted as he chased a small Filipino man down the street, "what can you tell us about your son's involvement in this terrorist activity?" The man, head low and holding his wife's arm, sidestepped the photographers and cameramen and ran into his home without a word.

The reporters had attracted a crowd in the mostly Filipino

neighborhood. Nur's sister decided to come out to read a short statement. She hoped to satisfy the reporters so that they would leave them alone.

"We lost contact with my brother more than two years ago," she said. "Suddenly, he just disappeared. We contacted Johns Hopkins where he was studying, but they knew nothing of his whereabouts. We went to Baltimore to check his apartment, and most of his things were gone. It didn't look like foul play, so we had nothing to go to the police with."

She was nervous, and the handwritten statement shook in her hands. She continued. "Months later, one of his friends told us that he had talked about working in the Philippines. That was the last we heard of him until his name was mentioned on television." She became emotional but proceeded. "We're saddened by what's happening around us, and we are shocked and humiliated that my brother might have had something to do with the epidemic."

"You lying Moslem bitch!" a neighbor cried from the gathered crowd, tossing a stone in her direction. "Your brother, your whole family, is disgracing and shaming the entire Filipino community. He should be hanged, along with all you Moslem pigs!"

The TV cameras were rolling. The overwhelming majority of the Filipinos were Catholic, and the Filipino Moslems were tolerated but often treated as outcasts by many in their own community. Others joined the chorus of insults, and Nur's sister was hit on the chin with an egg. She burst into tears, ran through the front entrance, and slammed the door. The networks had great headline footage.

"I'd feel sorry for them if I weren't feeling sorry for myself,"

Doreen told her husband. "Those poor people are being victimized for something they had nothing to do with. Why don't those reporters just leave them alone and let them grieve in peace?"

The cameras in Seattle were still rolling, with the field reporters making their commentary to the events just witnessed. Suddenly, a large SUV accelerated toward the gathering and a passenger began spraying automatic gunfire from an open window into the crowd. "Terrorists, go back to the Philippines!" someone yelled from the vehicle. The SUV sped down the street, shooting randomly at panic-stricken Filipinos diving into the ground. A small boy was shot on the head and an older woman crouched holding her stomach.

"God, the world is going mad!" Doreen exclaimed.

Frank didn't answer. He kept reliving the images on TV and feeling the pain and misery in the isolation rooms. He thought of a daughter who had gone terribly astray, of a dying couple holding hands, and of children who would soon be orphans. He got up and went to the bathroom. For the second time today emotion defeated him, but he could not let Doreen see him cry.

CHAPTER 15

As the number of victims grew, many people became consumed by fear. Entire families were leaving the cities for country homes or isolated cabins in the mountains where coming in contact with the virus was less likely. Many others had basements full of canned foods. They had locked their doors, not planning to open them to anyone until the outbreak was under control. Others were rushing to churches and making outrageous vows to God or to a favorite saint, vows that they would never be able to fulfill even if their requests were granted. Still others were looking for someone to blame and taking revenge on the Filipinos and other Southeast Asians.

The Seattle shootings sparked a rash of copycat attacks on innocent civilians in Filipino communities throughout the country. The violence had resulted in fourteen deaths by

Thursday. Filipino-Americans were as afraid of other Americans as they were of the virus.

"We demand protection," they shouted as they demonstrated in front of Seattle's town hall and in other cities.

To make matters worse, law enforcement had failed to apprehend and prosecute any of the attackers. The regular police were consumed by the medical emergency, and the military forces taking over crime prevention did not have the experience to deal with random hit-and-run crime. The racist thugs operated with immunity.

Although the shootings were getting ample media coverage, no one really worried or cared about them outside the Filipino community.

"It's their own fault," a white teenager shouted to a reporter covering the rampage. "The Filipinos started the whole mess, didn't they?"

"If they don't like it, they can go back to where they came from," said another, throwing a brick through a car window.

The disease-related deaths were increasing at an alarming rate, and that was the real worry for most Americans. Except for the violence in the Filipino neighborhoods, the army units patrolling the urban centers were preventing the most severe incidents of looting and lawlessness. Military logistics teams were anticipating bottlenecks in the distribution of essential items, such as food, medical supplies, and gasoline, and were succeeding in avoiding widespread shortages.

Civil libertarians criticized the President's declaration of martial law, the forced internment centers, and the use of the military for domestic law enforcement. But since they offered no adequate solution of their own, no one paid attention. The majority of Americans perceived the President's actions as appropriate and timely – a mighty enemy was loose right here at home and it made sense to deploy the military where the enemy was. The nation needed to be protected.

There were also plenty of opportunists taking advantage of the misery. Websites were springing up by the minute offering all kinds of wacky protection, everything from blessed icons to holy water to magical ointments to special vitamins guaranteed to fend off the disease. The Internet was the vehicle for the modern-day charlatans, and many were falling for it.

Still, amid the anxiety and the uncertainty, an eerie calm prevailed. Most Americans followed the progress of the disease with disbelief and some degree of helplessness, but accepted life one day at a time. So many were getting sick that no one could figure out how to avoid exposure, and people simply counted on the vaccine to protect them. Those not yet infected considered themselves lucky. Others perceived the events of the previous eleven days as a surreal situation, a movie set where someone would soon say "cut." Those out of work put things in perspective, deciding that unemployment was not a big deal as long as it didn't last too long and they managed to stay healthy. Those in quarantine prayed for it to be just a false alarm. The ones in isolation were the unlucky ones, who could do nothing but wait for a miracle.

"It's a different kind of war, but a war nonetheless," Russ Stone said in an interview. "In every war, there's always a heavy cost in casualties and hardship."

Americans were seeing the fatalities and feeling the hardship. Although scared, most accepted them with resilience and stoicism.

***

The same was not true in other parts of the world. In Europe, there had been no agreement on needed preventive measures, and actions by one nation were having negative repercussions in others. When France closed its borders, heated criticism ensued from Spain and Portugal, which became effectively isolated from the rest of Europe. The European nations were so interdependent for critical goods that no country was self-sufficient any longer. Not having access to French products or worse, not being able to use the French roads and rail system, quickly generated shortages for medical and factory supplies. The Spanish government threatened to pull out of the European Union if Brussels didn't force the French to reconsider.

"France's national security is more important than the future of a united Europe," the French foreign minister asserted.

The leadership of the European Union had no authority to force France or any other member nation to follow specific policies or guidelines and was not authorized to meddle in the internal affairs of sovereign countries.

"If we can't count on the Union in times of crisis, then we don't need it when times are good," the Spanish government replied. Spain pulled out.

This action increased the shortages. As this became apparent, there was a second run at stores and supermarkets, with people buying everything they could and aggravating the situation. TV and radio broadcasts induced similar reactions in cities where the shortages were still not a problem. Riots broke out, crowds became mobs, and throughout Europe people broke supermarket windows and stole anything they could carry.

"The virus is generating chaos around the world," Cecilia reported. "In many countries, law enforcement is failing to curtail violence and looting." As she spoke, images from Paris showed people hoarding purchased or stolen goods, then being ambushed and robbed by others in the street. The police resorted to deadly force to contain the mobs, with little success. A few people were hit and fell on a sidewalk, but others just ran away carrying their loot.

"Casualties are multiplying and we see no end to this nightmare," a French official was saying in an interview. "Emergency medical and police personnel have been vaccinated, but vaccines have already run out for the general population, including those in quarantine."

"What treatment do they receive?" the interviewer asked.

"None," the official replied. "We keep them for observation and to protect the general population." The image shifted to a terrified woman dodging bullets as she ran away from a quarantine center.

"And what care do you give the victims in isolation?

"Given the numbers, our hospitals can't provide any real treatment after onset of symptoms. Many victims know this and no longer seek help. They figure that if they are going to die, they may as well die at home."

The image shifted again to show an obviously sick man being forcefully removed from an apartment by emergency personnel in biological garb.

"In many cases,' the official continued, "family members do

what they can to make the victims comfortable, but others are simply abandoned for fear of exposure."

"People by the thousands are leaving the cities and looking for less crowded spaces in the countryside," Cecilia reported again. "They hope to join friends or family members still living in rural towns, but most are met with hostility." The television now showed roads in Italy and Germany crowded with overloaded cars and vans. In England, there were hastily prepared "Keep your distance" or "You're NOT Welcome" signs. In Spain, a menacing gun barrel peeked through a window.

***

As expected, the number of victims picked up in Rio. Health officials chose a luxury resort in a secluded section of Leblon beach to become the new isolation center. The 400-bed hotel was converted into a makeshift hospital exclusively for confirmed smallpox cases. Most of the available biological gear was sent to the resort for use by the medical staff. All knew that there was no room for carelessness. Inside the building, full protective clothing was mandatory at all times, and the entrance foyer and a pool-house at the rear were converted into decontamination facilities.

Bruce DuBois, the only survivor from the initial group of patients, was also moved to the hotel.

"You are doing well," Dr. Senna told him. "Just give it time."

Patients started arriving from every emergency room in the city. First it was a trickle, then a flood, and the emergency staff was struggling to keep up.

"I figure we can hold one thousand patients," Dr. Senna said.

"At this rate, it won't take long," Dr. Teixeira replied.

"I worry about the doctors and the nurses. The stress level will only get higher."

"They're here willingly. They'll be fine."

"They are only human. I wonder what will happen if one of us comes down with the virus," Senna said.

Meanwhile, officials took over a convention center in the southern outskirts of the city and converted it into a quarantine facility. They estimated that it could quarantine five thousand contacts. The individuals arriving were housed in groups separated by arrival date. If no one in a group were to show symptoms after seventeen days, the whole group could be released. But if someone developed the disease, the entire group needed to restart the clock.

"Without vaccines, there's no telling how long people will need to stay," a health official commented.

Armed guards were posted at all quarantine exits to discourage those inside from running away.

As the number of victims increased, so did the desperation. The stories coming from São Paulo and the images on TV added to the fear. Without vaccines, biological protection, and adequate facilities, many in the medical staff deserted from the city's emergency rooms and hospitals. WHO resources were spread too thin, police officers stopped responding to emergency calls, and ambulance drivers disappeared. The situation throughout the city became chaotic.

Looting and rioting broke out. The supermarkets were ransacked and were no longer operating. Long lines formed in the middle of the night in front of stores where bread, milk, and other items were expected in the morning. Fights were common if food finally arrived.

The city implemented mandatory curfews. Armed military personnel in the streets had orders to shoot to kill if the curfews were disobeyed. As in Europe, those who could were leaving the cities and spreading the virus. People were fleeing the disease, but mostly they were trying to escape the threat of starvation or murder. The wealthy minorities, not accustomed to hardship, most dependent on purchased goods, and most able to find shelter at their summer homes, were the first to leave. As a result, business and industry came to a standstill.

Unable to get help, many victims were going through the agonizing disease at home and infecting those around them. Many were left to die alone by their own frightened families, while some were murdered, like rabid dogs, by hysterical crowds.

***

At the General Washington Hotel in Morristown, all quarantined individuals had been vaccinated, but a handful had developed obvious smallpox symptoms: high fever, nausea, aches, and skin rashes.

"When was their contact with a sick patient?" Dr. DuBois asked.

"In all cases, days before the outbreak was recognized, sometime between Thursday and Sunday two weeks ago," Dr. Skarzinski replied. "Some were co-workers of the victims, others were in the emergency room when the first cases came in." He was very aware that he, too, had been in the emergency room in close contact with Sarah and Todd on that same weekend.

But he had worn gloves and a mask, hadn't he? Despite being vaccinated, Dr. Skarzinski found himself wondering about every little thing he had done during that first weekend.

"When were they vaccinated?"

Skarzinski checked the records. "Most on Tuesday, some on Wednesday of last week."

DuBois counted back. "Tuesday, Monday, Sunday, Saturday, Friday. It might have been too late. Waiting more than three days for the vaccine is dangerous."

"We just didn't know what was going on," Skarzinski replied.

"I know. There was nothing anyone could have done differently given the circumstances."

Like all other patients, the sick health workers were moved into isolation. The mood there was bewilderment – being diagnosed was practically a death sentence. Nationwide, it was now confirmed that the survival rate was no more than five percent. The patients knew it and received the news with crying, cursing, utter disbelief, or revolt. Several committed suicide upon feeling the dreaded symptoms.

Dr. DuBois completed his rounds. For the first time in his professional life, he wondered if he could keep his sanity. Each isolation room visit was an emotional challenge. The pain, the moans, the gruesome bleeding, the horrific wounds, the awful stench that seemed to get more unbearable each day, the anguish of the dying, and the desperation of knowing that there was nothing he could do were all accumulating, and he wondered how much longer he could go on without going over the edge.

He paid particular attention to the handful of patients who

appeared to be recovering. Whenever possible, he ordered those at the temporary facilities moved to the isolation rooms at the hospitals where additional care could be provided to help them recover.

As usual, he stopped to see Sarah. She was doing much better. She had large scabs on her face and body, but no more open wounds. She was walking gingerly through the isolation room and comforting other patients, living proof that you could survive and recover, even if her appearance were not much to look forward to.

"Great to see you up and about," the doctor said as he entered the room.

"I feel better. It's hard to walk because of the lesions between my legs and on the soles of my feet," she answered, speaking through her teeth.

"Are you eating okay?"

"Everything is pureed, not very appetizing. And I'm never hungry."

"You must eat in order to regain your strength."

Sarah walked back to her bed, and he spent some time checking her. "Everything appears to be going back to normal. The virus did a job on you, but you're healing nicely. Keep it up," he said, smiling.

She smiled back. It was good to see him. His visit was the only thing she looked forward to every day. This dear old man was her only connection to anything of emotional value.

Frank DuBois left the hospital and drove home. He was not prepared for what he found.

About fifty people had assembled in front of his property and had parked their cars haphazardly in the middle of the street. He couldn't understand what was going on. It was dark, and he couldn't see who they were.

Deciding not to meet them without knowing what was happening, he parked in the street about a hundred yards away. He cut through a neighbor's yard and entered the house through the rear. Doreen was in the living room, frightened and in tears.

"What's all the commotion out there?"

"They started showing up about one hour ago and have been shouting obscenities and threats," she said as she hugged him.

"Why?" Gently, he pulled away from her embrace to look at her face. "What do they want?"

"I don't know. It must have something to do with that damned TV report."

"What report?"

"They ran another program on the terrorists who spread the virus," she said, sobbing. "I didn't want to watch but couldn't turn it off. But then I couldn't believe what I was watching. They had a segment on Anne that made it sound as if we are somehow responsible for what she did."

"We?" Frank asked, incredulous. "We haven't seen her for ten years! She wanted nothing to do with us. How can we possibly be responsible?"

Frank started pacing. The shouts grew louder and they went upstairs to the privacy of their bedroom.

Doreen tried to explain the TV report, her voice trembling with disgust and sarcasm. "They found out about the work Anne did in high school with the orange peel extract, you know, the solvent to replace Freon. Because she worked with me on that, I am somehow responsible for her radical environmental tendencies. And because you're an infectious diseases specialist, it's obvious that she got the idea for bioterrorism from you."

"Those bastards!" he exclaimed, fists clenched.

A couple of days earlier, FBI agents had come to interrogate them. Frank and Doreen had spent four hours being grilled until the investigators realized that there was nothing they could tell them to help in their search for Anne. The DuBoises thought that was the end of it. They were wrong – they had forgotten about the media.

Outside, the mob yelled insults and pelted the house with snowballs. Then a TV crew arrived. Tragedy and violence were for reporters like blood for sharks – they could smell them from a distance and were immediately attracted. And as often happens, the camera fed the mob's fury. The noise increased and a number of demonstrators crossed into the backyard, banging on the doors and breaking glass. Suddenly, a rock came crashing through the bedroom window. Doreen screamed and held on to her husband.

Frank decided to confront the crowd. "I'm going downstairs to talk to them. They'll break all the windows if we don't do something."

"They'll hurt you. There's no use trying to reason with this kind of people."

Another rock hit the side of the house with a bang, then a third one came in through the already-broken window. Frank grabbed Doreen's arm and led her downstairs toward the front door. He opened it and reached the front steps, holding his wife's hand.

The group quieted down for a second. They didn't expect their targets to come out, but the surprise didn't last.

"Terrorists!" someone yelled.

"My brother is dead because of your daughter!"

"You and your daughter should be lynched!"

"How could you collaborate with those fucking Moslems?"

Frank was suddenly terrified. He had never seen anything like this and felt like a wounded deer cornered by a threatening wolf pack. Before he could speak, a baseball-size rock came flying from within the crowd and hit Doreen on the temple. She fell backwards. Frank bent over to tend to his wife, but the crowd assaulted him. He was kicked, punched, and hit over the head repeatedly until he passed out on the trampled snow of his front yard. The mob cheered, and heavy winter boots ran up the front steps to kick the bloodied head of the unconscious Doreen. The TV camera was rolling. Great footage.

Frank DuBois woke up in a hospital bed. His entire body ached, and at first he couldn't remember anything. Tight bandages wrapped around his ribs, and large gauze patches covered his chin, his left cheek, and the back of his head. Then he remembered and tried to get up, but a nurse held him down.

"My wife?" he asked with difficulty.

The nurse just shook her head.

***

Anne DuBois was in paradise. She was close to nature the way nature was meant to be, as secluded as she could be anywhere on earth. Maybe someday the whole world would be like this.

She had arrived with a new identity. The French language her parents had forced her to learn as a child and the four years of French in high school served her well despite her strong American accent, which she explained as French Canadian. No one knew enough about North American geography and regional accents to question her.

She had initially reserved a room at a small resort on the south end of Fakarava atoll. It was the low season for tourism, and she had no trouble booking the place. But the resort was expensive, so she looked for different accommodations. She found a tiny bungalow nested among palm trees by the lagoon in a secluded area of the island. The place was in need of repair and not very clean, but it was affordable and in an idyllic location. It never ceased to amaze her that the locals seemed oblivious to so much peace and beauty.

She planned to stay until the pestilence she had unleashed ran its course. She spent her days on the beach, walking, napping, or just staring into the lagoon's turquoise waters. It was indescribable, this sense of freedom, openness, and warmth, the breathtaking scenery, the warm winds ruffling the palm trees, and the unspoiled forces that had shaped the beautiful atoll over thousands of years. She enjoyed her meals sitting on the coral by the lagoon. The natural tropical aquarium would come alive with all sorts of marine animals, from small sharks to colorful little fish to huge moray eels fighting for the food morsels she tossed in the water.

She bought a bicycle to roam around the island and befriended a number of people, truly delighting in the almost-primitive way of life. One of her favorite hangouts was the pearl farm, watching the farmers carry out their tasks. It was hard work to tend the seeded oysters to ensure high-quality pearls and eventually harvest the shells and extract the precious nuclei. Tricking the oysters to produce something so unnatural was against her beliefs, but she marveled at the fact that a simple invertebrate creature could generate, given time, something so perfect and so beautiful as a pearl. She got to know the owner and spent time with the pearl farmers, sometimes giving them a hand.

Anne had no radio or telephone, but she knew that her team's plan was having the desired effect. Once the magnitude of the worldwide outbreak became apparent, the French Polynesian authorities quickly stopped all traffic among the hundreds of islands and atolls. It appeared that all islands were free of the disease with the exception of Tahiti Island, where Papeete, the regional capital, was located. No one knew how the virus had arrived, but some infected tourist seemed to be the likely carrier.

After a few days, the inter-island travel ban was lifted, but Tahiti and lands outside of French Polynesia were off-limits. Local law enforcement checked the origin of any boat entering their ports and forbade anyone from coming ashore without assurance that they were arriving from disease-free islands.

For the five hundred or so inhabitants of Fakarava, life went on mostly unperturbed by the turmoil around the world.

CHAPTER 16

By Friday morning, eleven days after the beginning of the vaccination program, rumors were rampant about the vaccine's failure to provide immunity.

Most medical personnel had been working despite the low-grade fever and the soreness of their upper arms, a small price to pay for the protection the vaccine was expected to provide. A few had experienced more severe side effects, like red rashes or blisters around their eyes, mouth, or genital areas, a likely result of accidentally getting some of the *Vaccinia* virus from the vaccination spot to other parts of the body. There were isolated reports of extreme reactions to the vaccine, like extensive blisters throughout the body, swelling of the brain, even heart trouble, but that too was expected. A number of hospitals had requested delivery of *Vaccinia Immune Globulin* and *Cidofovir*, experimental drugs reported to be effective in the treatment of severe post-vaccination complications.

But now doctors, nurses, medical volunteers, police, and firefighters were becoming sick in large numbers. They looked at the pus-filled blisters on their upper arms, clear signs that the vaccine should be working, and were baffled and horrified. The stoicism of the emergency response teams disappeared, and panic spread among those working directly with patients or manning the quarantine centers.

"The vaccine isn't protecting our people," Stone yelled into the phone. "Our emergency personnel are getting sick at an alarming rate, and those not yet sick are terrified. These people were vaccinated within a day or two of any contact with the virus and should be immune."

David Reiss didn't know how to answer. He had been suspicious and worried since finding out that the virus was genetically altered, but he had downplayed his concerns because that was all he could do. He could not issue a general warning – it would only add to the stress and create confusion, and there was a good chance it would be a false alarm. He had been monitoring the quarantine centers and emergency rooms and had seen vaccinated people coming down with the disease, but he kept explaining it on the basis of not getting the vaccine on time. He desperately hoped that the vaccine would still work. It was all they had.

But now there could be no doubt. It was apparent that those who received the shot were no more protected than those who did not. His worst-case scenario was confirmed.

"It has to be the genetic changes they made to the virus," he tried to explain. "As I told you before, we think they copied work done in Australia a few years ago, and whatever those bastards did must be allowing the virus to overcome the vaccine-induced immunity."

"I don't care what the virus does! What I need to know is what do we do now?" Russ Stone snapped. "We can't just let everyone die."

"There isn't much we can do."

"What do you mean, there isn't much you can do?" Stone screamed, exasperated. "You're the expert, for God's sake! You gotta give us something to fight with. The doctors, nurses, police, volunteers, everyone's contracting the disease. Those still healthy won't show up for work, and I can't blame them. How are we going to curtail this epidemic?"

"I don't have the answer," the CDC Director replied.

Yes, he was the expert but sadly, his expertise told him that they were helpless. This was not the time to sugarcoat the message. "The job just got much more complex," he said, "and we can anticipate a much greater loss of life than we'd thought. This thing isn't going to disappear soon. We need to expect this nightmare to last at least through the summer."

Stone uttered a profanity, but Reiss went on. "We don't have a vaccine, period. We're working with the Army and the pharmaceutical companies to test every antiviral drug in our arsenal but frankly, I don't hold much hope that we'll find anything effective against this virus. The best scientists all over the globe are dropping everything and concentrating only on developing a vaccine. The most advanced biological labs worldwide are working on it as their number one priority. Problem is, it'll take time."

"How much time? We don't have time!" Stone exploded in frustration.

He wasn't used to being denied. His success, first in business then in politics, stemmed from surrounding himself with the best professionals, providing them with clear direction, exuding confidence, and relying on his team to deliver results. Failure had never been an option. He was experiencing it now in the biggest challenge of his life, and he didn't know how to handle it.

Reiss didn't reply. Stone composed himself and asked, "With all those resources, can't we come up with something quickly?"

"Russ, it always takes nine months to deliver a baby, no matter how many people you throw at it. If this outbreak had started with a few isolated cases, we might have been able to stay ahead of it. But speed matters, and in this race the virus has an enormous head start. We're just trying to catch up to an avalanche, and the vaccine failure forces us to start from scratch."

Stone didn't answer. He was shaking his head. Reiss continued. "Initially, all the labs will do pretty much the same – search for something that may lead to an effective new vaccine. The time-savings will come from scientists sharing information. It'll avoid wasting time pursuing dead-ends and will speed up discovery by directing the work toward the most promising leads. But the process is never quick, even when we have the resources."

"God, this is worse than a nightmare! How are we going to control this epidemic?" Stone asked again, not expecting an answer. "Should we even be sending people into quarantine?"

That was another matter where the race against the virus had already been lost. The CDC had been madly rushing to deploy antibody and polymerase chain-reaction (PCR) tests aimed at early detection and diagnosis of the disease. Antibody tests could verify if anyone without symptoms had been exposed to the virus, and PCR tests could amplify DNA fragments of the *Variola* virus for rapid confirmation of infection. Both tests were to be used on victims' contacts and suspected individuals in an effort to limit quarantine to those in fact exposed to the virus. But the numbers had already mushroomed beyond any practical ability to screen those at risk. There were not enough kits, not enough staff, not enough labs.

"We don't have a choice, Russ. We need to protect the general population. If we don't quarantine those potentially exposed, they'll infect everyone around them."

"But locking them up in confinement centers is ensuring they'll be exposed," Russ retorted. "We already have plenty of resistance, the only thing that made quarantine tolerable was the protection expected from the vaccine. Without that, we'll have to drag everyone in and we'll have a rebellion to deal with."

"You're probably right, but what else can we do? As it is, we'll have hundreds of thousands, maybe millions of deaths in a month. It'll be much worse if we don't take drastic measures."

"So what do we do? Start shooting people if they don't want to stay in quarantine? This is absurd!"

"We'll need to take steps that were unimaginable just two weeks ago," Reiss replied. "But the stakes just became much higher. The folks in quarantine will have a hard time accepting the measures, but the population will understand them."

"I hope they do. In the meantime, I wonder how many of our emergency workers we're gonna lose."

"That will be a real tragedy," Reiss agreed. "I think many of them lowered their defenses after they were vaccinated. They assumed they were out of danger and took risks they wouldn't have taken otherwise. As they get sick, not only will we lose personnel we can't afford losing, but there'll be a huge psychological impact on the rest of the emergency teams."

"They simply won't show up," Russ Stone said. "We're already seeing it. Forget about interviewing the victims and looking for contacts. Our investigative teams are disappearing. Luckily, the number of new victims seems to have leveled off."

"Unfortunately, that will change. It's the calm before a bigger storm hits. Most of the new cases are still from the first batch of victims, those infected by the condoms. The second wave, those contracting the virus from the first victims, is only starting."

"How big will this thing get?"

"Very big."

"We had some projections assuming the vaccine worked, but now I'm at a loss."

"It'll be huge."

He should know. His agency was responsible for tracking the various infectious outbreaks around the world and had been collecting and analyzing data on the smallpox epidemic for the last eleven days. Although it was still too early to draw definite conclusions on propagation characteristics or mortality rates, his team had estimates on what to expect under various scenarios.

"It's possible that each wave will be an order of magnitude bigger than the one before. In other words, each smallpox patient could infect, in average, ten people or so," Reiss added.

Stone did the quick math. There were now approximately 120 thousand smallpox victims, a quarter of whom had already died. If Reiss's numbers were in the ballpark, they could expect more than a million new cases to start rolling in soon.

"We're not gonna make it," Stone said dejectedly. "We simply don't have the ability to handle so many patients without immunization. Our country's gonna collapse."

***

By late morning, it was apparent that Russ Stone was correct. Virtually all volunteers were staying home, and medical and law enforcement professionals were calling in sick in record numbers. The quarantine centers were left mostly unmanned, and many quarantined contacts, suddenly aware of the greater danger, left the centers. All over the country, there were reports of National Guardsmen using force against civilians trying to flee quarantine.

Hospitals became dysfunctional. Medical personnel reporting to work were immediately overwhelmed. While trying to protect themselves to avoid getting infected, they had to deal with a surge of new patients who demanded immediate attention. Additional National Guards were requested to maintain some order. Frightened guardsmen wearing biological suits were soon patrolling hospital emergency areas throughout the country. TV broadcasts showed scores of bewildered sick people waiting in frigid weather while armed troops prevented them from entering the hospitals.

Venkatraman came into Reiss's office with additional bad news. "Hospitals are closing their doors and not accepting new patients?" he said.

"Where?"

"Everywhere. They've been threatening for a few days, but with the latest rumors, they're shutting the emergency rooms and sending people away."

"They can't do that!"

"But they are. Some don't have sufficient staff to operate, others are closing because they're losing too much money."

"How can they be losing money? I've never seen so many sick people!"

"The medical insurance industry has been deliberating how to pay for the care of smallpox patients," Venkatraman explained. "It has now issued a statement saying that because the disease is an act of war, it's excluded by their policy clauses."

Reiss cursed.

"And the hospitals are left holding the bag," Venkatraman continued. "To make matters worse, the disease has affected normal revenue generating activities. All routine medical testing and non-emergency surgeries have stopped. Many patients normally seeking hospital care are staying away for fear of the virus. And many drugs are running out and not being replenished by the manufacturers."

Reiss shook his head. "We can't have that," he said. "The hospitals must remain open, or it'll make an impossible situation worse."

"Someone has to force them, but also give them a hand. Without money, staff, vaccines, and medications, they may as well stay closed."

***

Civil unrest picked up despite the presence of armed military. Neighborhood stores began demanding cash-only payment. People rushed to withdraw cash from their ATMs and banks. The ATMs were quickly emptied and some local branches run out of cash. When the news hit the airwaves, hysteria set in and the banks were inundated with withdrawal requests. By mid-afternoon, there was pandemonium in front of many bank offices, and branch managers were forced to close their doors for fear of violence.

That sparked another run at whatever was left in the supermarkets and within hours, most shelves were truly bare. Prices of many foodstuffs and other essential items quickly increased, in some cases doubling in a matter of hours. Many grocery stores closed, most for lack of products, some for lack of staff, and others counting on even higher prices as items became scarce. This proved to be a mistake – panic intensified and law enforcement was unable to maintain order. Pillaging spread from grocery stores to banks to other business, then it escalated to arson and random looting, particularly in inner-city neighborhoods. TV reporting spread the panic and fueled the frenzy. In some cases, armed troops used deadly force to control the mobs. In others, they refused to shoot unarmed civilians, even in the middle of the growing rampage. By Friday evening, lawlessness was the norm in Miami, Chicago, Los Angeles, Detroit, Newark, and Philadelphia.

The riots were at their worst in Filipino and Moslem quarters. What earlier had been mostly isolated drive-by shootings became an urban civil war, with gangs of white, black, and latino youths invading ethnic neighborhoods, setting homes ablaze, and making the residents scapegoats for the disaster. In Seattle, where the initial racial attacks had occurred, a new wave of violence left several dozen dead and countless others injured, to be treated by their desperate families who did not dare take them to the hospitals.

Meanwhile, the trickle of people leaving the cities became a flood, as had been happening in other countries. The roads were packed with loaded minivans and SUVs heading out of town. Interstate travel restrictions limited the mobility of panicked residents of places like Baltimore, Washington DC, Providence, even New York City. Nationwide, the situation was clearly out of control.

***

The President convened an emergency meeting of his National Security Council. The failure of the vaccine was a fatal blow in the desperate fight against the disease. The predictions from his experts were truly cataclysmic. And civil unrest, spreading like wild fire through the American cities, demanded immediate action. New, more drastic measures were needed.

Late Friday evening, the President addressed the nation for the third time since the beginning of the epidemic. With him were Russ Stone and Sam Atkins, the Secretary of Defense. The President walked to the podium with his head down. His tie was loose and his clothes disheveled.

"My fellow Americans. I'm sad to say that we've lost a major battle in the war against the disease. As the news media already reported, the biologically engineered virus is resistant to our vaccine. The smallpox immunization on which we counted isn't working.

"As a result, America is much more vulnerable than we hoped it would be. Additionally, the unrest that has flared up in several of our cities has added to the complexity of this disaster."

The President was clearly tired, with large bags under his eyes and new facial wrinkles that even make-up could not conceal. He continued. "Today, it is more evident than ever that this is a civil war, and we must treat it as such. In traditional wars, we send our military to the frontlines and support them with equipment, with our production facilities, and with our trust and prayers. They put themselves in harm's way, oblivious to their own well-being, indeed their own lives, to defend their nation. It's no different today, except that the enemy is more elusive and we're fighting the battle at home.

"We have three major tasks ahead of us. First and foremost, to fight the virus and take all steps necessary to prevent it from decimating our population. Second, to maintain order throughout the country. We can't permit panic and misplaced vengeance to transform our cities into battlefields. And third, to ensure the provision of essential products and services. We must avoid unnecessary suffering or death due to medical or food shortages."

The President straightened his shoulders, looked into the camera and went on. "To accomplish these objectives, we're putting into action a number of drastic measures to complement the martial law already underway. Because there is no more urgent business at this moment than the crisis at home, I'm ordering the return of all military personnel serving abroad and calling to service all national reserves. I'm ordering a draft of all essential medical and professional personnel needed to support critical emergency activities. I'm also ordering all branches of the armed forces, under the leadership of the Secretary of Defense, to immediately take over the essential functions required to deal with this national disaster.

"To survive this war, we must provide for the basic needs of the population. People need food, medical attention, and protection from mobs. We'll take all necessary steps to provide all three. Secretary Atkins will give you the details. In return, we ask every citizen of this great nation of ours to stay calm and serve when asked. And we need everyone to be patient."

The President paused, then continued slowly. "I will repeat: we're fighting a war and until it's over, our military will be in charge. It won't be life as usual. Our lives will be put on hold. Many will fall as casualties of this war. It serves no purpose to become upset, angry, anxious, or desperate. The situation is what it is, and the only certainties for the next few months are hardship and pain. To allow our emotions to take control will only make a bad situation intolerable."

The President moved aside and the Secretary of Defense came to the podium. Sam Atkins was a balding older man of average height with a pudgy face and a potbelly. The collar of his shirt was unbuttoned and his tie was loose and off-centered. He cleared his throat.

"To achieve the objectives outlined by the President, the following critical actions are being implemented.

"One, all hospitals will stay open, and all doctors, nurses, and trained medical personnel are mandated to report to work as usual. Also, doctors and medical professionals in private practice will report to the nearest hospital and will be assigned their duties as appropriate. Failure to comply will be equivalent to military desertion and will result in imprisonment.

"Two, all pharmaceutical companies will keep manufacturing and distributing key medications and medical supplies and take all necessary steps to make up for the loss of critical imported products. This order includes the suppliers to the pharmaceutical companies.

"Three, supermarkets will be identified in every community and will be set up as distribution centers for food and critical items.

"Four, food manufacturers are ordered to produce adequate provisions for the general population. The same applies to their suppliers.

"Five, farmers, including milk, eggs, cheese, and livestock producers, will continue normal operations. Wherever possible, increases in production or changes in product mix will be requested to make up for losses of imported foodstuffs.

"Six, electrical, water, telephone, and gas utilities will take all required steps to maintain distribution and avoid disruptions."

Secretary Atkins was sweating. He wiped his forehead with a handkerchief and continued. "The military will coordinate and enforce the provision of key goods and services. They will also secure the support of other required businesses, such as transportation and courier companies, inventory, warehousing, and logistics firms. Their request for support can't be denied without justification.

"Because of the difficulties already experienced by our financial and insurance systems, and because the law of supply and demand will create hysteria and confusion under these unusual economic conditions, a payment system based on IOUs will be implemented. Money or insurance won't be needed for food or for medical services. Everyone will be paid with IOUs, with prices frozen at end of February levels. An army logistics team will work with accounting firms and the IRS to develop a system for implementation and record keeping."

Atkins paused to wipe his face again. "To squelch the ongoing civil unrest and avoid future disturbances, we are imposing a general curfew nationwide. Except for those needing medical help and for key emergency personnel, every citizen must stay indoors from 7 P.M. to 7 A.M. Anyone violating the curfew without proper excuse will be arrested.

"These steps will be implemented immediately. Refinement will likely be needed as we move forward, and the decisions of the military authorities must be respected."

Sam Atkins looked back at the President, who returned to the podium.

"These measures may appear draconian, authoritarian, maybe even tyrannical, but they are necessary to contain the virus, maintain civility, and minimize loss of life. We need everyone to accept and follow them. May God bless and protect us all," the President said.

He left the room, ignoring the shouting of the press.

"We'll entertain your questions," Atkins told the reporters.

"Mr. Secretary, we are in effect turning our country into a military state. Is this constitutional?" the first reporter, a White House correspondent from one of the networks, asked.

Atkins couldn't hide his irritation. "We're at war here, and when you're at war, the military has the duty to fight the enemy. In addition, Congress has given the President the authority to use the armed forces to suppress civil insurrections and provide law enforcement in exceptional emergency cases. The present situation fully meets these criteria, wouldn't you think?"

"How about the press? Will it be subject to the curfew?"

Sam Atkins thought for a second. "I think a number of passes can be issued. I suggest that you obtain them before disobeying the order. We don't have time to waste with appeals and exceptions."

"How will the quarantine centers be managed? It appears that there's revolt from many of those confined," a network reporter asked.

"The quarantine centers are absolutely necessary to minimize the spread of the disease," the secretary replied. "We must remove potentially infected individuals from the rest of the population to avoid exacerbating what's already a catastrophe. Both medical and military personnel will monitor the quarantine centers and enforce the rules. Every possible precaution will be taken to avoid further exposing those already inside."

"But isn't it true that by being confined with people who were exposed, many unexposed contacts will end up contracting the virus?" the reporter insisted.

"We can't rule out a higher degree of risk for those in quarantine," Atkins answered. "But we must weigh this against the over-all risk to the population. When we do that, we have no choice but to enforce strict confinement for anyone who has been in close contact with a symptomatic victim."

"Doesn't that violate the civil liberties of those in quarantine?" the same reporter persisted.

Again, Atkins showed some annoyance. "We'll have to leave that debate for when this emergency is over. Right now, we're at war. As the President said, some of the measures may appear dictatorial, but we'd rather have a society left to debate their constitutionality than a wasteland of free dead people."

"Mr. Secretary, how are we going to reconcile all the IOUs when this is over?" another reporter asked.

Atkins was relieved that someone was changing the subject. "We'll still have an accounting system. Every business and every individual will have accounts receivable and accounts payable, except that there will be no cash."

"But why not just issue vouchers to those who need them?"

"Because it would not solve the problem. There's no way to provide the necessary goods and services to the entire population while accepting payment based on cash, credit, or even vouchers. Too many people will be out of work and too many products will be scarce. We just saw a run at the banks based mostly on hysteria. Medical institutions, insurance companies, the financial system, and a number of other businesses can't accommodate the extraordinary stress for very long. We need to take unusual actions to deal with an unusual crisis."

"Isn't the rest of the economy going to collapse? After all, nothing else is moving," the reporter insisted.

"What will happen to the economy, not just in the U.S. but worldwide, is hard to predict," Atkins answered. "I don't have to point out that we are experiencing a situation unlike anything else in recent history, even World War II. From our perspective, we are putting our capitalist economy on hold and reverting to a subsistence economy until we control the virus. As the President said, we need food, medicine, and protection. During a war, people don't need new automobiles, furniture, luxury items, expensive homes, plastic surgery, faraway vacations, or many other things that make up today's commerce and industry. We are also putting on hold education, travel, the financial markets, and a few other essentials. We will survive those disruptions, hoping that the situation is temporary and we can recover quickly."

"Mr. Secretary, any idea of when the virus will be under control?" a female reporter asked from the back of the room.

Sam Atkins looked over at the Secretary of Homeland Security. "Russ, do you want to answer?" he asked.

Stone came over to the microphones. "I've put the same question to the Director of the CDC," he started, "and I'm afraid that we don't have a good answer. Under the leadership of the CDC and USAMRIID, the DoD's laboratory for biological warfare defense, all major U.S. biological research labs are working on a new vaccine and other prevention and treatments. It's hard to tell when an effective vaccine will be available, but we expect it'll be a matter of months."

"Isn't that a long time to wait? Some experts predict that the number of infected patients will grow ten-fold every two weeks. We could all be sick in two months, couldn't we?" Reporters were people too, and most of them were as alarmed as the general population. The woman asking the question was no exception.

Stone thought for several seconds. He had the appearance of a KO'd boxer trying to regain consciousness. Then he answered the question, indirectly. "That's why the emergency measures outlined here tonight are so important for our survival as a society. We in government have more responsibility than most, but we're not supermen or wonderwomen. We're fighting an enemy against which we're poorly armed, and it will conquer us all if we don't fight it together. We're all soldiers going into battle. Some of us won't return alive, but we can't be cowards or we'll lose it. As the President requested, let's stay calm. Let's remain cool under fire, even when some around us are falling. If we follow the orders of those in charge and do our part, and God willing, we will overcome."

CHAPTER 17

It was four weeks since the first patients had been diagnosed. Dr. Senna and her team were bracing themselves for a third wave of infection and wondering how long they could hold on. Five other hotels had been converted into isolation facilities and they would soon be full.

The death of several doctors and nurses had sent shivers through the medical units in Rio, and even many who had vowed to stay had already disappeared. Dr. Senna was dependent on the support of the Brazilian military to staff the units.

"Seven hundred new patients today," Dr. Teixeira informed her. "At this rate, we'll fill one hotel every day."

"Make sure we double up all patients. It's not like they are going to infect one another," she said.

There were now over eleven thousand cases in the city, and counting. The isolation centers were wretched and pitiful places. Senna had initially figured the maximum capacity of each place at approximately three times the number of rooms, but that had been surpassed long ago. Patients were put two or three to a bed, and cots and mattresses lined the hallways and filled the conference rooms and resort suites. Pain and fear were stamped on the victims' faces, screams and moans echoed everywhere, and a stench of blood, urine, feces, and death permeated everything.

Most volunteers and soldiers appeared oblivious to it all. In a conventional war, with guns and grenades, there was often an adrenaline rush that conquered the fear in moments of danger. Here there was only willpower, and the underlying fright provided an emotional shield that allowed the workers to carry on their mission amidst the misery.

And there was no end in sight. The virus was spreading like fire through dry brush, and Dr. Senna was concerned that the rest of her staff might give up and desert. Or die. All were on pins and needles, wondering when and how they might make a mistake that would cost them their lives.

"How are our survivors doing?" she asked Teixeira. She had put him in charge of caring for the patients showing any signs of recovery and making sure they were getting the fluids, nutrition, and medical attention required to pull through.

"The American is doing well," he answered. "He's walking about and his sores are healing nicely. Some scabs are starting to fall off, and he can probably be dismissed in a few days."

"I know about Bruce. I mean the others."

"There are two hundred or so who already look like they're

going to make it. Not out of the woods, but just the fact that they're not getting worse is good news."

She nodded, but the situation was still hopeless. The next wave would likely swallow them all. It would be many tens of thousands of victims, then hundreds of thousands. From what she saw, and from reports from around the world, only a handful of those would survive.

The quarantine center had also run out of space, partly because very few people were being released except for the sick moving into the isolation. With the airlines grounded, city officials had converted the airport close to downtown Rio into a second quarantine camp, and a veritable tent city had been erected on the runways.

But order had broken down inside the camps. As the numbers grew and many developed symptoms, unrest followed. Most demanded to leave. Five men stole a vehicle and rammed through a fence out of the camp, only to be sprayed with bullets as they passed a police barricade. As a deterrent, they were left in the car by the side of the airport access road where they had been shot.

Dr. Senna had been disheartened for a couple of weeks, but a new idea had surfaced. "What if . . .?" she would ask herself.

When another colleague became sick, she decided it was time to act. "Ricardo, have you ever heard of variolation?" she asked Dr. Teixeira.

The doctor thought for a few seconds – the word rang a bell. "Yes, I have," he finally said. "I read about it when studying the history of the vaccine. Isn't it some kind of immunization using the live *Variola* virus?"

"Exactly. It's the intentional infection of healthy persons by implanting live smallpox matter under the skin. It's like a vaccine, but using the *Variola* virus instead of the *Vaccinia* virus," she explained. "It's thought to have started somewhere in Asia many centuries ago, then brought into Europe in the 1700s, before the vaccine was invented."

"Isn't the death rate very high?" Teixeira asked, trying to remember his medical history classes.

"Depends on what you compare it to." Senna was excited about explaining her idea to someone who would understand it. "If you compare it with a regular vaccine, yes, it's very high, maybe three percent fatalities among those inoculated. But if you compare it to the probability of dying from the disease during a major epidemic, it actually saves many lives. Armies in the New World in the eighteenth century were routinely variolated to insure that smallpox outbreaks would not devastate them during a campaign."

Teixeira was starting to guess where his colleague was going. It was an off-the-wall idea.

"What if we do the same thing here?" Senna asked, getting to the point. "What do we have to lose? Most of these people are going to die anyway."

"Claudia, I don't know enough about it, I need time to think. But if I remember correctly, they'd choose viral samples from people with mild symptoms to use in variolation. Nothing's mild about this outbreak. Even those who survive barely make it."

"That's true, but that's a risk I'm willing to take. That's all we have." Senna had thought about it and had a solution of sorts. "Back when people were doing this, they would use viruses from vesicles on a patient's skin, or from pus in the pustules, or from scabs on the healing sores. As you said, this outbreak is so virulent that I really don't know if it'll work, but I think we can use the scabs from healing patients. Maybe the viruses in the scabs of the survivors have mutated into a weaker strain."

"That's wishful thinking."

"I know."

"You're serious about this, aren't you?" Her resolve amazed him.

"Dead serious. I won't force anyone, but I'll try it on myself. The way this epidemic is progressing and given our continuous exposure, we're going to get infected eventually. And you know what'll happen if we come down with the damn virus."

"You need permission from the Department of Health to try anything like this. You could lose your medical license."

She flashed him a smile. "I don't expect to practice medicine if I end up dead. And if I don't, maybe I'll fulfill my Hippocratic oath of doing everything I can to save lives."

"And how do you plan to carry out this suicide mission of yours?"

"As you just mentioned, the American is almost recovered. I can take one of his scabs and insert some of it under the skin in my forearm. It's as simple as that. Then I'll go into isolation because I don't want anyone to pay for my foolishness if it doesn't work," she said with a look of determination.

She had made her decision but had not thought it completely through. This was a desperate act, maybe even irrational, and she needed to digest it further. She went to see Bruce DuBois.

She found him no longer confined to his room and walking down a hallway, wearing only a pair of shorts and socks. He walked with an uneasy gait and legs apart, the scabs covering his body making him look like some mutant reptile. He stopped to adjust the pillow of a fellow patient lying on a mattress on the floor. The woman groaned. Using his limited Portuguese vocabulary, he said a few words of encouragement and moved on to another patient.

"How are you feeling today, Bruce?" Senna asked in English.

"Much better, Doctor."

"You're turning into a social worker here," she said with a smile. She had developed a genuine affection for the young American. He was intelligent and caring, and just surviving the disease made him special.

"These people are beyond desperation."

"It's not just in here," she answered, more a mumble to herself than a reply.

He looked at the doctor and saw sadness and frustration in her eyes, but also a hint of a spark that appeared out of place. Behind her, a window allowed an inviting view of the ocean. "I wish I could at least go down to the beach," he said.

"Maybe in a few days."

He hesitated. She sensed that something was bothering him.

"What is it?" she asked.

"Can I ask you for a favor?"

"Sure."

"Can you make a phone call for me?"

There were phones in the hotel, but service had been lost in the city after a riot set fire to a building housing three telecommunication switches. Some telecom planner had placed most eggs in a single basket, which was now gone. The rest of the telephone network overloaded and crashed, and only one cellular carrier still provided sporadic service.

"Whom do you want to call?" she asked.

"My folks. I never called after leaving Chicago and I'm sure they're worried."

"I will be glad to, if I can get an international connection."

She, too, was worried. For almost three weeks, she had been unable to reach her son in London. She kept telling herself that Ronaldo was okay, but she was well aware that the virus was causing carnage all over the world and that the vaccine was now useless. Her own fears and the madness around her kept her from dwelling on it.

Bruce gave her his parents phone number, which she put to memory.

She examined him. The largest concentration of scabs was on his face, around the mouth, nose, and eyes. Some were starting to peel off but were held in place by the facial hair. He would certainly end up with disfiguring scars, but the alternative would have been much worse. With her gloved hand, she touched his healing wounds. She could pull off some scabs immediately and move ahead with her plan.

Then a thought struck her – why not ask for volunteers to be inoculated with her? She didn't have to try the experiment on herself alone or use unsuspecting individuals as guinea pigs. Maybe others would welcome the opportunity to take action and get rid of their anxieties once and for all. Even those who weren't ill were having a hard time coping with this Sword of Damocles hanging over their heads.

The more she thought about it, the more it made sense. Why not obtain some data from the experiment? If she inoculated herself and survived, what would that mean? She still would not have any useful information that could be applied to the population. But if she had a sample of . . . How big a sample will be meaningful? she wondered.

She drove to the airport quarantine center and showed her pass to the armed guards while glancing at the bullet-ridden car with the dead men still inside. If they're desperate enough to take the bullets, they're ready to accept my proposal, she thought.

She asked to meet with the latest arrivals and was directed to what had been a baggage claim area. Over a period of about thirty minutes, fifty people trickled in. Some were in tears, others were cursing, others seemed resigned to the situation. All were frightened and none wanted to be there.

"Thanks for coming. I'm Dr. Claudia Senna, the physician in charge of the isolation centers," she started. Several of them had sat down on a luggage conveyor while others just stood against a wall, arms crossed, staring with curiosity at the tired doctor with the short black hair and the expressive black eyes.

"As you know, this disease is turning out to be deadly for the vast majority of those infected," she said.

No one reacted. They already knew that.

"There's also a good chance that many of you have been exposed to the virus and will become sick over the next ten to fifteen days. That's why you're here," she continued.

"Or maybe we're not infected and will catch the fucking bug in this place," retorted a man standing in the back of the room, totally unconcerned about his foul language.

"I don't think it'll happen if you follow procedures and take proper precautions," Dr. Senna replied.

"Then why are you wearing that silly suit and we're not?" The man made a hand gesture to indicate his disregard for her opinion.

"I'm not here to argue with you about the situation," she continued, "but to tell you about something different I'm going to do. Then, I want to know if any of you is willing to join me." She paused and looked around. They were listening.

"What I'm about to do is an experiment, and I have no idea if it'll work. If it doesn't, it'll probably kill me." She paused again. She didn't want to mislead anybody. If they decided to join her, she wanted them to know that the risks were real. "But if it works, it'll make me immune to the virus and it may help develop a process to save other lives."

They were still listening. She explained the concept of variolation and the process she would follow for herself and for any volunteers.

"The experiment will be conducted at one of the isolation hotels. We'll use a separate building that used to be a restaurant. I'll take a few scabs from a survivor who is almost fully recovered and grind them into a powder. I will then make a small incision in the skin of the upper arm and insert some of it into the cut. The process is easy and straightforward."

"What will happen then?" a young woman asked. She had been tapped for quarantine after her sister was diagnosed with the disease. Her mother, father, and brother were also in the room.

"That's the part I don't know. The worst that can happen is that we'll get the disease and end up dead," she said, trying to make light of a serious possibility. Her audience didn't laugh.

"It's hard to tell," she added. "From the historical records on variolation, we know that those exposed to the virus as I just described developed symptoms that were much milder than in people infected naturally. I don't think anyone ever found out why."

"What you're telling us is that we'll become sick, but maybe we won't die," the young woman said.

"That's what I am hoping for," Senna replied. "Again, from the historical records, we know that some deaths occurred from variolation, but while the death rate for those randomly infected was anywhere from twenty-five to forty percent, it was around three percent for the variolated individuals. And once they recovered from any symptoms, people were immune to the virus."

"This outbreak isn't killing only twenty-five percent, lady. It's killing everybody," the man in the back of the room snapped.

"That's why I can't tell you what will happen," Senna answered. "This virus isn't exactly the standard smallpox virus, and it's possible that it will behave very differently. There's a good chance someone will die. Whether it's three in a hundred, or ten, or ninety-five, I don't know, but I believe that my chances of surviving the experiment are higher than if I were to catch the virus later. And given my job, it's probably just a matter of time. In view of your present situation, it's also a matter of time for some of you, and that's why I'm asking if anyone wants to join me."

There was silence in the room – it was a huge leap of faith.

"You're going to do this to yourself regardless of our decision?" the rude man wanted to make sure. Senna nodded.

"When will you know what reaction you'll have?" the young lady asked.

"It's hard to tell. If the inoculation site becomes swollen or develops blisters or vesicles after four or five days, it's a good sign. The blisters may spread up and down the arm and will leave a scar after they're gone, but that's a small price to pay. Or we may develop regular symptoms, and there's no telling what will happen then."

Again there was silence. Then the young women turned to her parents. Her voice was calm but determined: "Look mom, dad. I can't live with this anxiety, knowing that I'll probably get sick but not knowing when. If not now, it may be next month or next year, and no one seems to know how to stop this nightmare."

She took a deep breath and continued, "Dr. Senna is offering me a chance to get it over with once and for all. If I die, I die. If I don't, then I can live without this paralyzing fear. This virus, I can't see it or hear it or smell it, but I am terrified that it's going to invade me and destroy me from within. Living like this is harder than dying."

Several in the room had tears in their eyes. All shared her angst.

Twenty-three people volunteered to join Dr. Claudia Senna.

She arranged to have them moved from quarantine to the former luxury hotel. She then asked each one to sign a statement indicating that they were aware of the experimental nature of the procedure and the high risk of contracting the disease and perhaps dying, were submitting to the variolation procedure of their own free will, and would not hold any government or medical official responsible for the outcome.

With Teixeira's assistance, Senna removed two scabs from Bruce DuBois.

"Were you able to reach my parents?" Bruce asked.

In the excitement of her new project, she had forgotten. If she was going to call it had to be now, before she went into isolation. She headed to the decontamination area in the back, shed her protective gear, and exited the hotel building into an adjacent garden where only one month ago carefree tourists and business people used to sip *caipirinhas*, take a dip in the pool, or relax in the warm ocean breeze. The pool was now full with leaves, debris, and garbage, and the water had turned a murky green.

She sat on a stool at the pool bar and removed the cell phone from a pouch tied around her waist. The place had been ransacked days earlier and only a few broken bottles remained. She looked at the ocean, an immensity of sparkling deep blue interrupted by patches of turquoise. She could hear the waves crashing against the rocks and breaking on the beach below. Dr. Senna closed her eyes for a moment and imagined that the last four weeks had been a bad dream.

The broken bottles and the dirty pool were still there when she reopened her eyes. With a sigh, she flipped the phone open and punched the numbers from memory. She heard a busy tone and tried again. Eventually the call went through.

"Hello," a tired male voice answered.

"Mr. DuBois?" Senna asked.

"Yes."

"My name is Claudia Senna, a doctor in Rio de Janeiro, Brazil. I am calling on behalf of your son."

Frank's heart skipped a beat. "Is he alright?"

"Yes, he is fine."

His eyes were instantly wet. "Praise the Lord," he whispered.

"Why isn't he calling?" he asked after a moment.

"He has been very sick and is still in isolation."

"Smallpox?"

"Yes, but he is one of the lucky ones."

"Are you his doctor?"

"I am."

"And you're sure he'll recover?"

"Positive."

"When did he get infected?"

"Four weeks ago. He was one of our first cases."

Frank let it sink in. Then he relaxed a little and praised the Lord again. He thought of Sarah and imagined what his son's face might look like. "Is Bruce badly scarred?" he asked.

Dr. Senna pondered the answer. She decided that the truth was best. "I don't know if you've ever seen a victim of this disease," she said. "The virus mangles the body even on the survivors. Your son will show the scars, but he will live."

"I understand. I, too, have been dealing with the horror since the beginning."

"In what capacity?" she asked, curious.

"As a doctor. I guess Bruce didn't tell you."

He hadn't. They talked for a while, comparing notes. The measures enforced by the US government were preventing the level of anarchy seen in Brazil, but the advance of the disease was equally implacable in both places.

Frank did not mention Doreen's death – there was no reason to add to Bruce's burden. Senna said nothing about her project – the American might wonder what kind of lunatic was treating his son. They hung up with the promise to stay in touch.

Next she tried to call London, the millionth try in three weeks. As usual, all she heard was a busy tone. After several attempts with the same result, she gave up. "Keep him safe, Lord," she whispered, raising her eyes to the heavens.

She went back into the hotel to tell Bruce about her conversation with his father. Then she joined her volunteers to start the experiment.

Carefully, Dr. Senna grounded the two scabs into a fine dust, and with the bifurcated needle normally used for smallpox vaccination, she applied the powder into the upper arm of each of the twenty-four volunteers, starting with hers.

The variolation procedure had the feel of a religious ceremony. It was a secular baptism that would have a radical affect on their future and would transform them into different people. They could be committing suicide, albeit for a good cause, or they could be saving their lives and in the process the lives of others. Contributing to the ambiance were the prayers. "Jesus, into Your hands I commend my life," said one, paraphrasing the Gospel. "God, Thy will be done on Earth as it is in Heaven," added another. "Amen," all answered.

When they were done and realized that there was no going back, they all hugged in a show of solidarity and common fate. Some cried, others laughed, feeling like a new tribe or a new religious sect, with Dr. Claudia Senna as their spiritual leader. They were pioneers in a common adventure. No one knew how it would end but for now, they were glad they had joined.

***

Since arriving in Miami Beach, Raful had spent his days

walking the beach and trying to deny his guilt. The whole thing had been Shariff's idea, or Anne's, but not his. He had been a pawn in their hands, a spineless jellyfish snatched by Nur and dunked into their scheme until there was no way out. Nothing he could have done about it.

Nonsense, he told himself. He could have backed away. Why did he allow it to happen? The environmental troubles or the plight of the Moslem minorities weren't even his concerns, why did he let the others drag him in?

He tried to plead ignorance with his conscience. For almost two years, the epidemic had been an abstraction – nothing more than a fantasy, a mental exercise. Yes, he knew the potential impact, but he went along as an ostrich with his head in the sand and assumed that it would never happen. It was simply poor judgment.

Bullshit, he had to admit. He knew what the virus had done to Juanita and Consuelo. He was the one testing the latex and the lubricants, he was well aware of the purpose of his work, and he was nothing but a coward. Now that he saw the disease, the death, and the pandemonium sweeping the world, he couldn't rebut his responsibility.

This evening, he walked away from the beach, past the food distribution center, toward the shopping district where only a few weeks ago happy-go-lucky visitors purchased souvenirs, walked the streets gawking at the rich mansions of the wealthy, and relaxed with a Margarita or a beer at a sidewalk café. He had done everything he could to avoid seeing the misery and the pain, but now he needed to get close to the chaos and feel the suffering. The self-flagellation of confronting reality and accepting blame might cleanse him.

It was past curfew, but a dozen youths gathered, somehow unnoticed by the soldiers patrolling other parts of Miami. They moved slowly, peaking around every street corner, and their numbers quickly swelled as others ventured into the street. A body lay on the sidewalk partly covered by a mound of rotting garbage strewn about by dogs and raccoons. The man's face was under the trash, but his bare legs and arms were covered with open red wounds and he appeared dead. One youth tripped over him and a low groan was heard, but the man didn't move. The youngster spit in the body's direction and sprang quickly away as if pushed by an invisible jolt.

The group moved as a unit, a pack of hyenas ready to strike. Raful followed them, and in the poorly lit street he could feel the bottled-up tension ready to be released. Then it happened. The action went off so fast that it appeared synchronized, a band of starlings taking flight simultaneously in response to some unseen cue.

A garbage can shattered the glass window of an electronics store, and a crowbar forced the entrance to a jewelry place. Across the street, a brick smashed through a liquor store display. The mob rushed in to retrieve whatever they could find, ran away to hide the loot, and returned quickly for another load, often tripping over garbage and dropped items. Others waited outside to ambush someone carrying a particularly juicy prize. The hyenas had found a prey and were feasting in a chaotic frenzy, unfazed by the screaming of the burglar alarms.

Suddenly, machine-gun fire rang out, a string of rapid bursts in quick sequence. Several youths fell instantaneously, but the mob ran as a mass down the street, a herd of wildebeest seeking safety in numbers. Raful was pushed, tripped, got up, was pushed again, and moved along with the crowd, from time to time looking back to gauge the soldiers' advance. Someone broke the neck of a rum bottle, stuck a rag in it, lit it up, and smashed it through a display of oriental rugs. A second bottle found its way through a souvenir shop window. Flames immediately engulfed the entrance to both stores. Another burst of gunfire. Bullets whistled by, and a runner fell in the middle of the pack.

Raful found himself on top of a screaming young man. He thought about helping him, but the guns were getting closer. He split off from the group and sought refuge through the broken door of an apartment complex. His heart galloped in his chest and his shirt was soaked with sweat. He made his way to a first floor window and peeked out, feeling secure in the total darkness of the room. He could see the soldiers pursuing the mob with cadenced and deliberate steps. In their olive-green fatigues and black breathing masks with large muzzles and round plastic eyes, they resembled camouflaged bears hunting in a concrete wilderness. The injured man rolled in the middle of the street, but the soldiers ignored him and kept after the mob as if the chase, not the catch, were the objective.

Raful saw the action in slow motion, a surreal experience that he couldn't quite comprehend. The apartment appeared empty, and he didn't want to risk another encounter with the army during curfew. He decided to spend the night there. But as the mob and the soldiers veered down a side street, the flames took over the store next door. He watched as people ran away from the burning building and wailed in the street.

Minutes went by and no fire trucks arrived. The fire spread, first to the upper floors, then to adjacent buildings. Raful was forced to leave his hiding place and walked back toward his apartment by the beach.

"You there," a soldier yelled, stopping him. "Where do you think you're going at this hour?"

He thought quickly. "My home is in flames," he replied, pointing back. "I'm hoping to spend the night with a friend." The patrol team could see the red glow several blocks away and let him pass.

He moved on in a daze, his soul fluttering more erratically than the moths around the streetlights.

CHAPTER 18

"It's Day Forty-Four of the pandemic, and the tragedy shows no signs of subsiding," Cecilia Chapman was telling her audience. "Officials estimate that nationwide, the number of new cases is approaching two million daily, and the total number of victims is close to twenty million. One in every fifteen Americans has now contracted the virus. The number of deaths is around five million. Exact figures are difficult to obtain, partly because of the magnitude of the problem and partly because of increasing numbers of people dying at home instead of seeking medical help.

"With us from Atlanta is Dr. David Reiss, head of the CDC." Reiss's dark features showed up on the split TV screen, next to Cecilia.

"Doctor, how much worse can this epidemic get?" She was asking him the same question everyone had been asking for many weeks.

"As I said before, it's hard to estimate, but the disease has been growing exponentially." Reiss was matter-of-fact in his explanation. He had been forced to deal with the agonizing death of his friend and colleague, Dr. Venkatraman, and with his wife's struggle to survive. She was one of the lucky few and was now out of danger, but he had been so overwhelmed and frustrated that his mind was dodging emotion and resorting to facts only. He could have cracked but instead, he dealt with the tragedy by becoming emotionally detached. "If the next wave follows the pattern of the previous ones, we could have one hundred million victims by mid May," he added.

"That's a third of our country's population!" Cecilia exclaimed, uncharacteristically alarmed. "How can our medical system deal with so many patients?"

"We can't, Ms. Chapman," Reiss replied. "Ready as we were for a biological attack, we could never prepare for a virus as contagious, as deadly, and as unstoppable as this one. At all levels of government, we feel helpless because we can't do any more to protect the population."

He paused. Cecilia was still shaking her head. "And the sad truth is that we've done everything right," Reiss continued. "We could have stopped the disease with minimal harm if the vaccine had worked as expected, but it didn't. We have minimized the damage with martial law and the other preventive measures in place. When compared to other nations, we have held civic unrest to a minimum and kept the population fed and the medical establishment tending to the major emergencies. Except for the virus – we simply can't control the pandemic."

"Are you saying that the virus won't stop until we all get infected?" Cecilia asked with an incredulous look on her face.

"That could be close to the truth," he answered unemotionally. "The global effort to develop a vaccine is not moving as fast as we had hoped. Several of our best scientists have succumbed to the disease. Even if we had a vaccine today, it would still take some time to produce it commercially and in enough quantities to inoculate everyone. I fear that the virus will slow down only when the majority of the population has contracted the disease."

"If that's the case, why bother with quarantining people? Why not just let the disease take its course and get it over with?"

"We were hoping that the quarantine would slow down the progress of the virus. And I'm sure it did, more so than many people suspect given our abysmal situation. Slowing it down gained us some time to perhaps find a vaccine, but that hasn't happened. Yet, it has given us time to better prepare for what now appears to be inevitable: more sick people and more deaths than anyone ever thought possible. If instead of two million new cases we were getting ten million, think how much worse the situation would be."

Cecilia couldn't imagine how things could get any worse. Reiss took a sip of water and went on. "But we have already changed the quarantine rules. We stopped confining most contacts weeks ago for lack of quarantine space and due to the inability to monitor and care for those quarantined. The numbers are just too large. Right now, we are quarantining only individuals with a high probability of infection. This includes people who kissed, had sexual contact, or shared drinking glasses, needles, or eating utensils with patients after they developed symptoms. Then again, we find out about those only when they tell the emergency teams. We no longer have the resources to track them."

"Doctor, after initial reports of death rates above ninety percent, we are now learning that the rates are significantly lower, somewhere in the vicinity of sixty percent. That's no consolation, of course, but what are the real numbers?" Cecilia asked.

"Turns out that the vaccine is not totally ineffective, and we are once again advising non-vaccinated individuals to do so. The vaccine does not prevent contracting the disease, but it provides enough of a boost to the immune system to allow it to defend itself in almost half the cases. Both numbers are correct: the death rate is more than nine out of ten for unvaccinated persons, and approximately six out of ten for those vaccinated. When you look at it, the vaccine has already saved several million people and will likely save millions more over the next few months."

Cecilia finished her interview and Reiss's face disappeared from the screen.

"On another subject," she said, still subdued but going on with her bulletin, "Filipino authorities and FBI investigators have now identified the last two members of the group believed responsible for the epidemic. One is Raful Shomali, a Palestinian-born American biochemist who quit his job in Virginia two years ago and disappeared." A picture of Raful appeared on the screen.

"Shomali was raised in Chicago, where his family still resides," Cecilia continued. "The FBI believes that he may have returned to the U.S. in February, but has no idea of his whereabouts. If you have seen this man, please contact your local authorities or the FBI." Raful's picture stayed on the screen for a few seconds, with an 800 number displayed across the bottom.

"The other is Alexander Managadze, a microbiologist born in the Republic of Georgia, who spent many years in the Russian bioweapons program." Somehow, the network had obtained an old picture, and the face of a young Managadze now filled the screen.

"Investigators determined the identity of the two terrorists after combing through airline records for flights leaving the Philippines during the days preceding the outbreaks."

The camera returned to Cecilia's grave face. "Authorities believe that Managadze was the likely source of the smallpox virus, possibly smuggling it out of Russia's top-secret Vektor labs. But in a blow to the investigation, he was shot to death by a guard in Tbilisi before the investigators had a chance to interrogate him."

Cecilia shuffled some papers on her desk and continued. "In other news, memorial services were held this morning for the Governor of New Jersey, another fatality from the smallpox epidemic." Silent footage of the Governor shaking hands and waving filled the TV screen.

"The Governor was the first government official to recognize the devastating potential of the disease and led the nation in the implementation of preventive measures. He was tireless in his efforts, but in the end, he fell victim in a battle that appears futile. In this war, where we fail to celebrate the heroes because we are so busy grieving the fallen and worrying about ourselves, he was a true hero."

***

Sarah Wilson had been discharged from Morris General Hospital two weeks earlier. Her wounds had healed and all scabs were gone. She was weak, but she had recovered. More importantly, she was one of the few lucky people now immune to the disease.

Her scars were hideous, particularly the ones around her eyes, which made them appear as if each was focusing on a different spot. Her eyelids were irregular and rubbery shreds of skin, and the scars on her lips, nose, and cheeks were unsightly. Still, she was alive and had been more fortunate than most.

She had missed Dr. DuBois during her last three weeks at the hospital. At first, she couldn't understand why he no longer visited. She wondered if he was sick and in isolation somewhere and asked Dr. Skarzinski about him. The news had devastated her. Poor Mrs. DuBois! How could anyone do that to her?

And she had been dumbfounded by the news about Anne. There were no TVs in the isolation room, so she was oblivious to the events going on outside. Skarzinski was surprised by her reaction. "She used to be my friend," she told him as she explained her relationship with the DuBois family.

Frank DuBois had been released after four days in the hospital. He had suffered a concussion, two broken ribs, many bruises, and some internal injuries as a result of kicks to his abdomen, but he had been able to attend his wife's funeral. He was told to take it easy, so he stayed home feeling sorry for himself.

The call from Brazil came two days after Doreen's funeral. It had been bittersweet news – he now knew where Bruce was but worried about his condition and how he would make it home. Frank had already called repeatedly the number given to him by Dr. Senna, but all he got was a busy tone. Thankfully, the cameras and the thugs had not bothered him again.

Sarah decided to visit him. The roads were mostly deserted due in part to a gasoline shortage. Only a few designated gas stations carried it. Troops monitored sales, and priority was given to individuals employed in critical industries. Some sold their gas for cash at black market prices to those who couldn't get it legally. She still had an almost-full tank and could spare a couple of gallons to visit dear Dr. DuBois, who might need a friendly shoulder.

He was depressed but obviously pleased to see her. A few neighbors had come by to chat and keep him company, but he hated their pity and preferred the solitude. With Sarah, it was different. She was as scarred on the outside as he was on the inside, not counting her pain for losing Todd. And Anne, too. Sarah was traumatized by Anne's actions and was having difficulty adjusting to the idea that her childhood friend could be responsible for so much suffering and misery.

They talked for hours. Unimpeded by the disease or the biological suits, they could now hold a conversation. Frank talked about life without his daughter and how he had never gotten used to not knowing her whereabouts. And he spoke of Doreen – he missed her desperately. Eruptions of emotion interrupted their conversation as they cried together and held each other in silence. Ultimately, they also laughed together, remembering long-forgotten stories from Sarah and Anne's childhood. It all seemed so long ago.

It was a cathartic visit for both of them.

"Want to go shopping?" Frank eventually asked.

"Sure," she said, puzzled. No one shopped anymore.

Department stores and malls had been closed for weeks, and only essential items were still being sold. "What are we shopping for?"

"Groceries."

"Oh, sure."

They grabbed their jackets and left the house. A local supermarket was the closest food distribution center, about one mile from the DuBois home. They would walk there – a stroll would do them good. It was the middle of April, the air was still crisp but pleasant and spring was again awakening trees and fields. Nature was showing off its beauty, totally oblivious to the despair of the only species capable of appreciating it.

The supermarket was the new center of activities. People were tired of being out of work and cooped up in their homes, and those less afraid of the virus went to the store to share horror stories and shoot the breeze with friends and acquaintances. There were no handshakes, and everyone kept some distance from the others. Most wore surgical masks and gloves and some even donned breathing equipment, transparent visors, and plastic hoods. Two armed soldiers wearing biological masks walked about, but there was no sign of impending disturbance.

There was a short line at the store. Everyone stared as Sarah arrived holding Frank's arm. Most people had never seen the damage caused by the disease, and several approached to take a closer look. Even the soldiers were curious.

"Lord, what an awful bug!" one bystander exclaimed. "If it does this to a survivor, imagine the dead."

"God bless you, young lady," a woman in line said. "At least you don't have to live in fear anymore."

Inside the store, two more soldiers allowed people into the aisles at the same rate they were being checked out. Only a quarter of the shelves were stocked. Prices were marked, and people could buy anything available as long as they stayed within the $75 weekly limit per person. The variety was limited, but the quantities were adequate and no one had to starve.

Frank selected what he needed. Sugar was not available, but he found low-cal sweetener.

"This is fine, I'm not planning to bake a cake," he told Sarah.

They headed to the checkout counter where a clerk entered his social security number into a computer under the watchful eye of another guard. The clerk scanned his purchases, which added up to just over forty dollars. Frank signed a receipt, and they leisurely headed back home.

Children were out riding their bikes and playing in the cool spring afternoon. They wore no masks, just as they wore no helmets. Whatever fears lurked, some were hiding them well, even laughing, as children should. The adults, though, had long lost their laughter. All had friends or family members in isolation or already dead. Religious services were a daily occurrence for the thousands of deaths happening everywhere. Somber faces were the norm as everyone lived in fear, constantly checking for symptoms and interpreting every headache as the beginning of the end.

Frank convinced Sarah to stay for dinner. It had been a while since either had enjoyed a meal in friendly company. When she left, it was after 9 P.M.

She was violating the curfew and was stopped three times as she drove the twenty miles to her home. The checkpoints established by the military could be crossed only with special permits, or with employee IDs for specified companies. Sarah had neither, but the scars on her face granted her special privilege as far as the soldiers were concerned. She was allowed to pass with a mixture of pity and envy.

***

The Miami Beach police department received a phone call from a woman claiming to have seen the man on TV.

"What man?" the receptionist asked.

"The one they had a picture of just now," the elderly woman tried to explain. "They said he was one of the people who spread the disease. I couldn't understand his name when they said it."

"You mean you saw one of the terrorists?"

"Yes," the woman replied. "I saw him two or three times in the food lines."

"Hold on, ma'm," the receptionist said. She had not seen the news, and no one had told her anything about a terrorist. She summoned a sergeant who picked up.

"Ma'm, you think you saw one of the terrorists, is that correct?"

"That's right, just yesterday, right here in Miami Beach."

"Give me your address. We'd like to talk to you to get more information." The sergeant took down her name, address, and phone number and called the FBI.

Two agents were at the woman's apartment in less than forty minutes. She was quite positive on her identification of the man, but they knew that many such tips were simply cases of wrong identity. She did not know exactly where the man lived, but she had seen him walk toward a motel two blocks from the beach.

The woman's tip paid off. The motel manager immediately recognized the photograph.

"Yes, he's one of my guests and has been here for several weeks. I have only two paying guests, you know," the man said, including information the agents didn't care about. It was actually a surprise that he had any guests at all.

"What do you know about him?"

"He paid cash and in advance, so I don't have a registration form. But he calls himself Rafael."

Rafael, Raful. The agents looked at each other. Close enough. "Which one is his room?"

"Number 217, the corner apartment. It's one of only four with a mini-kitchen."

The agents headed toward the second-floor apartment and knocked on the door. There was no answer. "Do you know if he's in?" they asked the manager.

"I didn't see him leave. He stays in there most of the time, but sometimes he goes for a walk on the beach." The day was warm but misty, not a good beach day. They knocked again.

Still no answer. "Do you have a key?" one of the agents asked.

The manager took his key ring, looked for the right key, and opened the door. He walked in ahead of the agents. His stomach suddenly lurched, sending him back into the hallway where he threw up his lunch, white as a sheet.

The agents stepped back. They pulled out their service revolvers, eased the manager aside, and went in. They, too, quickly turned white.

There, hanging from a hook in the ceiling, was Raful Shomali. His belt was wrapped around his neck, his purple-tinged and swollen tongue hung from his mouth, and his eyes bulged in his contorted face. His crotch was still damp and a foul odor filled the room. He had soiled himself in his death struggle.

On the kitchen counter, the agents found a note scribbled on a piece of paper. "I am so sorry."

CHAPTER 19

For several days, the results had been very promising. Claudia Senna had waited impatiently, but now she couldn't wait any longer. It had been seventeen days since the inoculation. She could trust the results.

Of the twenty-four variolated individuals, twenty-one were not and had never been in grave danger. Some, she included, showed only a number of swells and blisters around the application spot. They were healing rather nicely and in another week, only a few harmless scars would remain in the upper arm. The bulk of the group bore an extensive array of blisters and wounds from the shoulder to the elbow, and several had developed nausea, fever, chills, and aches. But the symptoms had subsided and they were recovering.

Three had not been as lucky. They had developed internal bleeding and large rashes. Two of them experienced extensive hemorrhages and were probably not going to make it. The third one was still in doubt.

Although heartbroken about the last three, Dr. Senna was elated by the outcome of her experiment. Twenty-one people were now immune to the virus, virtually scar free, and out of fear. She had something to celebrate and more importantly, she had reinvented an ancient practice that could save lives. Even if three people died, a death rate of just over twelve percent, it was a far cry from the chances for the general population if nothing were done.

The news spread through the entire staff at the isolation and quarantine centers. Everyone wanted to be variolated. Senna proceeded to inoculate anyone who asked, following the same procedure. Eighty-two doctors and emergency workers were inoculated, including Dr. Teixeira.

"How can I help?" Bruce asked. His wounds were fully healed. The scars were unsightly around his mouth and eyes, but the beard and the long, disheveled hair covered the others. He was also stuck in Brazil for the time being. There was no telling when air travel would be restored, and all commercial and leisure boats had been docked.

"How much medical training do you have?" Dr. Senna asked.

"I'm a sociologist and I've had extensive emergency preparation. I was a member of one of Chicago's volunteer first-aid squads."

"Excellent. You can help me roll out a variolation plan," she replied.

Her affection for the young American had grown. Not only was he a survivor, he was also the son of another doctor fighting the merciless virus in another hemisphere. And somehow, by helping him, she hoped that someone would give her own son a hand, should he need it. She had been unable to reach Ronaldo since the beginning of the madness and was very concerned.

She invited Bruce to stay at her apartment after his release, and he became her sidekick.

"I want to variolate anyone going into quarantine," she told him.

"It's a very tall order," he answered. "The numbers are overwhelming."

Health officials were still hoping against hope that some miracle would save their city from complete collapse, but only a fraction of all contacts was being identified and quarantined. Even so, the capacity of the two quarantine centers had been exceeded, and a soccer stadium was now being used to accommodate the overflow. Because of the stifling heat, tents were set up as shelters from the sun, and water hoses were available to cool off. Conditions were less than ideal, but it was the best anyone could do. Armed guards patrolled all exits.

The first people had arrived in the stadium three days earlier. This was ideal for Senna's plan – if infected, they were early in the incubation cycle, and inoculation, assuming it worked like the standard vaccine, might still prevent the onset of the disease as it had for the initial twenty-four.

She called Rio's health administrator and explained her experiment, the preliminary results, and her plan. After gaining the proper authorization, Senna, Bruce, and a number of volunteers headed to the stadium with their powdered scabs and a supply of bifurcated needles. The volunteers were some of the people she had variolated and who were now fully immune. They had been trained to apply the virus and were glad to be of help. They were hugely grateful to Dr. Senna and did not waver when she asked for their support.

They briefly explained their mission and convincingly displayed the healing blisters in their arms, the only remnant of a procedure that had saved their lives and freed them from fear. Bruce's scars were further evidence of the viciousness of the virus, and he was a survivor.

They established four variolation stations in the hallways of the stadium. The number of needles was insufficient and they needed to be recycled. Pots of boiling water were setup at each station to disinfect the needles after each use. In five hours, Senna and her volunteers variolated almost four thousand individuals.

Word of the experiment quickly spread, a glimmer of hope in a truly desperate situation. Due to the nature of their assignments, soldiers, police, doctors, and other emergency workers still on the job were contracting the disease at catastrophic rates. Hospitals were useless for lack of staff. The military patrolled some parts of the city in a futile attempt to maintain order and in search of the sick, but even they did not venture into many neighborhoods. Most victims just died at home.

"The city is a wasteland!" Bruce exclaimed, as he and Dr. Senna rode in the back of a police car on their way to her home, a penthouse overlooking Lagoa Rodrigo de Freitas, the scenic lagoon in the center of Rio. Dr. Senna no longer ventured to drive and relied on a police escort to commute within the city.

They passed a food truck and were almost swallowed by

the crowd chasing it. The armed forces were bringing in truckloads of grains and other items, but only the use of deadly force prevented the mobs from stealing the trucks. However, the troops were unable to protect those who received food rations once they left the distribution area, and many were robbed, beaten, even killed for a few pounds of beans or potatoes. Most law, order, and civility had broken down, and large portions of the city were controlled by gangs of youths.

The car drove through a part of downtown where arson had already destroyed an entire city block. The skeleton of a colonial church and charred concrete walls were all that remained. To the south, a cloud of smoke drifted from a hillside toward Leblon and Ipanema, obscuring the sky and the famous beaches.

"Rocinha is ablaze," explained the policeman in the front seat, referring to the slum that 150,000 people called home. "No one is even trying to put the fire out. Without a major thunderstorm, the whole *favela* will burn," he added.

"Where will those people go?" Dr. Senna asked.

"The military is setting up campsites in open fields outside the city and moving entire neighborhoods into the temporary camps," the policeman answered. "There, they hope to maintain order and provide food without gang interference."

As they approached the apartment, an army unit was fishing corpses from the lagoon and wrapping them in plastic sheets. The population was dumping the dead wherever they could, and many bodies could be found in city canals and by roadsides.

"It's a miracle that some other epidemic didn't break out already," Dr. Senna said.

As they exited the car in front of her apartment, she looked up. The immense statue of Christ the Redeemer towered half-mile above them. She thought about saying a prayer but defiantly, decided not to. Tears of rage swelled up in her eyes. Either He couldn't see or didn't care about the misery going on in His city, what kind of God was He?

***

Without alternatives, Brazilian officials quickly decided that they had nothing to lose by adopting Dr. Senna's procedure. All healthcare, military, and law enforcement personnel were ordered to be variolated. If Rio and São Paulo were mostly lost, maybe they could still save the cities not directly targeted by the terrorists, like Belo Horizonte, Fortaleza, Porto Alegre, and the rest of the country. The nationwide implementation of a procedure tried on only twenty-four subjects and which included three fatalities was the clearest indication of official desperation.

Within days, every Brazilian city had setup variolation centers. In addition to the emergency personnel, priority was given to people in quarantine centers where quarantine was still being enforced. Variolation was not immediately mandatory for the general population because of the significant risk of death, but health officials were encouraging it. Politicians, doctors, and celebrities appeared on TV being inoculated and urging everyone to do the same.

As the first to be variolated in large numbers, the people in the soccer stadium were being anxiously monitored. After twelve days, medical officials became convinced that they had made the right decision. Over eighty percent of those inoculated were relatively symptom-free, and the appearance of their arm wounds suggested that they were not in danger. The condition of the others was more uncertain, and many would probably not survive. Still, sacrificing a few people to save the vast majority was a compromise that made sense. It would also help eliminate fear and remove the uncertainty about the future, allowing the country to pick up the pieces.

***

The conditions in many cities in all continents was no different from that in Rio de Janeiro. The virus was rampant, and government officials were giving up and allowing the pandemic to flame itself out. In some places, more than a third of the inhabitants were already infected. The medical profession and police forces were being decimated, the population was starving and hysterical, and lawless gangs controlled the neighborhoods.

In addition, utilities were out of service and bodies rotted out in the open for lack of gravediggers, coffins, body bags, or anyone with the courage to handle the pestilent corpses. Even the soldiers were deserting or refusing to obey orders.

In Southeast Asia, outbreaks of cholera killed many that the smallpox had spared. Sanitary conditions were nonexistent, as government social services had stopped many weeks ago. Food and water supplies were disrupted, and the population combed through dumps and mounds of garbage in the streets looking for scraps. Famine was widespread and cats, dogs, even the rats that fed on the garbage became meals. Decomposing bodies were commonplace, feeding rodents in cities, fish in lakes and streams, vultures in fields and by roadsides, and flies everywhere. The fetid smell of garbage and rotting flesh permeated everything. Government officials, long overwhelmed by the pandemic, were helpless to search for the source of the cholera.

Zamboanga was no exception. The smallpox virus had found its way to the southern Filipino city of half million people shortly after it spread out of Manila. The fragile infrastructure and the lack of response coordination rapidly spelled chaos for the population and overpowered any effort to maintain law and order. Death was so common that no one noticed the difference when the first cases of cholera appeared. Water contamination was almost certainly the culprit, but no one was bothering to find out. Whatever it was, *Vibrio cholerae* was thriving in it and being ingested by many.

Shariff Usman and Nur Ahmad were living in a house just outside the city with other MIIGro militants who were unaware of their role in the ongoing epidemic. They were initially elated about the spread of the virus. But as it reached their city and killed the poor Moslem minorities they aimed to save, there was neither joy nor a sense of accomplishment.

"Anyone coming down with the disease leaves the house," the group leader ordered.

They all agreed. It was a tough rule, but they were tough men. When two of them developed headaches and fever, it was immediately assumed that they had contracted the smallpox virus. The sick men were asked to leave. When one refused, the leader shot him.

Within hours, three others came down with the same symptoms, including Shariff and Nur. They left the house and looked for an empty home, although they suspected it was not smallpox. They were immune to the virus, weren't they?

The answer came quickly. Severe diarrhea and vomiting

ensued – it was not smallpox. They felt weak, achy, and generally miserable. Over the following twenty-four hours, the diarrhea did not stop and the quantity of fluid they expelled was astounding. They became severely dehydrated and needed to replenish their body fluids. But both were too weak to move, the pain was overwhelming, and there was no one to help them. Shariff lay in a pool of feces and urine, tucked into a ball. Ultimately, he went into cardiac arrest and stopped breathing. Nur just lay there in a stupor, unable to move, and feeling life slip away.

The two men, who thought themselves immune to the pandemic they had unleashed, were dead on the sordid floor of an abandoned house, victims of another disease against which their immunity was useless.

***

The Brazilian experiment became news around the world. Once the results from the soccer stadium became known, health officials everywhere rushed to learn more about the procedure and scrambled to implement variolation centers of their own. Most countries just copied the Brazilian model.

Not everyone was inoculated. Many were not ready to subject themselves to a procedure with such a high probability of death. They chose instead to wear their facemasks, stay away from crowded places, and do everything possible to avoid infection. Maybe someone would soon develop a safer vaccine. Or maybe the virus would just mutate and disappear like epidemics had done in the past.

In addition, not everything went smoothly in the variolation programs. In the rush to implement the procedure, technicians were often improperly trained. At times, the skin was not completely punctured and the variolation did not take. In other cases, appropriate post-variolation precautions were not followed and variolated individuals ended up carrying the disease home to family and friends who had chosen not to be inoculated. Oftentimes, needles were reused without proper sterilization, exposing otherwise-healthy individuals to blood-borne diseases.

Still, people by the millions were variolated in hundreds of cities around the world.

***

After dozens of attempts over a period of weeks, Bruce heard the phone ring. Finally, he thought, as he waited for what seemed like an eternity.

"Hello," Frank DuBois said.

"Dad? It's Bruce."

Frank was immediately overcome. "Praise the Lord," he said. "How are you, son?"

"I'm okay, now. I managed to survive smallpox, no small feat. How are you?"

"Still alive. I've managed to stay healthy, also a major achievement."

"And mom?"

Frank sat down on the sofa, not ready to answer. For the last month, he had been so concerned about simply hearing from Bruce that he had forgotten about how to break the news to him.

Bruce noticed the silence. "Is mom okay?" he repeated, anxiety setting in.

Frank still didn't answer. How do you tell a son that his mother has been murdered?

"Hello? Hello?" Bruce shouted, thinking he might have lost the connection.

"I'm here, son."

"What happened to mom?" He was now sure that bad news was coming.

"She's passed away, almost two months ago."

"Oh, my God!"

They were silent for a minute. Bruce was dealing with the sudden heartache, a pain sharper than any virus could ever inflict, and Frank was helplessly feeling his son's sorrow.

"How did she die?" Bruce finally asked, his voice trembling.

"The epidemic," Frank lied. He could not tell Bruce the whole truth. The blow would be too much, and it would lead to other questions that he was not ready to discuss. He would tell him someday, hopefully face-to-face, after the pain dulled.

Neither man spoke for a while, as Bruce wept. Frank heard his son wail and blow his nose, and the knot that had been lodged in his chest for weeks squeezed tighter.

"Does Anne know?" Bruce eventually asked.

"I doubt it."

"Have you heard from her at all?"

"No."

Bruce was not surprised by the laconic reply. His sister had been an emotional thorn for over a decade, and mom had probably carried it to the grave. If he only knew.

Again, there was silence between them. Bruce struggled to compose himself, but suddenly he was also concerned about his father. The old man had to deal with the death of his wife without a familiar shoulder to lean on.

"How are you holding up, dad?"

"Work keeps me busy."

"How bad are things at home?"

"Indescribable. The cities are tinderboxes ready to explode," Frank answered.

"You should see Rio. It's a war zone after the war."

"Except that the war is far from over. What started as waves of victims has turned into a tsunami with the power to overwhelm every defense."

"You should implement variolation," Bruce said. "Dr. Senna came up with the idea, and it appears to be working. The Brazilian authorities have made it mandatory."

Frank had heard about the procedure, but not about Dr. Senna's role. Small world, he thought. He knew that American health authorities were discussing it, so he was immediately interested. They talked about it for a long while, with Frank asking details and Bruce providing them. Bruce expected the connection to drop at any time, but it held up. When his phone battery started beeping, they had to hang up.

Dr. DuBois felt relieved and excited for the first time in what seemed like ages. Relieved about his son, and excited about the news he had heard. He picked up the phone again and called Atlanta.

***

In most American cities, the forced calm provided by troops in the streets and helicopters in the sky was breaking apart.

"In Chicago, gangs set fire to mountains of garbage piled up in the streets," Cecilia Chapman reported. "The fires quickly spread to homes and businesses and blew out a major power station. In Los Angeles, a blaze destroyed a telecommunication switch."

Similar occurrences were taking place all over the country. Riots were breaking out in many places. The soldiers were seeing so many from their ranks falling prey to the disease, and so much misery in the streets, that they couldn't shoot unarmed civilians any longer. Instead, some were joining the looting and the rioting, and the situation was deteriorating out of control. As a result, sections of many metropolitan areas were left without utilities, and no one would fix them anytime soon.

The living conditions were horrendous. Many were getting sick and dying in their homes, and the moaning and stench inside apartment buildings became overpowering.

"The population is being advised to boil their water, as bodies have been found dumped in reservoirs," Cecilia continued.

Inside the prisons, death and fear sparked violent revolts that the guards were unable to contain. The entire inmate population at a number of correctional facilities, including a maximum-security prison in New Jersey, had escaped. Hospitals and their staff, despite government mandates, were no longer functional as doctors and nurses were dead, sick, or too scared to report to work. With more than a quarter of the population infected, there was nothing anyone could do to bring about any semblance of normalcy.

Amid the despair and the helplessness, a religious phenomenon swept the country. The deaths, the suffering, the scarred survivors, and the fear led millions back to their religious beliefs. God was the only possible refuge for their misery, the only One who could release them from suffering.

Churches filled up despite warnings from health officials and some religious leaders – the faithful refused to believe that God would allow them to get sick in His house of worship.

Most impressive was the revival of TV evangelism. The Reverend Charles Haywood preached repentance and sacrifice as the only way to appease an angry God and bring an end to the pandemic.

"The disease is God's wrath upon a sinful civilization," the Reverend would tell his nationwide TV audience. Then he would quote directly from the Book of Revelations. "Depart from Babylon my people, as to not take part in her sins and receive a share in her plagues, for her sins are piled up to the sky and God remembers her crimes."

Reverend Haywood developed a huge following of new converts. His sermons were filled with condemnation of sexual promiscuity, material wealth, and selfishness. "How did God bring about this plague?" he would ask rhetorically. "Through prostitution, and through the use of contraceptive devices intended to defeat God's purpose for the sexual act. It's a sign that the Almighty is angry because of our sins. Until we start to believe in Him, to follow His commandments, and to love Him above all things, He will not let go of His wrath."

The reverend pointed out the evil deeds and the uncaring nature of the modern society that had provoked God's retaliation. "The pursuit of pleasure and instant gratification has become our god. Do we love Him above all things? Of course we don't. We love our money, we love our big houses, we love our fast cars, and we love our comfort. For our comfort, we kill our unborn children, we put our elderly and sick in nursing homes, and we look the other way when we come across a homeless widow or a child in need of adoption. With all our comfort and wealth, we don't even bother to thank and praise Him. God has decided to throw some discomfort our away so that we will remember Him."

The millions listening to Haywood truly believed that they were culpable. They prayed and cried with him as they tried to purify themselves for the pending coming of a vengeful God. Many made vows of poverty and chastity. Others vowed to dedicate themselves to the service of the Lord. Yet others inflicted pain on themselves, fasted for weeks, whipped themselves, slept on hard floors, walked with pebbles in their shoes, or knelt for hours in front of a cross, hoping for an end to the pandemic.

***

U.S. government officials had learned about the Brazilian experiment and were seriously considering it. They knew that many countries were already moving ahead with implementation plans and, given the hopeless situation, it was the only thing that made some sense.

"What do you suggest, Dave?" Sam Atkins asked on the phone.

"The Brazilian procedure is the only way I see of deterring this virus and saving those of us still healthy," Reiss replied.

"Even if it kills ten percent of those inoculated, as the Brazilians are reporting?"

"Maybe it won't. Most of our population has been vaccinated. The same way that the vaccine is reducing the death rate of those infected, it may also provide some protection to those variolated."

"You think so?" Atkins asked, hopeful but skeptical.

"It's a good possibility. We don't have hard data, but we have anecdotal information from Brazil. Frank DuBois's son is in Rio and participated in the variolation experiment. They have talked, and it seems that the few emergency workers who had previously been vaccinated ended up with much milder reactions from the variolation procedure."

Atkins pondered the information. "Any educated guesses as to what the death rates from such a procedure could be here in the U.S.?"

"I don't really know, Sam," Reiss replied, scratching his head. "If it's half the numbers reported in Brazil, it could be down to five or six percent. But even if it's ten, it'll save many lives if we move quickly."

Within a few hours, the President was on TV. He was visibly tired and appeared to have aged decades. The virus had hit home, and not only because it was killing the people he was sworn to protect. The Secretary of Homeland Security had fallen victim of the disease, and the President's own daughter was battling it. He rested an elbow on the lectern as he looked at the camera.

"My fellow Americans. I don't need to tell you that the catastrophe devastating our country has mushroomed beyond our scariest nightmares. Health researchers around the world have been unable to develop effective tools to defend the population against the bioengineered smallpox virus, and the pandemic is well on its way to destroy every society on the planet.

"However, there is some hope. It's a procedure that, while far from perfect, has the potential to save lives and eventually halt the progression of the disease. It's called variolation, and its implementation is similar to the vaccine that many of us received."

The President paused. He was reading from a sheet of paper instead of using the teleprompt. He looked at the camera and continued. "Variolation isn't new. It's a centuries-old procedure employed by many societies before the invention of the vaccine. Among others, General George Washington ordered his soldiers variolated after smallpox outbreaks weakened his troops. And variolation isn't one hundred percent safe. Some will likely contract the disease and die. It's a price we have to pay given the devastation the virus is generating and frankly, because we don't have an alternative.

"As soon as possible, variolation stations will operate at all food distribution centers throughout the country. All military, police, fire, medical, and emergency personnel are ordered to be variolated. This order doesn't extend to civilians, but I strongly urge every healthy person to take advantage of this opportunity to save his or her life. If the majority of the population is inoculated, we can stop the spread of the virus and look forward to restoring normalcy in our society."

As the President ended his address, the first lady and several cabinet members came into the pressroom. They rolled up their sleeves and a nurse scratched the scab powder under the skin of their forearms, right in front of the cameras.

The President again faced the camera. "It's this simple," he said. "We wouldn't do it if we didn't believe that this procedure will increase the odds of saving our lives. Do yourself a favor. Go out to your food center and get variolated. And may God protect us all."

CHAPTER 20

Life in Fakarava remained tranquil, but there were exceptions. The handful of guesthouses stayed empty as the South Pacific high season arrived, and their owners were hurting. Also, the pearl farm, although operational, could find no outlet for its product. It survived for a few months but eventually it ran out of capital, with most of its value locked in the inventory of cultured South Sea pearls with nowhere to go.

By July, the owner, a burly, dark-skinned man going by the name of Gaston, was getting desperate. He contacted a middleman in Tahiti and convinced him to risk a trip to Fakarava in exchange for a large discount. The world pearl market was depressed, but it would rebound, wouldn't it? They agreed to meet a couple of miles offshore to avoid detection. With the transaction concluded, the pearl farm continued its operation.

Two weeks later, Anne met Gaston during one of her visits.

"Anne, come on over. I have something to show you," Gaston said, inviting her into his office at the end of a wooden pier overlooking the pearl farm.

She parked her bike and followed him inside. He wanted to show her two particularly large and flawless pearls that had recently been harvested.

"Look at them. They're exquisite," he said. "Each pearl is unique. Finding a good match for a particular one is very difficult, but these two are not only rare in size and luster, they're also a perfect match, which makes them a very valuable set."

Anne admired the pearls using a special magnifying lens. They were truly beautiful. "How did you find such a wonderful match?" she asked.

He laughed. "It takes some luck, of course, but it also takes Marie's expert eye." He took Anne to an adjacent room where a large Polynesian woman was sorting pearls according to color, size, shape, luster, and flawlessness. Each pearl was given a grade, which in turn would determine its price.

They chitchatted for a few minutes while Anne observed Marie's work. She didn't stay very long. Gaston was feeling a bit under the weather, and she didn't want to catch a cold.

Three days later, Gaston was very sick. His mild fever had turned into severe headaches and vomiting. When his vomit became bloody and a rash developed on his torso and limbs, someone suspected the dreaded disease ravaging most of the outside world. A call was placed to health officials in Papeete and within hours, a doctor in full biological gear arrived in Fakarava. He soon diagnosed Gaston as the first smallpox case in French Polynesia outside of Tahiti. Somehow, the travel restrictions had been violated and now another five hundred people were at risk.

The following day, two health technicians arrived with orders to variolate anyone who had contacted the victim. Several employees of the pearl farm were inoculated, but no one thought of the young foreigner. Anne was unaware of the events, having spent the previous few days in her bungalow and at the nearby beach.

She learned about poor Gaston during a bike trip to the grocery store in town. A full week had passed since he had shown her his precious pearl set. She became immediately concerned, but said nothing. Would she be hoisted by her own petard? She had always thought it was possible, but had assumed that it was not very likely. She had carefully planned her isolation from populated centers. Although she knew that the highly-contagious virus would find its way to unusual places, she never thought that this pristine, almost-empty island, in a remote corner of a vast ocean, might become exposed.

She had been wrong.

Over the following days she pondered her predicament. What would she do if she had been infected? Nothing, she decided. She would accept it as the big girl she was. Her actions were changing the world, so the least she could do was to die courageously. If the virus could find her, it was only proof that her plans were succeeding. No one could hide and no place was safe, just as they had intended.

Days later, she felt ill. Her head and back ached, and she was nauseated. She locked herself in the small bungalow and lay in bed. A high fever ensued and her whole body began to hurt. Within days, she was vomiting blood and the surface of her body had the texture and feel of someone stung by a swarm of killer bees. The pain was agonizing, as her skin appeared to split in sheets from the underlying tissue. Her eyes were squeezed shut with bleeding wounds and she became blind. At times, the pain was so severe that she would pass out, only to wake up minutes or hours later to another bout of pain.

Ultimately, blood oozed from her mouth, anus, and vagina as the virus ate away at her internal membranes. Except for short periods of unconsciousness, she remained alert through the ordeal. The blindness and the pain brought a thought from the depths of her conscience. Did I cause this much suffering to so many people? She mused. But she quickly replaced that thought with another one. It's for the good of the planet. The death of a suffocating species will allow others to flourish.

She wondered about her parents. Had the virus affected them? What had happened to them in the middle of the chaos? But she set those sentiments aside. She wouldn't allow for last minute mushiness. They, too, were part of the problem. She felt no remorse.

The virus kept feasting on her body. Her lungs filled with blood and she struggled to breathe as the lining of her throat, intestines, rectum, and vagina disintegrated. Finally, her heart gave out.

Several days went by. The owners of the bungalow realized that they had not seen their tenant for some time and went to investigate. As they approached, they saw Anne's bicycle leaning against a tree. The sun was bright, reflecting between the palm trees on the blue-green waters of the beautiful lagoon. Warm trade winds blew in from the water and caressed the skin. It was paradise.

Then the stench overpowered them.

***

"It's not completely over, but I believe we can stop worrying about just controlling the disease and start taking steps to restore a normal way of life," Sam Atkins was saying. "From a practical perspective, we have the pandemic under control."

"Mr. Secretary," Cecilia Chapman asked, sitting in front of Atkins in a television studio. "Are you saying that the population no longer needs to be concerned about the virus?"

"To some extent, yes. We estimate that over eighty percent of our people have either been exposed to the disease or have been variolated. Of course, the other twenty percent are still at risk and as vulnerable as before. But from a medical perspective, we can manage that now. New infections are at a level that we can handle with the emergency measures still in place."

"Are we keeping variolation mandatory for the victim contacts?"

"Of course. The benefit of variolating those who have contact with infected persons still outweighs the risks," Atkins replied. "As you know, we were very lucky with the results of variolation. It was a stroke of luck that the procedure was tried and actually worked. We were also very fortunate that the initial vaccine provided enough immunity to significantly reduce loss of life. The casualties from variolation in the U.S. hovered around five percent, half the rate in most countries."

"What do you think would have happened without this procedure?"

"It's hard to tell, Cecilia." Atkins had thought about that many times and had a pretty good idea, but it was too painful to discuss. "What happened was enough of a catastrophe. We caught a lucky break and are grateful for that. It allowed us to halt the uncontrolled spread of the virus and get our arms around that particular problem, but we still have a lot of work to do to put our society back together."

"How long will the military forces stay in the streets?" Cecilia asked.

"Until the social ramifications of the pandemic are under control, local governments are again functional, and law enforcement agencies can take care of law and order. As you know, police and EMTs were devastated. They were in the forefront of the fight, and when the vaccine failed they were the most vulnerable. In some places, half of them are dead and the rest are emotionally and physically devastated. They are war heroes who gave their lives in defense of the population. Until those agencies are reorganized, restaffed, and retrained, our armed forces will provide those services."

"Wasn't the military equally affected?"

"Not to the same extent, in part because they already knew that the vaccine wasn't effective when they were mobilized. They were able to take precautions that the initial response teams had not. Our soldiers used the same equipment they would have used to protect themselves from a biological or chemical attack in the battlefield. Although we didn't have enough for everyone, what we had kept most of them healthy."

"Mr. Secretary, we know that some military units suffered unusually high levels of casualties." This was a touchy issue with the military authorities, but she was not going to let the Secretary of Defense off the hook. "Rumors abound that those units may have used defective batches of protective gear, and that the manufacturer had been aware of it. Do you care to comment?"

Atkins tried not to squirm, with little success. "I'm aware of the rumors, but we have no evidence that they are actually true. While some units were hit harder, it's too early to blame the equipment. Obviously, we are investigating, but let's not forget that we were forced to use everything we had available to combat the virus. We protect our soldiers in every way we can, but they are conditioned to die if necessary to defend the country. It's a professional hazard, if you will, and many died in the line of duty. All in all, the military units were affected at about the same rate as the general population."

"As we reported several times, there were instances of soldiers panicking or deserting, and certainly not doing their job," Cecilia said. She had reported extensively on soldiers joining or even leading the rampage in the streets during the height of the pandemic, but she was not going to point that out again. Atkins knew it and didn't need to be reminded. "How's the military leadership going to deal with those soldiers?" she asked.

Atkins was perspiring under the lights in the studio. He wiped his forehead and then replied. "In the same way we would deal with them if they were in a battlefield in Afghanistan or Iraq. We will punish the deserters or traitors according to military rules. That said, we don't want to take a bad situation and make it worse. The war we've been fighting is unlike anything our soldiers ever encountered. First, it's at home, and it's much more difficult to maintain dedication and discipline when you are forced to go against your countrymen. Soldiers are trained to defend them, not repel them. Second, the real enemy is invisible and more deadly than most enemies in the battlefield. It's everywhere, but you can't shoot at it. You can only try to prevent it from attacking you. It's easy to panic in such a situation. And lastly, we must remember that these are very young people, many barely out of their teens, and they were as scared as everybody else. After weeks of chaos without an end in sight, some of them simply snapped."

"What do you think will happen next?"

Atkins tried to cross his chubby legs, but was clearly uncomfortable. "We still have a huge job ahead just to ensure proper living conditions and feed the population," he answered. "The military logistics teams are still coordinating food production and distribution, and they'll need to do so until commerce and industry are back on their feet. We're coordinating, and in many cases performing garbage collection and clean up duties. We finally caught up with the interment of all the dead, quite a number still unidentified."

He shifted in his chair, set both feet back on the floor, and continued. "There are still bodies out there in shacks, in the woods, in rivers and ponds, in abandoned homes, that we haven't found. But at least we've cleaned out the streets and parks, the residential areas, and of course the hospitals and isolation centers. We're fairly confident that the sanitary conditions are again adequate, but we need to keep our military around until the cities are back in operation."

"Do you think we'll ever learn the identity of all the victims?" Cecilia's own sister was one of those unaccounted for. She had been away in school when the virus appeared, and the family had not heard from her since.

"We took all possible steps to identify those we buried or

cremated. Given the numbers, it wasn't feasible to identify everyone, and we didn't have the time or the resources to be thorough. We also couldn't keep decomposing bodies around hoping that someone would show up to identify them, so we noted any unusual physical condition, where, how, and when the bodies were found, took photographs and DNA samples, and kept some of the personal items found on the victims. It was a gruesome task that our soldiers handled with dedication and respect."

Sam Atkins paused to collect his thoughts, then continued. "Right now, our most important job is to take care of the living. We have millions of children being taken care of by volunteer groups. Some are orphans, others are probably abandoned and others are separated from their parents. As you know, we tried to isolate every infected person as soon as the individual showed symptoms. Often, it was a parent with children at home and, more frequently than we'd like to admit, those children became lost in the shuffle. Sometimes the parent died, or the child got sick before the parent recovered. But the grim reality is that many children will need parenting and their parents aren't there."

"There are many parents who lost children. Do you think the orphans can be adopted?"

"That would be ideal, but I don't have to tell you that it won't be easy. We're inviting every parent who lost a child to adopt another one. We're pretty sure that we'll even be able to match the age and sex if they want to. We're not trying to replace a child, but perhaps we can reconstruct broken families and give some children a chance at a stable environment."

Cecilia was about to ask another question but Atkins

continued. "And let me make another point," he said. "We have an equally large number of elderly left alone and helpless. Some were self-sufficient before the disease, but are too weak now to care for themselves. Our responsibility as a society is to take care of them."

"How about the emotional toll on the rest of the population?" Cecilia asked, thinking of herself and millions like her. She was one of the invisible victims, even though she had not contracted the disease. She had been vaccinated and variolated, was immune and scar-free, but she was not well. She had lost a grandmother, two cousins, several friends, and probably a sister. She felt constantly tired and depressed. She had trouble falling asleep and would wake up bathed in sweat or crying for no apparent reason. Internally, she was an emotional wreck who put up a front every day for her TV audience.

"We're not even thinking about that yet," Atkins said. "Most people will carry the emotional scars for the rest of their lives. They'll have to deal with the nightmares and the pain on their own, just like the European and Japanese victims of World War II. It's the tragic legacy of war. I hope that, as our society gets back to normal, support groups will be formed and psychologists will be available to help people cope. For now, we're just trying to survive."

"I understand that there is much work to be done to take care of the living, but as you mentioned, we need to get our economy moving again. To do it, the administration needs to lay out a framework for recovery. What are the next steps?"

"The administration is struggling with that issue." He wasn't the best person to answer the question, and he knew it.

"We're just now getting our arms around what has been a human tragedy. Our country has lost almost a quarter of its people, which means that we're now back at the same population level of the 1960s. We put our economy on hold while trying to save lives but when this is over, the economy won't be what it was at the end of last year. We'll need to take precautions to avoid an economic tragedy equal to the human tragedy. Major changes will take place in industries and commerce, but we must avoid economic chaos. There'll be tremendous instability and it'll be difficult to decide what to do, but the economy will recover. What we can't do is allow the free markets to immediately dictate where we end up because it would be devastating to the nation."

"What you are suggesting is that the government will adopt a strong interventionist policy," Cecilia said. "Do you also mean that the administration won't reopen the stock markets and the banks anytime soon?"

"I didn't say that," Atkins replied. "We need to reopen the banks since we can't get other businesses going without cash and financing, but we must prevent them from going bankrupt the day they open. The administration is studying various options, but drastic and even unpopular decisions will be required. Again, we're facing situations never encountered before, and we need to come up with alternatives that were never tested. What those will be is still being debated."

CHAPTER 21

It was the middle of October and Frank DuBois was driving back home after spending the morning at Morris General. The days were again getting shorter and the trees were putting on their annual fall display of yellows, browns, reds, and purples. Many suburban lawns, normally green and manicured, were now an unkempt mess of knee-high weeds and grass sprinkled with papers, bottles, and other garbage. Here and there, a homeowner had cut the grass, but the Latin American immigrants who used to come around during the warm months to mow the lawns had stayed away.

The children, still not in school, played in the yards and streets, but the mood was far from happy and carefree. Most had lost mothers, fathers, siblings, or friends, and many exhibited the gruesome scars of a death struggle they had won at a tremendous cost. Dr. DuBois heard the chatter and occasional laughter, but underneath there was a sadness that eyes and faces could not hide.

Neighborhoods were being uprooted by people trying to get their lives back in order. Everyone had lost someone to the virus. For most of the spring and summer, people had put their futures in limbo, hoping to merely survive the pandemic. Now that the worst appeared to be over, the survivors were evaluating their options, picking up the pieces, and making difficult decisions.

Frank parked his car in the driveway and walked into his home.

"Good afternoon, Doctor," Sarah said, raising her misshapen eyes from the book she was reading. "How are things at the hospital?"

"As well as can be expected," he answered with a shrug. "It'll take years before we get back to normal. We lost too many good people and it'll be a long while before we can replace their expertise. The medical staff will be in short supply and overburdened for years to come."

"They paid a terrible price for doing their job."

DuBois nodded. "I still don't know how I managed to escape."

"You were very careful and very lucky, that's all," she said. "Are there still many new cases?"

"A few. There are still pockets of the disease. We're seeing three or four cases a week, and the emergency teams are busy checking their contacts to determine if they've been exposed or variolated before, but the numbers are manageable."

Frank went into the bathroom to wash up and looked in

the mirror. He had aged noticeably over the last seven months. His hairline had receded and he was now all white, and the bags under his eyes extended almost halfway to the edges of his mouth. And the aging wasn't just in appearance, he really felt old. There was a perceptible shake to his hands and his walk had slowed considerably. At fifty-nine, he looked ten years older.

He missed his wife more than he ever thought possible. They had been each other's pillars of strength, particularly after Anne's departure. When Doreen was murdered, he was left grieving for a loving wife who had been taken away and for a prodigal daughter who had turned into a veritable monster. Then he worried about a son recovering from the dreadful disease. In the weeks after Doreen's death, he had found little meaning in his life and had wondered how he would survive the ordeal.

Then Sarah had called, a soul whose needs equaled his. Their conversations and walks were therapeutic and her visits provided some degree of healing. In many ways, she was slowly replacing the daughter he had lost, and he found purpose in helping the sweet, lonely, disfigured young woman.

She, too, found pleasure in helping the old man. His house was becoming a tomb and added to his depression. He used only four rooms, and the nine-room home developed a musty smell, with dust accumulating on the hardwood floors and furniture. During one of her visits, Sarah spent the day vacuuming, dusting, and cleaning.

"What would you say if I were to move into one of your empty bedrooms?" she asked during one of their walks.

"I'd be delighted." He had already thought about it but

hadn't expected her to suggest it. "But you don't want to share a house with a crabby old man."

"Don't be silly. You're the closest thing I have to family and right now my only friend. I think you, too, can use some company."

"What will you do with your apartment?"

"I haven't thought about that yet. Maybe sell it."

"Good luck! Have you noticed how many 'For Sale' signs are out there?"

"I may just turn it over to the bank. The way home prices are coming down, my mortgage could be greater than the value of the apartment."

That was the cruel reality. Every block had one or two homes for sale, not including the foreclosed properties. The real estate market plunged as soon as the administration tried to reopen the economy to regular commerce. People had assumed huge, low-interest mortgages in the overpriced house market of the previous five years, but the upheaval caused by the pandemic, the massive unemployment rate, and the abrupt decrease in population created an unprecedented house glut. Already, a large number of mortgages greatly exceeded the value of the homes that secured them. Asking prices were down seventy percent from a year ago, and still no one was buying. Most people were not yet ready to make major decisions. In addition, no one knew where the bottom would be.

"At least my home's paid for," Frank said with a sad smile. "The equity is dropping, but life is such a mess that my net worth isn't really a major concern."

Less than one year ago, he would have agonized over the loss of so much property value, or that he couldn't sell the shares of stock in his retirement plan, or that the banks seemed to be going bankrupt and he would be at the mercy of the FDIC to recover some of his savings. But now, money wasn't part of the things that were important to him anymore. Except for the disfigured woman walking next to him and a son stuck in a foreign country, nothing else really mattered.

They walked for a while without speaking, just enjoying the pleasant fall weather and admiring the autumn colors.

"Have you thought about plastic surgery to correct your eyelids?" he asked after several minutes.

The question surprised her. She would like to correct her spooky gaze, but with the epidemic still lingering and the uncertain economic conditions, she didn't think it would happen anytime soon.

"I've thought about it, but aren't all doctors and medical facilities tied up with real emergencies?"

"Not necessarily. Plastic surgeons have been filling gaps in medical assistance, but several are itching to get back to their craft. Some are already looking into the possibility of repairing scarred victims, and many operate out of their private clinics. I have several friends who are very good, and I can look around for you, if you want, maybe even get you a special rate. After all, you're special, you were the very first survivor," he added with a tender smile.

"I'd like that," she said, smiling back. Maybe then she would be able to walk around without the stares. Initially, she had worn her scars as a badge of honor, a symbol of survival, and a reminder of how lucky she had been. But as the months went by, she became self-conscious, hid her eyes behind dark glasses, and tried to conceal her scars under heavy layers of make-up. She had not returned to the office partly because of the way she looked, believing that her appearance, her eyes in particular, would be a distraction to co-workers and interfere with her ability to do her job. The only person to whom she could show her face without embarrassment was Dr. DuBois.

"I'll do some digging," he said.

Again they walked a couple of blocks without speaking.

"Have you reconciled your IOUs yet?" Sarah asked as they headed back home.

IOU payments for food and essential items had stopped for all who could afford them. People now could withdraw up to one thousand dollars per week from their bank accounts and write checks of up to five hundred dollars. They could also use credit cards, although most had been cancelled by the issuing institutions. IOUs were now accepted only for medical emergencies and in case of demonstrated need.

The administration of the IOU accounts was the responsibility of the IRS and many people were disputing their balances. Often, pertinent records could not be found, as record keeping had not been a major priority during the pandemic. It would take years to reconcile every dispute, if ever.

***

Until late summer, the war on the disease had consumed all efforts and fear had paralyzed citizens and government officials alike. No one seemed concerned about the November elections, even after nineteen senators and a larger number of representatives had died from the virus. But once the pandemic subsided, politicians suddenly realized that this was an election year, and the airwaves were filled with a cacophony of messages. The many holes in the political world would be filled in the forthcoming election, three weeks away. In addition to the presidential selection, more than half the seats in the Senate and the majority of the House of Representatives were up for vote. Besides the deceased and the ones at the end of their terms, many lawmakers had decided that they were not up to the challenges ahead, or were too tired, or still grieving from personal tragedy, and were voluntarily giving up their seats.

There was nothing routine about this election. The huge sums of money usually spent by the candidates and their political parties were absent. The political machines and the thousands of volunteers that normally rallied behind popular candidates had failed to organize, and the pre-election campaigning was being done almost exclusively on the radio and TV. The broadcast stations, without new shows or sports events to present, were only too happy to allow the politicians to explain their ideas on talk shows and news programs.

Reconstruction ideas were all over the place. Rebuilding the economy was the number one priority, with proposals ranging from complete isolationism, to some form of protectionism, to reconstruction based on a worldwide recovery. Some advocated taking free-food distribution a step farther: free government provision of all essential services, like food, shelter, education, and healthcare for everyone. Others supported an immediate stoppage of all free services to eliminate dependence on handouts and force people back to work.

There was no guarantee that the incumbent Republican would be re-elected. The nation had been a battlefield in a war that had been clearly lost. Now that fear had subsided, there was an overwhelming sense of frustration. No specific group or nation had been made to pay for unleashing the tragedy that had created so much devastation and had so utterly changed the world. The fact that the current administration had effectively minimized the damage was no consolation for a dejected population.

The Democratic opponent was successfully convincing the voters that the Republican hard line on terrorism had misfired and was responsible for the catastrophe. In the Democrat's argument, the pandemic was the result of a misguided policy. By focusing on rogue nations and threatening to use military power against specific targets, the administration had splintered organized terrorist groups into small independent cells which were, in aggregate, more powerful, more dangerous, and more difficult to track and control. The consequences were evident.

However, the surprising front-runner was an independent fireball by the name of Rachel MacDowell. An elegant, middle-aged woman with short brown hair, aquiline nose, and large expressive brown eyes, she called herself the "candidate for common sense." Although college educated, she had stayed home to raise her boys. From home, she had launched a successful cosmetics company that was now defunct like many others. Her husband and younger son had succumbed to the disease and her other two sons, both waiting for the university to reopen, often accompanied her to TV interviews and public appearances.

MacDowell didn't have many specific plans on how to get out of the mess. She stressed that the problems were so severe and the challenge so enormous that any preconceived ideas would be thrown out the window when facing reality. She pointed out that neither Republicans nor Democrats were better prepared to run the country than anyone else.

"The last thing the country can afford is for ideology to prevail over common sense," she emphasized during one of her television commercials. "There is a need for drastic decisions and for policies that can shape the future of our nation for generations to come. To allow partisan politics to dictate these decisions would be a travesty."

***

Cecilia Chapman's "Outbreak News Bulletin" was on. It remained the most widely watched news program, but its focus had shifted from the progression of the disease to its social and economic implications, and it was the preferred forum for politicians and so-called experts. The upcoming elections provided plenty of discussion.

"Almost eight months after the beginning of the outbreak that ravaged the world, the social, economic, and political ramifications are difficult to assess, but the year's events are certainly shaping the election landscape. With us today is independent presidential candidate Rachel MacDowell." The camera shifted from Cecilia to the candidate. "Mrs. MacDowell, welcome to our program."

"Thank you, it's a pleasure to be here," the woman said with a smile. She was attractive and confident, and her appearance and demeanor were undoubtedly part of her appeal to the voters.

"Mrs. MacDowell, the presidential campaign has focused on the measures we must take at home to rebuild the nation. Yet, we don't live in a vacuum, and international relations will be important in shaping the economy and maintaining peace at home. Do you expect any significant changes in the international balance of power as a result of the pandemic?"

"Without a doubt," the candidate said, adjusting her glasses. "One of the things we saw was that every nation was left on its own to fight the virus. All nations, including the rich ones, were so overwhelmed by the magnitude of the problem that there was no room to help anybody. As a result, we're already seeing a resurgence of nationalistic movements in many countries. In addition, the wide deployment of military forces to combat the virus, primarily in nations with recent totalitarian tendencies, is very troubling. The combination of economic chaos, irrational nationalism, and totalitarian regimes led to much of the turmoil of the twentieth century. It could happen again."

"You mean another Hitler or Stalin?"

"Exactly," MacDowell replied, nodding emphatically. "Europe is in shambles, both economically and politically. A united Europe, which appeared to be a reality at the beginning of the year, no longer exists. Each country fought the virus alone, and the various governments are now consumed in dealing with their own social and economic messes and aren't even attempting a combined recovery plan. Some countries have no diplomatic relations even with their neighbors. Spain, Italy, and Greece are dusting off their old mints and re-issuing the national currencies they had chucked a few short years ago. Others may follow. It's a clear message that they have no intention of rejoining a united Europe."

"Is the European Union the biggest casualty of the pandemic?" Cecilia asked.

"It's a big one, but not necessarily the biggest." Rachel MacDowell was composed and believable. "The main victim could be world trade. And I don't mean during this past year, but in the future. With the enormous population reduction worldwide, there's a huge labor loss and, more troubling, an irreparable skill loss. It'll take years before critical skills are adequately recreated. As a result, most nations will direct the available skills toward sheltered industries aimed primarily at the needs of the domestic market. If the nationalistic sentiment I mentioned earlier takes hold, we may see a resurgence of protectionism in many places. Several countries, like Brazil for instance, have already announced that they won't repay their foreign debt and are renationalizing key industries, which they had privatized over the last decade. These countries see the collapse of a world economy and want to deal with the reconstruction of their economy without foreign interference."

"The trend you describe is obviously disturbing," Cecilia said. "In the past, nationalism and protectionism went hand in hand with expansionism and aggression."

MacDowell was nodding as Cecilia spoke and didn't even wait for her to ask a question. "We all know that the best way to diffuse trouble at home is to appeal to the nationalistic sentiment and to start trouble abroad. No nation is going to recover quickly from this catastrophe, but the population will soon demand quick fixes. What a crazy dictator can do then is anyone's guess. Given the number of countries with nuclear and chemical weapons, there's ample reason to fear another major disaster. Of course, we all know what a few nuts can do with a rudimentary biological lab."

"Do you see any particular nations poised to take advantage of this global chaos?"

The candidate took a sip from a glass in front of her. She put the glass down and thought for a few seconds. "A few. North Korea is of particular concern," she said. "With their philosophy of self-reliance, they came away from the global pandemic relatively unscathed. The terrorists didn't target any of their cities, and as a closed society, the number of infections was relatively small when the rest of the world was dying. The authorities also realized the catastrophic nature of the disease, and as a military regime with limited internal mobility, they already had the conditions to effectively identify, isolate, and quarantine victims and their contacts. Therefore, they had by far the lowest mortality rates of any major nation, and the pandemic barely impacted their economy and society. If they were already an 'axis of evil,' they are now a stronger evil. We don't know their intentions, but they certainly can be a major threat to their neighbors and to world peace and recovery."

"Mrs. MacDowell, the President called back most of our military in order to deal with the domestic crisis. How does that affect our ability to respond if a nation decides to start trouble?"

MacDowell pondered the question. "There's a new world reality, and we need to get used to the idea that the U.S. can't police the planet," she finally said. "Our troops are deployed where they are most needed, and that's right here at home for the time being. Clearly, this will present an opportunity for rogue nations to again contemplate expansionism or divert attention from their domestic difficulties. But they could be making a huge mistake if they think we won't react. We're hurt, but not dead. We remain the most powerful country on earth, and we'll take whatever action is necessary to protect our interests."

"If you're elected, do you see the U.S. getting involved if a traditional ally becomes the target of a major aggression?"

"I don't know what my administration will do in situations that haven't yet happened. Our priorities will be our domestic problems. If anyone attacks us, we will respond. Beyond that, it will depend on the particular circumstances. We'll do what makes sense," MacDowell replied.

Cecilia decided to challenge the candidate with a different question.

"Great wars have always changed the course of history and often induced major transformations in the character and intrinsic values of societies," she said. "This was a major war, perhaps even greater than the Civil War and ending without a victory. How do you think it'll change us as a nation?"

The candidate laughed. "That's a great question! Many volumes will be written to answer it over the next hundred years. Even with the benefit of evidence those future historians will probably be wrong, so I won't presume to have the answer at this time." MacDowell thought for a few seconds, took another sip of water, then continued. "Here's a hypothetical outcome, maybe more plausible than most of us would want to believe – the great social experiment of the second half of the twentieth century comes to a disastrous conclusion."

"What do you mean by that?"

MacDowell removed her glasses. "Let me try to explain," she said. "America has been an open and trusting society. We welcomed every citizen of the world, every religion, every culture, every color, every language, and respected them all. We've been the land of the free and the land of opportunity and we extended both freedom and opportunity to the hungry, the tired, the prosecuted, and the opportunistic. In exchange, we expected other nations and cultures to accept and respect us. And they did. They also admired us and often tried to imitate us."

She shifted in her seat and continued. "As we became the most powerful nation on earth, it was often said that America couldn't dominate the world but could and should lead it. But power is corruptive, and powerful nations, like powerful people, often make mistakes. We frequently took over-assertive positions that alienated our friends, and as a condition to our help and friendship, we placed demands on the world's nations – to treat the world community and their people in accordance with our perspective on human rights, social justice, and fair play.

"On September 11, we were badly hurt, not so much physically but psychologically and emotionally. Suddenly, we realized that there were people out there who didn't buy into our value system, who didn't like us very much, and who were dead serious about causing us pain and disrupting our way of life. But we failed to recognize that it was not irrational hate confined to just a few extremists, but a groundswell of resentment for our success and sometimes arrogance."

Cecilia listened to the candidate with some surprise. She had clearly thought about the subject and was eager to articulate her thoughts.

"Then the virus arrived and the ensuing catastrophe will force us to rethink the practices of our society," MacDowell continued. "The world obviously doesn't want to be either dominated or led. Maybe America will abandon the idea that it should be the leader. Should it be our business how other cultures treat their women, their children, or their prisoners? Or do we have the moral high-ground to demand that other nations disarm when we have larger stockpiles of arms of mass destruction than any other country?"

She took another sip of water and went on. "Many values and ideals that we took for granted at the end of the century were shaken on September 11, but now they have been cracked by the events of the past year. Questions that we used to abhor are being asked again, not by extremists or bigots but by mainstream America. Should we keep admitting all kinds of people into our midst or should we close our borders? Or should we be selective? Do we want to keep pushing the idea of globalization or should we clam down, take advantage of our resources and ingenuity to feed and please our people, and the hell with the rest of the world? Should we tolerate nonconforming views? What price are we willing to pay to maintain the civil liberties we cherished until a few months ago? Do we want to preserve our right to privacy and free speech or should we resort to new technologies to monitor the whereabouts and expression of our citizens?

"How will this experience change us as a nation?" Rachel MacDowell asked, repeating the question. "I don't know, but let's carry this hypothetical scenario to its extreme conclusion, maybe not too farfetched given the numbers of people advocating it." Her tone became sarcastic. "We isolate ourselves as a nation. We take the necessary steps to recover and provide a comfortable living for our citizens. We implement draconian procedures to control the malcontents in our midst. We stop all immigration from undesirable cultures. We relinquish any interests abroad so that no nation can threaten them. We stop all international cooperation and intervention to avoid having them perceived as self-serving meddling. In return, the terrorists forget about us and leave us alone."

Rachel MacDowell looked squarely into the camera. "Is this what we really want?"

CHAPTER 22

February 23rd, the first anniversary of the smallpox outbreak, went unnoticed.

There were no monuments, no memorials, no special services. There were no speeches condemning the terrorists, or commending the heroes who had saved lives, or remembering the lives that had been lost. It was just another day in a new reality. The world had changed. Everyone, from the politicians to the clergy to the average citizens, was still learning to live under a hardship unimaginable only one year earlier.

Police departments were again staffed and partly trained, and schools had reopened at the beginning of the year. Those were the only two signs of normalcy on this first anniversary.

The severe winter had taken another toll on a population struggling to reshape their lives. Even though food distribution remained adequate and essential items were still available for free to those without a job, a large number of people, mainly elderly, had been unable to reach the distribution centers during the snowstorms and cold spells that had plagued most northern states. Worst yet, hundreds of people had frozen to death, some for lack of heating oil and gas, others for lack of technicians to fix broken heaters or because social services were unable to respond.

The economy struggled to develop some rhythm. Bilateral trade agreements were being negotiated, mainly for export of foodstuffs, but international commerce was still non-existent. Many industries depended on foreign materials or parts for their operation and were scrambling to develop domestic alternatives, but critical skills or equipment were often unavailable.

The recovery of the capital goods markets would be a long time in coming and a number of industries were not even trying to recover. Many hotel and resort chains, most of the airline companies, and two of the big automakers had declared bankruptcy. The construction industry was stopped given the excess of housing and office space, and telecommunications suppliers and semiconductor manufacturers, already weak before the pandemic, had not yet resumed operation.

Underscoring the economic problems was the collapse of the banking industry despite the government's effort. With federal help, the banking system had been poised to absorb huge losses from commercial and personal real estate loans when the bankruptcies of major corporations and the losses from international investments sent them over the edge. The stock exchanges, which had reopened on the first business day of the year, quickly dropped to the levels of the late 1940s.

The few industries that had been kept afloat by government-mandated emergency measures – food, medical, pharmaceutical, energy, and other essentials – were trying to lead a recovery of sorts. Agriculture was the only flourishing business. People needed to eat and imports were non-existent.

Unemployment was at levels not seen since the Great Depression. Job openings produced lines of applicants that stretched for blocks, and wages for unskilled labor collapsed below the minimum-wage level. Families already hurt by the epidemic couldn't extricate themselves from poverty and dependence on handouts. Many left major industrial areas for rural communities, some hoping to start small farms, others filling in for the migrant farm workers blocked from entering the country.

A class of new poor was created, coming from the upper and middle classes. Most people with savings and retirement plans in real estate or securities saw their investments become worthless. With their high-paying jobs eliminated, their skills not immediately useful, and their wealth gone, suicides were not uncommon.

Adrift in the chaos, people looked to God as the solution to their distress. The Reverend Charles Haywood's following was larger than ever. His daily sermons and prayer programs had one of the highest ratings on TV. "Apocalypse" groups formed all over the country and people came together to listen to the reverend, perform acts of contrition, and pray as a group. The destitute believed him. He was a modern-day prophet showing the way back to the Lord. God had to be very upset; there was no other explanation for the continued misery.

***

Sarah sat in the living room as Dr. DuBois prepared tea in the kitchen. He preferred coffee, but coffee and sugar, not considered essential items, were now very expensive if they could be found. The evening was cold and a light snow had begun to fall. Sarah had gathered firewood from the woods behind their property, and a cozy fire was crackling in the fireplace.

"It's been a year since we bumped into each other again," she reminded him as he walked into the living room and handed her a cup. She sipped her tea. He had sweetened it with honey, still readily available.

"Nothing personal, my dear, but I wish it didn't have to happen." He gave her a faint smile and sat in the recliner by the fire. He turned the TV on with the remote control.

Reverend Haywood was preaching. "Revelations says, "I saw the dead, the great and the lowly, standing before the throne. All the dead were judged according to their deeds. Anyone whose name was not found written in the Book of Life was thrown into the pool of fire." This prophecy is being carried out in our day. Satan was released to deceive us, and we allowed ourselves to be deceived. We keep ignoring the needs of the helpless, the sick, the old, the orphans, and the hungry. The Lord is punishing us. Without repentance, without penance, and without compassion, He won't find our names in the Book of Life."

"He won't find our names because He's already forsaken us," Frank said sarcastically. He changed channels.

Cecilia Chapman was reading the news. A major electronics retailer had reopened its first store in Cincinnati, only to see it vandalized by a gang of youths. A nuclear power plant in New

York had been close to a meltdown because officials had insisted in keeping it running without enough qualified technicians. Per-capita consumption of alcohol was way up from a year ago. Los Angeles residents were still waiting for telephone service. The President was proposing sending surplus grain to central Europe where famine was rampant, even though regions of Africa, Asia and South America were even more desperate. The new Moslem regime in Indonesia had re-annexed East Timor and threatened to invade the Philippines in support of their Moslem minority, and the U.S. was considering whether to interfere to support the Filipino regime.

On the positive side, one airline was resuming flights to several cities that had been without air travel for a year, and the baseball commissioner had announced that, after missing an entire season, spring training would start in April.

When the news was over, Frank switched the TV off.

"You look so much better," he told Sarah.

"Thanks to you. At least people don't look at me like I'm some Halloween freak," she replied.

Frank had convinced a colleague to perform free plastic surgery on Sarah's eyes. She was repaying the favor by doing his paperwork and updating patient files. Her eyelids had been reshaped and the major scars around her mouth and eyes minimized. The evidence of the disease was still there, but the pale, pretty face was back.

Frank pushed his recliner back and picked up a book. His eyes fell on the framed picture hanging on the wall above the TV, one from earlier times and much happier days. The four of them as a family, with him in the middle, his right arm hugging Doreen's waist and his left holding a five-year-old girl with dirty blond hair flowing down her shoulders. Her tiny arm was wrapped around his neck and her round cheek was pressed against his. Doreen's hand rested on the shoulder of an eight-year-old boy standing in front of them. All were smiling.

He couldn't hold back a tear and a quiver of his lip. Sarah saw it and felt sorry for him.

"I went by my old home this morning," she said as unemotional as she could. "It's still standing but showing all the signs of nineteen years of neglect."

He didn't react. She went on, "Ever since I left, I've had nightmares of demons in white suits and face masks. Every time something good happens, I dream that they are coming back to take it away."

Frank DuBois remained silent, just staring at the picture.

Sarah looked at him and added, "I can't explain her actions and I can't forgive them. But the Annie I knew would never do anything so awful. I often wonder what demons haunted her."

The old man closed his eyes. He, too, could never explain it, but how could he not forgive? "Wherever you are, my angel, I hope you're at peace," he said quietly..

CHAPTER 23

Sarah rushed to the door as soon as she heard the car outside.

"Bruce called," she said as Frank walked up the front steps.

"Damn, I missed him again," he replied, frustrated.

Bruce had called only twice in many months, and both times he had left the same message on the answering machine. He was okay, Dr. Senna was helping him, he had traveled outside Rio to make the call because the city still didn't have phone service, he didn't know when he would return to the U.S. because there was no international air travel, he hoped that dad was coping with the tragedy, and he missed dad.

"No, no, you don't understand. He's on his way here!" Sarah said excitedly.

Frank stopped. "When?"

"Tomorrow. He's in Miami and will be arriving in the morning."

Frank displayed a broad smile. It was the best news he had heard in over a year.

He stayed home the following day. Only one airline had resumed direct flights between Miami and the New York area. He called it and learned that a flight would arrive just before noon. The only other flight would arrive in the evening. He fought the urge to jump into his car and drive to Newark airport.

"Relax, Dr. DuBois," Sarah said with a smile as Frank paced the kitchen floor. "He won't arrive any sooner just because you're anxious."

"Do you think he got on the flight?"

"Relax. He would've called if he didn't."

She was also thrilled that Bruce was arriving. As a thirteen-year-old, she had had a tremendous crush on him. She never mentioned it and he never paid her any attention, but she was excited nonetheless and wondered if he would remember her. This morning, she had spent more time than usual with her hair and make-up.

Frank was peeking through the window when a taxi arrived. He ran out the front door and met Bruce on the driveway where they stopped in each other's arms. Tears of joy and relief swelled up in Frank's eyes, and father and son held on for a long while.

"It's great to see you, dad," Bruce said finally.

Frank wiped his eyes with his sleeve, a little embarrassed when he saw a woman standing behind Bruce. She was tanned and elegant and smiled as if she knew him.

"Dad, this is Dr. Claudia Senna. She was my guardian angel for the last fourteen months. I doubt I would've made it without her."

Frank extended his hand and Claudia grabbed it with both of hers. "It's a pleasure to meet you, Dr. DuBois," she said. "Your son is too kind."

"It's the truth," Bruce replied. "I would've starved or been murdered if Dr. Senna hadn't taken me under her wing."

"The pleasure's mine, and please call me Frank," Frank said. She was still holding his hand and smiling warmly, a tenderness he found fascinating.

"I convinced Dr. Senna to come with me," Bruce added. "She needs a break. She has been working non-stop since the beginning of the epidemic."

"I can relate to that," Frank replied, his hand finally free. "Let's go in the house."

Sarah was watching them from the front porch.

"Hello, Bruce," she said smiling.

He stared at her with an inquisitive look. The pale smile was familiar.

"Sarah?" he asked, uncertain.

She nodded. "Welcome back," she said.

He noticed her scars, and she noticed his. There was an immediate bond that needed no words. They had suffered the same agonizing disease, had survived against the odds, and had been marked as a reminder of how strong they could be.

"It's nice to see you," he said. "What are you doing here?"

"It's a long story," his father answered.

"I have all the time in the world," he replied. "But first, can Dr. Senna try to call London from here?"

"Sure," Frank said, directing Claudia to the office adjacent to the living room. He closed the door to give her privacy.

"She has been trying to reach her son since the beginning of the epidemic," Bruce explained. "It has been impossible from Brazil. One of the reasons she came was to try to reach him from here. If she can't, she'll fly to London to look for him."

Something else they had in common, Frank thought. He knew too well the angst of not knowing the whereabouts of a child.

He examined his son. Bruce had aged and was much thinner. His beard, now black and gray, was longer to hide the damage to his face and neck, but his brown eyes still sparkled despite the scars that framed them.

Claudia came out of the office twenty minutes later. "Ronaldo is alright," she said, trying to smile but on the verge of tears.

Bruce hugged her, and for a while she couldn't speak. "He has been as worried as I have, but unable to reach me," she said after collecting herself. "He has tried the phone, e-mail, the Post Office, but nothing has been working between London and Rio."

They sat in the living room to catch up on the events of the previous year. The story was longer and more painful than Bruce suspected. He still didn't know about his sister's role in unleashing the disease, or the truth about his mother's death. Frank spared no detail. At times, the memory of the events was too painful and Sarah took over the narrative.

Bruce was numb. He left them sitting in the living room and disappeared into his old bedroom upstairs. They let him go.

Claudia recounted the events from Rio. The tidal wave of infections, the civil chaos, the city destroyed, the variolation experiment. She modestly downplayed her role, but Frank was truly impressed by the guts required to carry out such a desperate plan. She told them about Bruce's work after his recovery, first in the rollout of variolation and later coordinating social assistance to the hundreds of thousands of orphans and homeless. Frank was proud.

Bruce came out of his room when Claudia was finished. Pain dulled the sparkle in his eyes, his lips were tumescent, and his scars were redder. The invisible wounds had just gotten deeper and would take longer to heal than the visible ones.

"I need some fresh air," he said. "Why don't we go for a walk?"

They walked outside.

"I'm so relieved that dad had someone to lean on during this nightmare," Bruce told Sarah as they strolled down the sidewalk. "You don't know how grateful I am."

"We needed each other," Sarah replied. "Everyone needed someone else in order to survive." She recounted her own ordeal and her losses, with silence at times speaking louder than words.

Behind them, Frank and Claudia compared their experiences fighting the same invisible enemy and worrying about their children. They would never be the same, but life would go on. The events were so recent and yet, they could belong in a different lifetime.

Claudia wrapped her slender arms around Frank's elbow as they walked. He felt her warmth and a hint of perfume from her hair, and he sensed an unexpected spring in his step.

The pleasant April afternoon was a welcome change from the lingering winter in New Jersey and the sweltering heat in Rio de Janeiro. The cherry trees and dogwoods were in full bloom and the squirrels were searching for the acorns they had missed in the fall. Children passed them on their bikes and roller skates, again laughing carefree. As it should be.

ABOUT THE AUTHOR

J. A. Lourenco is an accomplished scientist and international manager. He writes for fun.

He holds a B.A. (Kean University), M.S. (Seton Hall University), and MBA (The Wharton School). He has published numerous scientific and strategy papers, holds 5 patents, and has successfully managed an international division of a major U.S. corporation.

J. A. Lourenco grew up in Portugal, resided in Brazil as a corporate expat for the better part of three years, and has called New Jersey home for most of his adult life. He is married with three children.

He invites you to visit his website, http://www.scriptor.us, for additional information, including details of his last book, *On the Banks of the Zambezi.*

On the Banks of the Zambezi, based on a true story, captures the factual experience of those who lived through a pioneering, daring, dangerous, and eventually futile effort to carve out a living in the undeveloped interior of Africa during the Portuguese colonial war, a turbulent period of history which led, in the mid 1970s, to the independence of five separate nations.

The book portrays, through the eyes of a white child whose parents settle in the interior of Mozambique to run a general store catering to the local Chisena people, a family's struggle to rebuild their lives and business, in spite of sickness and death, only to have their lifestyle destroyed again by forces beyond their control. The experience of growing up white in a remote black environment is portrayed vividly, as is the primitive life of the locals, the disparity of opportunities for the white settlers compared to the native blacks, and the build-up of war from a rumble to a tragic reality.

In addition, *On the Banks of the Zambezi* depicts the transition from a colonial war led by the distant Portuguese government to an equally senseless but even more vicious civil war within the newly independent Mozambique, and the toll on the lives of all residents of the new nation. The book is a story of life, death and survival in the midst of hatred and adversity by whites and blacks alike. *On the Banks of the Zambezi* is a piece of history that is mostly unwritten. It is a tale that will appeal to anyone who has survived the adversity of war or has experienced life outside the main stream, and especially to anyone with a passion for Africa and its history.

The author invites your comments via email to lourenco@scriptor.us

Made in the USA
Middletown, DE
05 February 2016